A Hand for the Duke

Books By Meredith Bond

The Merry Men Series
An Exotic Heir
A Merry Marquis
A Rake's Reward
A Dandy in Disguise
My Lord Ghost
My Gentleman Thief
Under the Mango Tree
When Hearts Rebel
A Spanish Dilemma

The Storm Series
Storm on the Horizon
Bridging the Storm
Magic in the Storm
Through the Storm

The Falling Series
Falling
Falling for a Pirate

Chapter One: A Fast, Fun Way to Write Fiction
Self-Publishing: Easy as ABC
"*In A Beginning*", a short story featuring Lilith

A Hand for the Duke

The Ladies' Wagering Whist Society
Book One

Meredith Bond

Cover Art by QuarterbackTB, https://qtbdesign.wixsite.com/qtbdesign

Logo by Anjali Banerji

Edited by The Editing Hall, http://theeditinghall.com

Published by Anessa Books
http://anessabooks.com

To all those who make it possible for others to do what they do.

This includes my wonderful beta readers: David, Emmanuel, Venette, and Judy. My daughter and husband, both of whom make it possible for me to do my work every day, but also lent particular help on this project. And, of course, my editor who is the silent writing partner I just can't do without.

PROLOGUE

~March 1, 1806~

Tina Rowan could barely breathe. Her legs trembled with every step forward.

Her foster-father wanted to have a word with her.

How many bruises would she come away with this time?

Most of the time, she managed to stay out of sight. Out of sight, out of mind. Throughout her childhood, she'd kept in his good graces, merely by keeping out of the house as much as possible. At first, it had been tutoring with the vicar, who'd been kind enough to not only teach her but allowed her to spend hours in his library reading everything she could. He'd understood her need to stay away from her foster-father and had abetted her in every way possible.

When Mr. Rowan had apprenticed her to the local seamstress, she'd spent her days and sometimes well into the night sewing. He'd been happy because she was earning money, and every penny she earned made him richer.

But now... Now, she wondered, what more did he want from her?

"Sit down," he said, by way of greeting when she walked into his bedchamber.

She did so immediately, sitting on the edge of his bed—the only place for her to sit.

He paced for a moment before stopping directly in front of her. He smiled.

Tina felt a cold bead of sweat roll down her back between her shoulder blades.

"Congratulations, my dear," he said, holding the unnatural smile on his face. "You are to be married."

"What?" she breathed. She'd not heard a word of this—not a whisper from anyone in the household. Had they not known? Or she supposed it was simply that they didn't care. One would have thought growing up in the household would have endeared her to this family that raised her, but no, they'd only felt contempt for her and hadn't once felt the need to hide it. She thought her foster-mother held some affection for her. Her four foster-siblings had made it abundantly clear throughout her life that they felt nothing for the illegitimate child who'd been thrust on them.

"You'll be marrying Caleb," he said, naming his eldest son.

"But..." She stopped. She didn't dare argue, or could she? It was merely a question of how badly he'd beat her if she did. But surely there had to be a way out of this. She couldn't, *wouldn't* marry her foster-brother. He was cut from the same cloth as her foster-father.

He was not a nice man.

"When you marry him, your monthly allowance will go to him," her foster-father said, the smile fading from his lips.

Oh. So that's what this was. He wanted to keep her allowance—the money her biological mother paid for her upkeep.

"You just want to keep the money in the family," Tina said to confirm her suspicions.

He stared at her neither confirming nor denying it.

"But if I marry Caleb, he'll get the money, not you," she pointed out needlessly, but she was thinking this through, looking for a way out. "What if I could ensure *you* continued receiving the money?"

She would do anything, anything at all to keep from marrying her brute of a brother.

Her foster-father narrowed his eyes. "And just how would you do that?"

"I could... I could work and—"

"You do work, but you are twenty years old. Lady Norman expects you to marry. If you do, it's going to be to Caleb."

"Lady Norman has said she wants me to get married?" Tina asked. Her biological mother hadn't said anything to her when they'd met just the week before at the seamstress's shop. Tina had made Lady Norman three gowns. She'd been very happy with them and very happy that Tina had made and designed them. But not a word about marriage had been spoken.

"She hasn't," her foster-father conceded, "but it's just a matter of time. You're twenty!"

"Perhaps I can forestall her..." Tina suggested.

"You need to marry. You *will* marry Caleb. End of discussion!" Her foster-father turned to leave. He wasn't a man of many words, and he was not used to being argued with.

"What if I earned even more money? What if I... I went to London and worked? I could send you the same amount Lady Norman has been paying you... perhaps with an additional ten percent," Tina said quickly before he left the room.

He stopped.

Slowly he turned back. "And how do you propose to do that? She pays me a good sum."

"I could work as a journey-woman. A seamstress. I've learned a lot in the two years since I've been apprenticed to Mrs. Little."

"You wouldn't earn that much as a seamstress." He shook his head. "No, you'll marry Caleb."

"I could if I weren't just a seamstress. I-I design dresses too. I could become a-a modiste. To the noblewomen. To the ladies of London Society," she said, pulling straws out of thin air.

It *was* true that she had been designing dresses for a little while. Mrs. Werthing, the vicar's wife had always allowed Tina to look through her fashion magazines, so she knew something of what the current trends were in London.

"Lady Norman was very happy with the dresses I made for her last week, and I've made dresses for quite a few others who've all admired my work," she added for good measure. "Lady Norman paid five guineas for each dress I made her."

Her foster-father narrowed his eyes at her at the mention of the money.

"If I make enough dresses, I could afford to pay you," she said.

"Twenty percent."

"Twenty? What? No! I still need to be able to live and living in London is expensive. Ten." She couldn't believe she was arguing with this man. Her boldness surprised her.

"Caleb will be happy to take you to wife."

"Fifteen. It is all I can afford." To be honest, she had no idea how much she could afford, but it sounded reasonable.

"How will you get started? You'll need a patron," he pointed out.

"Lady Norman will help me, I'm sure."

He nodded. "Fifteen plus what she already pays me. You have two months to start paying. If I don't get my money on time, I'll tell the newspapers the truth about you, you little bastard, and who your mother is too." With that, he walked out of the room.

Tina's jaw dropped. He would let the world know the truth? That would destroy both her and Lady Norman. She would have no choice but to marry Caleb—she couldn't imagine anyone else would have her.

And he only gave her two months! No one could get a business started and profitable in two months! It would take an absolute miracle!

Not only that, but she hadn't yet asked her biological mother if she would actually help her. She could only pray that Lady Norman would. Otherwise, she was going to have a lifetime of black eyes and tip-toeing around an angry husband.

CHAPTER ONE

~March 24, 1806~

Tina stood clasping and unclasping her hands. Even from where she stood in the game room of Lady Norman's London home, Tina could hear her mother greeting her guests as they came into the drawing room. With merely a collapsible wall separating the two rooms, it was easy to hear everything. Of the twelve who Lady Norman had invited, seven had agreed to come.

Tina was rather happy it was a smaller group. She wasn't used to a large number of people. Seven or eight women seemed like a reasonable number. If all of them bought dresses this afternoon, Tina's new business as a modiste would be made—assuming they liked what she created.

This whole past month had been like a dream. Her mother had done so much more than Tina had ever expected of the woman who'd given her up less than a week after she'd been born.

Lady Norman had spent time with her, telling her all about the women of the beau monde, how they expected to be treated, even who the leaders of society were and what they wore for different occasions. Growing up in her little village of Northram Commons, Tina hadn't experienced any of this, hadn't even been aware that one needed a different dress to go out for a drive in a carriage than what one wore to visit friends. It was a whole new world for Tina, but she'd studied hard and committed everything her mother had told her to memory. She'd even spent a week studying her mother's copy of Debrett's, so she would know that Miss X was the daughter of Lady Y and not to call the daughter of a viscount Lady Firstname, but Miss Lastname, whereas the daughter of a duke was always Lady Firstname.

It was dizzying, the rules and conventions, the names and titles. But she'd spent her time studying it all. And when she wasn't doing that, she was studying the latest fashions and creating dress designs. Her mother had bought all of the fashion magazines and given her old copies as well, so Tina could learn the designs for the various types of dresses her clients would need and even advise them on the latest fashions.

Now, as the folding wall in front of her was pulled open by the two footmen, she would put all of that hard work to the test. Quickly, she placed what she hoped was a welcoming, confident smile onto her face. She and Lady Norman had worked on that smile for nearly a quarter of an hour, practicing to get it to look as if she were sure of herself rather than dyspeptic.

The guests were all sitting around Lady Norman's elegant drawing room with its golden sofa, blue brocade chairs, and inlaid wooden accent tables. All the ladies were well dressed, naturally, but it was immediately evident to Tina's discerning eye that not all were wearing what flattered them the most. There was even one young woman who looked positively ill thanks to her jonquil gown.

"May I present Miss Tina Rowan?" her mother was saying.

Tina was so overwhelmed by all the eyes on her and magnificence of the scene that she almost missed her cue. For a moment it all felt surreal, like a fantasy she had never imagined possible. She recalled herself and dropped into a curtsy before launching into her practiced speech.

"Good afternoon, ladies. I know that Lady Norman has already thanked you for coming, but I would just like to add my thanks as well. I invite you all to come and see the fabrics I have here. You should have already had an opportunity to see some of the fashion plates I have prepared for you, but if there is something that you've seen elsewhere, please know that I will do my utmost to recreate what you have in mind. I do hope I have the opportunity to work with you all." She gave another little bob and a smile.

The ladies all sat staring at her for a breath, and then a few got up to examine the material Tina had laid out on a card table next to her. Lady Norman's footmen hadn't removed any of the furniture of the game room but merely rearranged it. The only change to the furnishings had been the addition of the full-length cheval mirror from Lady Norman's dressing room so that the women could hold the material up and imagine what they would look like in a dress made from it.

Eventually, all of the women joined her in the gaming room. Most were talking amongst themselves, but one young woman about Tina's age with auburn hair and strikingly pale blue eyes came up and fingered a yellow silk saying, "My father wishes I were more concerned with my attire. It's one reason why I came today." She looked up and smiled at Tina. "I'm afraid such things as dresses and fashion just never interested me."

Tina returned her smile and felt herself relaxing a little. "I can understand. I don't know that I would have become so interested if I hadn't been apprenticed to a seamstress from a young age." She picked up the material the woman had been eying. "If you would permit me, my lady?" Tina asked. She unraveled a swath of it from the bolt. "This yellow would bring out the blue in your eyes and the pink in your cheeks. Just look in the mirror, if you would?" She placed the material over the lady's shoulder and directed the woman's gaze to the mirror. It really was a stunning color on her.

"Oh, yes! My goodness, I've never worn yellow before. I'm afraid I never really liked the color, but... My, it does do all that you said it would."

Tina tried to hide a grin of triumph. Her first sale!

She shifted the material so that it stretched across the woman's slender chest. "If you would imagine this with a square neckline and then caught just below your bosom so the skirt falls elegantly to the floor." Tina tilted her head seeing the dress already made in her mind's eye. "Would you consider a small train? This could be a lovely carriage dress or even something you might wear for visiting."

"I was wondering if it could be a ball gown? I don't have very many," the lady said. "I know young ladies are supposed to wear white, but it just makes my hair look horribly red."

"It's because you're not wearing the correct shade of white." Tina put down the yellow and unraveled a creamy white silk. She gave the material a twist and draped it across her chest so that the twist fell between her breasts. "Some pleating here to emphasize your lovely shape and a sleeve capping of this material then shifting into a cream lace." Tina adjusted the gown in her mind.

"When you are finished with Miss Hemshawe," another young woman said, coming up to them, "I would like to have a dress made." She had been looking at a bolt of fine sprigged cotton with green and pale purple flowers that would have looked nice on Tina herself because she was blonde and fair, but it absolutely would not work with this young lady's darker coloring. Tina would recommend another sprigged muslin she had with deep pink and blue flowers instead.

"Yes, of course, Miss," Tina said. She gave the woman a friendly smile before turning back to her current customer. "Six small buttons going up the back covered in this same material," she continued. "And pleats below to provide that elegant short train. May I sketch something up for you quickly?"

The woman looked a little dazed but gave a small nod. Tina removed the material and picked up her sketch pad, which she had kept handy for such an occasion.

"Before you wait on Miss Sheffield, Miss Rowan, I would like a gown of that blue cotton in this style," another woman said. She held up one of the fashion plates Tina had left out, but it was a morning dress intended for a much younger woman. It would require a bit of altering to be appropriate for the middle-aged woman holding the drawing.

"Yes, my lady, I'll be with you in just a moment," Tina said, suddenly feeling rather overwhelmed.

Very quickly, she did a rough sketch of the gown that had been in her mind for Miss Hemshawe.

"That's amazing!" the first young woman exclaimed, looking over Tina's shoulder. "What an incredible talent you have, Miss Rowan."

Tina turned and gave the woman a true smile. "Thank you, my lady. Would you be interested in commissioning this gown?"

"Yes, I would, thank you," the woman said. "But I'm the daughter of a baron, not my lady," she added with a kind smile.

"I do beg your pardon!" Tina said, quickly. She was already making faux pas. Thank goodness, Miss Hemshawe didn't seem to mind.

"That is very pretty, Miss Hemshawe," said an older woman with fair hair in a complicated coiffure and very large brown eyes. She was a larger woman who obviously enjoyed rich food. Making a dress that complemented her figure would be a bit of a challenge, but Tina could do it.

"Do you think so, Your Grace? I know so little about fashion," Miss Hemshawe said, looking to the older woman for approval.

"Yes. It will be very flattering, and goodness knows you could use a new ball gown. I think I saw you in the same one twice within the past few weeks, did I not?"

"Oh, dear. I do have two gowns that are nearly the same color. Could it be that you mistook the two for the same dress?"

"I suppose that is possible," the duchess conceded.

A small black and white dog with a feathered tail and long floppy ears nosed over, sniffing at the material.

"Can I interest you in a gown, Your Grace?" Tina asked, so proud of herself for remembering not to say 'my lady' to a duchess.

"Me? Oh, goodness, no! I have used the same modiste for the past fifteen years. I am not interested, thank you. However, judging from the dress you made for Lady Norman, you do fine work." She turned and looked about. "Mrs. Aldridge! Please remove your animal at once, it is getting amongst the fabric!" She called out. "Disgusting creature," she added under her breath.

Tina picked up the little dog. "Oh, she's a darling! I don't think she would hurt anything, would you?" she said, scratching the animal behind her ears.

The pup had slashed pale brown markings that looked like eyebrows over huge brown eyes, making her expression look very worried. She turned and licked Tina's nose before laying her head on her shoulder. "Oh! How sweet!" Tina said, unable to contain a giggle as the dog's whiskers tickled her ear.

Another older woman in a violent violet gown bustled over. "Is my little Duchess being a naughty girl?" she said in a baby voice.

The true duchess winced. "*Must* you call her that?"

"But that's her name!" Mrs. Aldridge protested, reverting back to her true voice.

Tina laughed. "You named her Duchess?"

"Actually, I didn't. My husband did. She always expects everyone to wait on her, and she is quite regal in her bearing. Of course, she is a Cavalier King Charles Spaniel, a breed created 'specially for the royal family. Naturally, she is a duchess."

The real duchess shook her head in disgust and walked away.

Tina did her best not to laugh, but Mrs. Aldridge and Miss Hemshawe clearly had no such qualms. They both burst into giggles.

"Well, she is adorable," Tina said as she handed the dog back to her owner.

"Thank you. As soon as you are finished with Miss Hemshawe, I'd like you to take my measurements. I have exactly the sort of dress I want in mind. It's one that I saw in *La Belle Assemblée* last month."

"Oh, I've seen the new magazine. It has beautiful and quite forward-thinking gowns. I'd be honored to make one for you, madam," Tina said. "Although, I'm afraid two other ladies are ahead of you in their requests that I create a gown for them."

Mrs. Aldridge didn't look thrilled at having to wait her turn, but nodded and said, "When you're ready." She turned and walked over to speak with some of the other ladies who had sat down at one of the card tables. A deck of cards had been produced, and it looked like they were preparing to play a game of some sort.

It was an odd thing to do at a fashion party, but Tina supposed those women had no need of new gowns. It was all right, she thought. She currently had four gowns to make, and there might be more coming as there were still other ladies looking through her fashion plates and the material.

Tina was busy measuring Miss Sheffield when she heard the footman announcing the Earl of Ayres. Why would Lady Norman have invited a gentleman to a party where the focus was on fashion and dresses?

Tina exchanged a look with the young woman who just shrugged. Clearly, she was as confused as Tina.

CHAPTER TWO

"Lord Ayres, what a pleasant surprise." Tina's mother could be heard greeting the gentleman.

"Good afternoon, Baroness," the man said. There was a pause as Tina supposed, the gentleman bowed to the lady. "You did say for me to visit this afternoon?" he asked as if he was reminding Lady Norman of this.

"I did?" Tina's mother asked.

"Yes, unless I got the date wrong from your letter, but I'm almost positive you had said today," he said with a little laugh.

"You received a letter from me? But I never..." she gasped. "I confess I wrote a note, but then I didn't mean to send it. I, er, I was going to revise it and change the date before I did so. It must have accidentally gotten mixed in with the invitations I sent out for this afternoon. I do so apologize, my lord."

"Oh, no worries, no worries at all." There was a pause. "It looks like you're having quite a lovely gathering."

Tina continued to measure Miss Sheffield even as she heard the man come closer. "Your Grace, how lovely to see you again. Lady Sorell, Lady Blakemore,

Mrs. Aldridge. Goodness, what excellent company!" The man gave a little laugh. "But I seem to be interrupting something that looks distinctly feminine."

"Yes, it is." Lady Norman sounded flustered. "I do beg your pardon, Lord Ayres, that letter should never have been posted!"

"Not at all, not at all. And what have we here?"

Tina stood up from where she'd been bending over her sketchbook, making note of Miss Sheffield's measurements. The gentleman was arrayed in the finest coat of bottle green with tan breeches and Hessians that shone so brilliantly you could almost see your reflection in them. His waistcoat was tan with lovely green, and gold embroidery and his neckcloth was a confection that must have taken him at least an hour to create. He was, in short, the best-dressed gentleman Tina had ever seen.

He also had intensely green eyes and, although his face was beginning to show his age—which had to be somewhere in his forties—he was still a very handsome man with light brown hair only lightly sprinkled with gray. His eyes creased with the smile that spread across his face.

"Miss Sheffield, that blue material will look absolutely stunning on you," he said. He then turned and took a glance at the drawing Tina had made of the dress she would produce with the material now draped over Miss Sheffield's shoulder.

"Ah, excellent, excellent," he nodded. "I like the line, but to be most flattering to the lady, you might want to raise the décolletage just a touch." He picked up her pencil that had been laying on top of the sketchbook and made a few adjustments. "You see, while it is a little higher—"

"You gave it a scooping shape," Tina said, looking at how he'd adjusted the sketch.

"Yes. That way it will be more flattering to her lovely figure," he said, giving her a smile.

"Yes, I see. It doesn't need to be quite so low since it has that pretty shape."

"Exactly! Although I do like the underskirt showing there. That's a very nice touch, Miss..."

"Rowan. Tina Rowan, my lord." Tina dipped into a curtsy.

"Tina is opening a new modiste shop," Lady Norman said. She'd been hovering in the background, but now moved forward.

Tina paused as she looked at her mother. She looked oddly pale but had bright spots of color on her cheeks. If Tina didn't know better, she'd think the woman was nervous or scared, but why would she be afraid of this gentleman? He seemed perfectly nice, and he certainly had an excellent eye for fashion.

"Is she? And you are helping her get started with this little gathering?" he asked, turning to Lady Norman.

"Yes. She lives in the little village near Norman Abbey. She made this dress for me, and I just *knew* she had to come to London," Lady Norman said as if it had been her idea that Tina try to start a business for the *ton*.

Lord Ayres paused and inspected Lady Norman's dress. "Yes. Yes, I can see a great deal of potential."

"Potential, my lord?" Tina asked, stepping forward and looking over the dress her mother was wearing.

"Yes. It's quite fashionable, but maybe not *quite* right for its wearer?" He stood back and placed a hand to his chin as he thought about it.

Tina took a closer look herself, and then it hit her. She grabbed a box of pins she'd kept on the gaming table and pinched together the back of Lady Norman's dress, pinning to hold it so that the shoulders of the dress sat closer to the lady's neck. "And then perhaps letting out the skirt just a touch to create more flow."

"Yes! Brilliant! That's exactly it! That will make it flatter her more and stand out as an exceptional gown," he said, standing back and nodding his approval.

Tina had never really thought too much about using clothing to emphasize the better features of a lady's figure, but even doing something so simple as what she'd just done with Lady Norman's dress did just that—and it made all the difference! The dress was no longer hanging on the woman, but actually doing something to make her look more beautiful.

Tina turned to the gentleman. "Thank you, my lord." She put true gratitude into her words, and clearly he heard it for he nodded his head graciously before taking Lady Norman's arm and walking with her to the door.

What an incredible man! He had a knowledge of fashion better than many women and dressed himself to advantage as well. Tina could hardly take her eyes off him even as her mother saw him out.

"Miss Rowan, when you are ready," Miss Sheffield said quietly, startling Tina out of her reverie.

"Oh, I do beg your pardon!" Tina said, returning to her customer.

"He is quite magnificent, isn't he?" Miss Sheffield giggled.

"He is! And his knowledge and understanding of clothing is impressive," Tina agreed.

~March 24~

The Duke of Warwick shuffled the papers on his desk around, but he couldn't find what he was looking for. He rearranged everything into neat piles, one for each of his six estates, but it *still* wasn't there. Finally, he gave up.

"Martin, where is that report from Hanley?"

His secretary looked up from his own desk to Warwick's right. It was an odd situation, sharing a study with his secretary. At his country estate, Martin had his own room just off of the duke's study, but here in town there simply wasn't the space. Luckily, it was a good-sized room they shared.

Martin stood, grabbing a piece of paper from the corner of his desk. "It's here." He handed it over.

"Hadn't you just given this to me?"

"Yes, but then I took it back."

Warwick looked up at his secretary. He could never tell when the man was fooling with him or when he was being serious. His high, sharp cheekbones and laughing blue eyes always gave the impression of good humor, even when he was serious.

He'd known Martin nearly his entire life— Martin's father had been secretary to Warwick's father. They'd grown up together, even sharing a tutor, although when Warwick had gone to Eton and then Oxford, Martin had continued studying under his father and had eventually gone to a smaller university.

"Yes," Martin said as if reading Warwick's mind. "I gave it to you, then took it back just so you would have to ask me for it again."

Warwick frowned at him.

Martin laughed. "I needed it in order to complete the budget you asked for," he admitted, sitting back down at his desk.

"Ah. Thank you." Warwick gave a little laugh and a shake of his head. He looked through the report once more, looking for particular indicators that would guide him in his planning for the following year.

The two men lapsed into silence as they both returned to their work until a knock interrupted them.

"Come!" Warwick called out.

His sister, Margaret, slipped into the room, opening the door just wide enough to allow her through.

Warwick gave her a welcoming smile. "What are you up to today?"

"I just... Do you have a minute?" she asked, approaching his desk. "Good afternoon, Martin," she said, pausing by his secretary's desk.

The man had risen to his feet. "Good afternoon, Lady Margaret," he said with a small bow.

"I don't mean to interrupt your work..." she began. Warwick noticed that her pale blue eyes looked unusually shiny as if there were tears in them threatening to fall.

"You know I will always make time for you. Is there something wrong?" Warwick said, standing up and moving toward the sofa near the fireplace and indicating his sister join him there. The heat of the fire was a little warm for him, but he was certain his sister would be glad of it. He sat at the farther end of the sofa, allowing his sister to take the side closer to the heat.

She folded her hands in her lap. "It's just..." She paused, blinking rapidly but keeping her gaze fixed on the dark blue carpet at their feet.

"Margaret, whatever it is, you know you can talk to me," he said gently.

She took in a breath and said, "I think I'd like to return to Warwick."

"What? But you're here to make your debut. I've already sent in your name to the Lord Chamberlain to be invited to the next drawing room held by the queen. And you only have two more years to find a husband," he said, confused by her sudden change of heart. They'd discussed this a number of times over the past few months, and finally, he'd gotten Margaret to agree to enter society.

He was still furious at his father for stipulating in his will that Margaret be married by the age of twenty or else forfeit her dowry. The crafty man had even accounted for all the ways Warwick himself could have averted this with the threat that if he even tried, all of the family's estates but the one property entailed to the dukedom would go to his second cousin and heir. It would leave Warwick with almost no income. He would be, essentially, a duke in name only.

No, Margaret truly had no choice but to make her entrance into society and do her best to find herself a husband. Warwick was determined she would marry no one she didn't truly care for, ergo the need for her to start looking sooner rather than later. He swore to do everything he could to help her, including escorting her to every social occasion. It was going to be awkward, and a tad unconventional, but for his sister he would do absolutely anything.

"But you haven't yet received the invitation to the queen's drawing room, have you?" she asked.

"Well, no, it's not actually been announced yet, but I imagine it can't be too far off. And you've already made great headway on planning your ball, haven't you?" he asked.

"Yes," she hedged. "Cousin Sonora has been a wonderful help in guiding me with that."

"Then? What's the problem?"

"I just... I don't know... I just don't feel ready, that's all," she said to the carpet, now not meeting his eyes *and* beginning to wring her hands as well.

Warwick placed one of his hands over both of hers, stilling their movement. Her worried gaze flicked up to meet his. She had beautiful, expressive eyes. When he was younger, he'd always wished his had been the same color as hers rather than the dull brown that his eyes were. They did both inherit their mother's rich brown hair though, complete with its silly curls that looked beautiful on Margaret but ridiculous on himself. He knew carefully tousled curls were all the rage for men; he just didn't think it made him look as serious and imposing as a duke should be. His father had always bemoaned his curls as well, saying that Robert would have to work even harder to look somber, so as to be taken seriously when he became duke. He'd done his best.

"Why this sudden bout of nerves?" Warwick asked. "Has something happened? Has someone said something?"

"I met with Cousin Sonora's modiste today," Margaret said in a near whisper.

"Yes?" Warwick prompted his sister when she fell silent again. "And is she going to make you a beautiful gown for the ball? I suppose you need one for your court appearance as well?"

Margaret shook her head. "Florence had to ask her to leave."

Florence was Margaret's maid. "That was very bold of her. Why did she do this?"

"She... she..." Margaret started to blink rapidly.

"You can tell me, Margaret," Warwick said, trying to sound as encouraging as possible while not allowing the sudden fury that had ignited in his chest to show through his words.

"She said that it would be difficult to dress me seeing as how I was so skinny. She said she would need to pad the bosom, and I might have problems managing the panniers of my court gown. Oh, and she thought I should wear the same gown to my ball as I did to court! Panniers, Warwick! To a ball!"

He shook his head. "I'm an ignorant fool, my sweet. What are panniers?"

"They're the frame that holds a lady's dress out to either side. They were fashionable fifty years ago. Mrs. DuBois thinks they're still worn at court."

"Oh! That! Good God, no! I mean, I don't know what ladies wear to court, but they certainly don't wear, what are they? Panniers to a ball," he said, thinking about this. He'd had to be presented to the king after his father died and he'd taken over his duties as duke, but that wasn't the same thing as a young lady's court presentation.

"Feathers," Martin added. "Ostrich feathers, I believe it is."

"What is ostrich feathers?" Warwick asked.

"What women have to wear to court," Margaret answered for him. "They have to wear them in their hair. Cousin Sonora says the queen is very particular about what one wears, but no one, absolutely no one, wears her court dress anywhere else but at court. Even I know that!" Margaret said becoming more forceful. Warwick took this as a good sign.

"It's been nearly thirty years since Cousin Sonora made her debut. Clearly, this modiste didn't know what she was talking about," Warwick agreed.

"Not to mention that you aren't skinny," Martin added.

"What? No! Of course she isn't," Warwick agreed immediately. "You say Florence threw the woman out?"

"Yes. I was so surprised at her nerve, but after the mantua-maker had gone on for a good five minutes or more about my atrocious figure, Florence got up and apologized before saying she was afraid the lady would have to leave. Can you believe it? She told her to leave!"

"Good for her. Martin, have we given this woman a raise recently?" Warwick said, turning around to address his secretary.

"I don't know, but I'll be certain that she receives one," he answered making a note on a piece of paper off one side of his desk.

"I fully support giving Florence more money. She is truly a gem. But I still wish to return to Warwick. I… I don't think I could face coming out now. And who would want to marry a scrawny young woman such as myself? Maybe in another year I can put on some weight or, or exercise more, or—" Margaret began to flounder as her eyes filled once more with tears.

CHAPTER THREE

"Margaret, don't you dare! You have a lovely figure, but more than that, you are a sweet, intelligent person. Any gentleman would jump at the chance to marry you—and not just for your dowry. That woman was wrong. Don't give her another thought," Warwick said, pulling out his handkerchief as one tear began to make its way down her cheek.

Margaret accepted it from him and then swiped at her tear. She proceeded to twist and turn the piece of cloth in her hands. "But she said—"

"Where did you find this awful mantua-maker?" Warwick asked, cutting her off.

Margaret blinked a few times while looking up at him. "Cousin Sonora has used her for years."

"Well, it sounds as if the woman ought to retire. She is out of date, and rude as well. No, you need to find someone else."

"But I don't know anyone else," his sister cried.

"We'll find someone for you," Martin said.

"Yes. Martin will find someone for you. Someone young who knows the proper fashion for both court and ballroom."

"Wait, *I'm* going to find someone?" Martin asked, clearly not happy with this turnaround.

"Yes. You did just say that you would," Warwick said.

"No, I said we, meaning *you*," Martin argued.

"Me? I don't know any mantua-makers." Warwick didn't even bother to turn around to address the man. Instead, he gave his sister's hands a squeeze. "Martin will find someone for you. Don't you worry. There is no need for you to return to Warwick. You'll do just fine with the right woman."

"Cousin Sonora would be a lot happier—" Margaret started.

"I don't care what Cousin Sonora wants. She is here to chaperone you, and so she will." That came out a little more strongly than he intended, but their cousin was turning out to be a lot less useful than he'd hoped.

"She truly dislikes being out in public. It makes her itchy, she says." A twinge of humor lit Margaret's eyes, much to Warwick's relief.

"Itchy?"

She nodded. "She even begins to scratch at her arms if we're out of the house for more than a few minutes."

"That's ridiculous!" Warwick said.

"It's actually sort of funny. Oh, I know I shouldn't laugh at her affliction, but honestly, have you ever heard of such a thing?"

"Never. I think she's making it up. She just doesn't like being in public," Warwick said, shaking his head ruefully. If there were anyone else who could chaperone his sister, he would happily call on them, but there was no one. His father's sister had passed away a number of years ago, and his mother hadn't had any close female relatives.

"It's quite possible. I can't blame her. I don't love being out in public either, and now I'm going to be the very center of attention at this ball," his sister said, beginning to look worried once more.

"I know you don't like so much attention, but you *do* love to dance. Just think of all the fun you're going to have," he offered.

"I don't—" she started.

"Now who is being silly? You *love* to dance! I've seen you do so any number of times when Mama invited people over," he argued. True, they'd been very small gatherings, and only close friends had been invited, but he distinctly remembered watching his sister laugh and have fun as she danced. It had made him happy just to see her begin to come out of her shell.

"Yes, but Mama's not..." Tears filled his sister's eyes once more.

It had merely been two years since their parents had succumbed one after the other to influenza. A more difficult winter they'd not had in years. Margaret herself had gotten sick, but thankfully recovered, being young and in excellent health. Their parents had not.

"I'm here with you, Margaret. I promised you that I'd be here, didn't I? And have I ever not kept a promise?"

"You've always been wonderful," she admitted.

"Then you've got nothing to worry about. You continue on with your preparations, Martin will find you a mantua-maker, and everything will be fine."

"You know, I don't think I've got time to go about searching for the right woman. I've got—" his secretary started.

"The budget can wait, Martin. We only have two weeks before the ball," Warwick reminded him. "You will find a modiste today."

"*Wie Sie wünschen, Mein Herr,*" Martin said, standing and clicking his heels together as he bowed low.

Warwick just frowned at his man, but Margaret began to giggle. "I do love it when you do that. Do you still remember your German, Martin?"

"*Natürlich, Ich werde meine Mutterspache nie vergessen,* Lady Margaret," he answered, giving her a little wink.

"*Ausgezeichnet. Ich hoffe, Sie tun es nie,*" she answered.

"I have no idea what you two are saying, you do know that?" Warwick interrupted.

Margaret giggled, and Martin gave her a conspiratorial wink.

"You know I learned the language myself just so you would have someone to speak with, aside from your father. Especially since *someone,*" she turned and looked at Warwick, "refused to do so."

"I was learning French, Latin, Greek, and Italian! I refused to learn yet another language," Warwick protested.

"But you could have spoken it with Martin, and no one but the two of you would have understood each other, like we just did," she argued.

"And you," he pointed out. "You would have understood us."

"Well, yes, and me." She gave him a broad smile. "But that means Martin and I have a secret language you will never understand."

Warwick sighed. "So, what did you two say to each other?"

"Oh, nothing," his sister said, clearly pleased with herself.

Martin laughed. "I will do my utmost to find you the best modiste in London, *meine Dame.*"

Margaret lost a little of the happiness in her eyes at the reminder but accepted his words with a nod of her head. She gave Warwick a little kiss on his cheek, then left the room.

As soon as she was gone, Martin turned back to Warwick. "Where the hell am I going to find a mantua-maker? I haven't the least notion about ladies'..." he waved his hands ineffectually in the air, "*things.*"

Warwick stood. "I haven't the foggiest. What did you and Margaret say to each other?"

Martin sighed. "Nothing of import, but I know you, and you're not going to stop asking until I tell you."

"No." Warwick waited for an answer.

"I told her that I would never forget how to speak German, and she said she hoped I never would. Are you happy?"

"Yes." He sat down at his desk.

"Wait, I've answered you, now how am I supposed to find a modiste?"

"I told you. I have absolutely no idea. I don't know about these things either. You figure it out." Warwick went to go back to his work. This was why he had a secretary, to do that which he simply didn't have time to handle—like finding a modiste for Margaret.

"But she's *your* sister!" Martin protested.

"Yes, and I'm *your* employer."

~March 25~

Christianne stepped down from her coach outside of Layton's drapery shop at Covent Garden. Unlike most ladies, she wasn't at all tempted to go into the shop to peruse the latest poplins. Unlike her daughter, sadly, she had no interest in fabrics and fashions. No, she was more of a people person, and in particular, people who she cared about.

She, therefore, proceeded next door and climbed the stairs to the first-floor flat above the bank where she'd managed to secure lodgings for her daughter. Tina herself answered on the first knock.

"Don't you have someone to answer the door for you?" Christianne asked after they'd gotten through the regular pleasantries and she'd been admitted into the drawing room. The room smelled like cotton, and it was no wonder—aside from the small seating area, most of the room was taken up by a large table covered with bolts of material. More stood against the walls, carefully arranged by color.

"No. But that's all right, I don't need anyone. I've hired a daily to clean and cook in the afternoons," Tina said, sitting on the lovely new pale green sofa Christianne had insisted on buying for her. Tina indicated she should take the comfortable matching chair.

"You will tell me if you need any funds," Christianne said, giving her a warm and, she hoped, motherly smile.

Tina smiled back at her indulgently. "I think you've done more than enough already."

"I could never do enough. You're my daughter," Christianne said, wanting to reach out and touch her. She was too far away, however, so she simply had to convey her love through her eyes and hope that Tina would recognize it. They had only just begun to get to know each other, and Christianne wanted so much to have the opportunity to continue to do so.

The problem was that Tina was still so reserved around her. Christianne was doing everything she could to make her feel more comfortable. She had lavished time and money on the girl, and now, she supposed, she just had to be patient and allow for all that she'd done to take root in her daughter's heart.

Tina's gaze dropped to the bare wooden floor at her feet. "I appreciate all that you've done."

"Stop. We agreed that you were not going to continue to thank me, didn't we?" Christianne reminded her.

"Yes, we did." Tina looked up and gave her a timid smile. "However, I cannot *not* thank you once again for hosting that party for me. Four dresses were ordered and not one of the ladies who ordered them asked how much they would cost!"

Christianne laughed. "No, naturally, they would not. I only invited those who I knew could easily afford the most expensive gowns. You should feel free to charge them handsomely."

"Oh no, I couldn't!"

"No, truly, you must. If you charge too little, they'll think that the quality isn't good."

"But if I charge too much, they won't come back and order more or recommend me to others," Tina argued.

"That's true. You should charge just a little higher than average so that they feel they're getting something special. I should think about twice what I paid for the gowns you made for me," Christianne said, thinking it through.

"Seriously? *Twice*?" Tina asked, shocked.

"Oh, absolutely! Those were ordered from a little village seamstress. These gowns were ordered from a London modiste. It's completely different."

"But I made your gowns the same way I'm going to make these. Although, I will go to these ladies' homes for their fittings rather than ask them to come to me."

Christianne shook her head. "That makes no difference. The point is where you are and the fact that your services are exclusive to only the best of the *haute ton*."

"But they aren't—"

"Yes, they are. You be sure to tell your clients so. Everyone likes to be thought the best of the best." Christianne lifted her chin to emphasize her point.

Tina laughed. "I think I'm beginning to understand. No matter whether it's true or not, I will tell my clients that the dresses I make are exclusive to only the best, the highest members of society."

"Exactly! Now, do you think you'll be able to finish the dresses you have orders for within two weeks, by the start of the season?"

"Oh yes, without any problems. I should be able to contact the ladies who ordered them and arrange to go to them for fittings in a week."

"Excellent. I'm still quite thrilled you got so many orders," Christianne admitted.

Tina gave her a smile and a little shrug. "I was actually hoping that with seven ladies present, I would get more."

"Well, these things always start off slow. Truly, these women are taking a chance on a complete unknown merely on my word."

"Yes," Tina said slowly. She kept her eyes lowered, but Christianne could see a frown was creasing her forehead.

"Is there something on your mind, Tina?" Christianne asked. She couldn't help feeling as if there was something her daughter wasn't telling her. She'd gotten this sensation a number of times over the past few weeks as she'd helped Tina prepare for her London debut, but so far she hadn't had the nerve to ask.

When her daughter looked up, her eyes were glassy with tears. She quickly blinked them away and started to shake her head.

"There is something! I knew it, and I've known it ever since you came and asked me to bring you to London. Tina, you can tell me anything! I know I've told you that before. Please, trust me," she said, practically pleading.

Tina closed her eyes for a moment. "I'd hoped to sell more gowns. I *need* to."

"Need to? I don't understand. If it's the money I've advanced to you..."

"It's not the money. At least, it's not I who needs it or...or wants it."

"Is there someone else?"

Tina sniffed and looked away. "My foster-father," she said very quietly.

"Mr. Rowan? What need does he have for money? I've paid him well every month since you were born."

"Yes, but he wants more, or at the very least not to lose that to which he's become accustomed.

Apparently, you told him when you handed me over to him that the money wasn't for him, it was for me, to pay for my upkeep."

"That's right. I didn't want him to think of the money as his, but as yours," Christianne agreed.

"And you said that you would go on giving me this money for the rest of my life."

"Yes. I've always planned on supporting you."

"Well, *he* wants to continue receiving that money. The only way for him to do so is for me to be his responsibility," Tina explained.

"Well, yes, but you aren't any longer. You're an adult and therefore your own responsibility," Christianne said.

"Right, which is why unless I pay him as much as you gave me, plus another fifteen percent, which he figured I would earn from my business, he's going to force me to marry his son, Caleb, who will then get the money as my husband." A tear slid down Tina's cheek, but Christianne could barely breathe.

"The nerve of that man!" she finally managed. "But he couldn't possibly force you to do that."

"He can. He threatened to write to every paper in London telling them of my parentage if I didn't. We'd *both* be ruined!"

"Blackmail!" Christianne nearly screeched.

Tina could only nod sadly. "Now you see why I need to earn more money, why I need to get more business. He gave me two months to make my business profitable enough to give him what he wants. If I can't, he'll come and drag me back to Northram Commons to marry Caleb."

"Two months! But that's not nearly enough time!"

"I know, but he didn't give me the opportunity to argue with him."

Christianne collapsed back against the sofa. "What are we going to do?"

"Get me some more clients."

Christianne was silent while she furiously tried to think of how to do that. Perhaps another party? But no, she'd already tapped out the meager store of ladies she could possibly ask. This was what came from keeping apart from society for too long.

"I've already made friends with the shop girls and the owner at the drapers next door. They've agreed to recommend me to any customers who ask."

"But that's wonderful!" Christianne said, sitting up again.

"I hope so."

"And word is bound to spread as more and more people come to town and see your beautiful work," Christianne offered.

Tina managed a little smile, the brave girl. "Quickly, I hope." She paused for a moment. "Can I ask you a question on a different topic, something that's been nagging at me?"

"Of course!" To be honest, Christianne had had more than enough of the current one.

"Who was that man who joined us at the party?"

CHAPTER FOUR

Christianne could not meet her daughter's eyes. She opened her mouth to speak but then closed it again, unsure of what to say.

That was your father didn't seem quite right, especially since she hadn't even had a chance to tell Liam about Tina's existence. She had to do that before she could tell Tina. It was the *right* thing to do.

Christianne had been mortified when Liam had shown up at her party—mainly because she'd completely forgotten about the letter she'd written and hadn't intended to send. On the other hand, it had been extremely gratifying that he'd come with apparently no reservations or ill-will toward her despite the fact they hadn't seen each other for nearly ten years and hadn't spoken properly since... Well, since Tina had been conceived twenty years ago.

And then to see him interacting with his own daughter without any knowledge of who she was—it had been heartbreaking she hadn't been able to say anything to either of them. Christianne had had to bite her tongue more than once to keep from shouting out the truth in front of everybody.

She nearly laughed. Wouldn't *that* have been a juicy scandal to start off the season! But, no, she'd managed to control herself and get rid of Liam as quickly as possible. But what to tell Tina now? She couldn't tell her the truth—not until she'd spoken to Liam.

"Lord Ayres is an old friend of mine," she said, keeping as close to the truth as possible. "It was so embarrassing that he showed up that afternoon. I'd written to tell him when I was coming to town and invite him for a visit, but I'd meant to change the date in my letter before it was posted. The footman must have seen it on my desk and picked it up with the other invitations." She shook her head and forced out a little laugh. "It will be fine. I'll speak with him soon and apologize."

"He didn't seem to mind at all," Tina said with a giggle. "And I appreciated his thoughts. He has the most incredible eye for fashion—certainly better than any man I've ever met."

Christianne's laugh was honest this time. "Indeed! He is well known for that eye. He has been considered one of the best-dressed gentlemen of the *ton* for over twenty years."

"My goodness! That's impressive," Tina exclaimed. A knock at her door interrupted whatever she was going to say next, however.

She jumped up to answer it, and Christianne could hear her speaking to another woman who seemed to be asking about her services. It was time she left anyway.

She got up and joined Tina as she was letting the other woman into her home. "Miss Rowan, thank you so much for your time. I do look forward to seeing what beautiful creation you have for me," she said with a wink to Tina.

"Oh, thank *you* so much, Lady Norman. I will be contacting you shortly," Tina responded, playing right along.

"Oh, hello, Lady Moreton, how lovely to see you again," Christianne said, greeting the other woman.

"Lady Norman, it is a pleasure. I just came by because I saw the exact material I want for my new gown, and it's just at the draper's next door. I've purchased what you will need, and they said they would have it delivered to you later this afternoon," Lady Moreton said.

"That's wonderful! Thank you so much for letting me know," Tina said.

"Of course," Lady Moreton said.

"I'm finished here. Shall we walk out together?" Christianne said, tucking her hand into the crook of Lady Moreton's arm. Perhaps she could convince the young woman to spread the word of Tina's designs sooner rather than later.

~March 25~

Warwick was nearly finished with his plans for five of his estates for the following year. He had one more to do.

He'd just pulled forward the budget and reports from the previous year and bent his mind to the task when Martin came into the study and threw himself into his chair. He reeked of an alehouse, leaving Warwick no doubt as to where he'd spent most of his afternoon—hopefully gathering good information.

Warwick looked up and waited. He knew that he'd get an earful in just a moment. Martin could never keep anything to himself for long.

"I give up," the secretary said finally. "I can't do it."

"What—"

"You know, there aren't a lot of things I can't do," he said, interrupting Warwick.

"Indeed, I do know—"

"And it's not for lack of trying, I can assure you," he said, cutting him off again.

"Of course not." Perhaps if he kept his responses short, he wouldn't be interrupted again.

"What? Is that it?" Martin said, turning on him. "Aren't you going to ask what it is that I can't do?"

Warwick had a sinking feeling he knew what Martin was talking about, but clearly his secretary needed to unburden himself. "I was about to, but—"

"I feel like the world is conspiring to keep this information from me," Martin said as if Warwick hadn't said a word.

Warwick couldn't take it anymore. He started to laugh. He was almost certain Martin was doing this on purpose. He certainly wouldn't put it past him.

"What's so funny? You try finding the best modiste in London! In fact—you *do* have to do this, Warwick. I can't. Honestly, I've tried. I've spoken to at least fifteen different people and have gotten so many shrugs of ignorance, I can't tell you."

"Ah! That's where I thought you were going, but I did want to make sure," Warwick said, leaning back in his chair.

"What else would it be?" Martin said, feigning outrage. "Did you possibly think there was anything else I *couldn't* do? Truly? *Your Grace?*" The last words were spoken with such feelings of hurt Warwick almost started laughing once again.

With some effort, he kept his amusement to himself. "No! Absolutely not. I know you to be a remarkable person, able to take on any task that is set before you. It's why I thought you'd be able to achieve this one little—"

"*Little*! Are you kidding me?" Martin jumped up from his chair. "Have you any idea? No, clearly you do not. Well, I dare you, I *dare* you to discover who this paragon of female fashion is because I can tell you that I cannot."

Warwick steepled his fingers together and thought about this. Who could he possibly ask? What female did he know who would be able to recommend an appropriate modiste for his sister? "Ah!" He stood up. "I know exactly where to find out."

He headed for the door.

"Wait! You aren't even going to tell me where you are off to?" Martin objected.

Warwick turned around and graced his secretary with a smile. "I will be paying a visit to the Duchess of Kendell, my good man. *She* will know who can make a ball gown for Margaret."

"Oh, sure, flaunt your noble connections in my face!" Martin called after him. "And don't forget, Margaret needs a gown for court as well!"

Warwick laughed and sent one footman running for his hat and another to inform the stables that he was in need of his phaeton.

Within a quarter of an hour, Warwick was knocking upon the Duchess of Kendell's front door, and less than two minutes after that he was shown into her esteemed presence.

"Warwick, how lovely to see you!" the duchess said, holding out her hands toward him.

He bowed over them and placed a chaste kiss on the back of one.

"And to what do I owe this unexpected pleasure?" she said, sitting down and indicating that he do so as well. She gave a nod to the footman, who was still hovering near the door.

"I'm afraid I've not come on a social call," he admitted. He adjusted his coat a touch. Somehow the duchess always managed to keep her drawing room stifling hot. He glanced in the direction of the fireplace, and indeed, there was a large blazing fire dancing away.

"No, I hadn't thought so. You never do, you know, but you might consider it every so often," she said, with a twinkle of amusement in her large brown eyes.

"Yes, you're right, I should. I apologize," he said.

"It's quite all right. Knowing how busy Kendell was, I can imagine that you don't have a great deal of time to go visiting old friends—with the emphasis on *old*, of course."

He gave a laugh. "You are *not* old!"

"I am exactly the same age your mother would have been had she not been taken far before her time," the duchess said. A sad smile trembled on her lips. "We came out together, you know. Of course, I couldn't stand her at the time, especially when she managed to attract the attention of your father almost the moment she set foot into our first ball."

"But you showed her, you got your own duke, didn't you?" he said, smiling fondly at her.

"Ha! Yes, I did. And I'm certain I wouldn't have been nearly as happy with Warwick as I was with my dear, sweet Kendell."

A maid came in bearing a tea tray. They waited in silence while everything was set out for them. The duchess poured and offered Warwick a slice of seed cake, which he accepted gratefully realizing that, once again, he'd missed the mid-day meal. He really had to ask Margaret to keep him from doing that.

"Now," the duchess said, settling back with her own cup of tea, "what can I do for you?"

He quickly swallowed his mouthful of cake and said, "I am planning on bringing Margaret out this season."

"You are? Why, that's wonderful! Who do you have sponsoring her?"

"My cousin, Lady Sonora, will present her at court. The rest I will do myself. Poor Sonora hates being in public and absolutely refuses to attend even the quietest of parties. She agreed to the Queen's drawing room, as that is the one thing I cannot do, but other than that..." He gave a little shrug.

"Oh, dear!"

"Yes. Sadly, she also seems to have an unreasonable fear of mantua-makers—which is what brought me here today. I was wondering if you knew of anyone you could recommend to make some gowns for Margaret. She'll need a court dress and one for her coming out ball, and maybe others as well, I don't know."

The duchess carefully placed her now empty teacup down on the table in front of them, and Warwick reached for a second piece of cake while she considered his question.

"I wouldn't recommend that she go to my woman. She's older, and I believe caters to us old folks. I've been going to her for years, but Margaret needs someone younger, more...current, I believe."

Warwick nodded his agreement even as he chewed. "Do you have anyone in mind?"

A smile slowly spread across her delicate features. "As a matter of fact, I do. I was introduced to just such a person only a few days ago by Lady Norman. She found a very talented young woman in her village and has set her up here in London. I think she would be perfect for dear Margaret. She's just starting out and so is at the very forefront of style—trying to make a name for herself, you know."

"But is she good? Could she make gowns appropriate for my sister?"

"I believe so. And, if I remember Lady Margaret correctly, she's a rather...sensitive girl, isn't she?"

"Yes," Warwick said with a sigh. It wasn't Margaret's fault. Their parents had never paid their daughter any attention, and somehow she'd just faded away into the background. He said nothing of this to his mother's friend, not wanting to speak ill of the dead.

"Well, this young woman seems like she would be perfect for a girl like that."

"How do you know?" he asked.

She paused to think about it for a moment. "I'm not entirely certain, to be honest. It was just a feeling I got from speaking to her and watching her work." She gave a decisive nod. "Give her a try. I'm not sure where she's located, but I'm certain that you'll be able to reach her through Lady Norman."

~March 26~

You are cordially invited to attend the first meeting of the Ladies' Wagering Whist Society.

Christianne had been pleased and a little amazed at the response she'd gotten to her invitations. She'd only sent them four days before the gathering, and almost immediately she'd heard from nearly everyone. Eventually, every single invitation had been accepted. Even Miss Hemshawe, who had been given only a very quick introduction to whist at Tina's fashion party, had responded positively.

The same seven women who'd attended Tina's gathering had been invited to join the Whist Society. With little to do while Tina had discussed dresses with individual ladies and taken measurements, some of the other women had sat down with a deck of cards and proceeded to play a hand of whist. They had enjoyed themselves so much that when Claire, Lady Blakemore had suggested forming such a group, everyone had agreed the idea had merit. Now, even a week later, clearly they were still interested.

Christianne welcomed all the women into her drawing room. Once everyone had been served a cup of tea and offered a piece of cake, she looked around for a moment just to confirm the impression she had come away with after their last gathering.

She'd felt an unusual camaraderie among the ladies, and indeed, even today as she watched, Lady Sorrell and Lady Moreton seemed to be deep in conversation over some serious topic. The two youngest ladies, Miss Sheffield, and Miss Hemshawe, were giggling together, and the three older ladies Mrs. Aldridge, Claire, and the duchess seemed to be comparing notes regarding this season's crop of girls making their debut. She wasn't certain about how well the duchess and Mrs. Aldridge were getting along. No matter what one said, the other seemed to have an opposing opinion. Claire was doing a fine job of mediating until she caught Christianne's eye and gave her such an exasperated look that Christianne laughed and called for everyone's attention.

"Ladies, thank you all for coming this afternoon. I assume that you are here because you're interested in joining the Ladies' Wagering Whist Society." She paused as many of the ladies agreed, either verbally or with a simple nod of her head. "And as I always believe in giving credit where it is due, I must thank

Lady Blakemore for coming up with this idea the last time we all gathered together."

Claire returned Christianne's nod and gave everyone else a polite smile.

"Since there are precisely eight of us, this works out very well. We'll be able to form two tables."

"How often do you expect we should meet, Lady Norman?" Lady Sorell asked.

"Yes, that's an excellent question," Lady Moreton agreed. She was usually very quiet, but Christianne was happy to see that she felt comfortable enough in this company to speak up.

"Would once a week be too often?" Christianne asked. "We could make it every other week, but then I worry we would forget or become confused as to whether it was an on week or an off."

"No, every week would be much easier to manage," the duchess proclaimed.

"And if for some reason someone can't come?" Miss Hemshawe asked.

"You'll be forced to partner with me the following week and believe me, you don't want that!" Miss Sheffield said bursting into giggles.

A few other ladies also laughed, although the duchess and Claire merely shook their heads with condescending smiles at the girl's silliness.

"If any are missing, we will rotate people in with each hand," Christianne proposed.

"Scoring will be a little tricky, but it's possible," Claire agreed.

So far, everyone was in accord. This was definitely an auspicious beginning.

CHAPTER FIVE

"Speaking of scoring, you named the group the *Wagering* Whist Society. Is there to be wagering?" Mrs. Aldridge asked, stroking her little Cavalier King Charles Spaniel. It was always within her easy reach if not actually in her lap.

"I was thinking that it would make the game more exciting if there was," Christianne said.

"I only have my quarterly pin money, although sometimes it is supplemented with winnings from a race or two," Miss Hemshawe said, unabashed to admit that her disposable income was limited.

"You actually wager on races?" Lady Moreton asked, sounding fascinated and a trifle horrified.

"Oh, yes! It's much more fun that way," Miss Hemshawe replied with a little laugh.

"And your father is aware of this?" Claire asked with a disapproving sniff.

"Of course! He always knows about the best races and escorts me to them. He places my bets for me," Miss Hemshawe said, her bright blue eyes going wide.

"We don't have to wager for money," Lady Sorell offered. "We could simply keep track of points."

"But then how does one win?" Miss Hemshawe asked. "Someone must."

"And *what* does one win?" Miss Sheffield asked immediately afterward.

Fully conscious of the fact that both the younger ladies were new to the game, Christianne explained the way scoring worked. "Each team gets one point for every trick you take after the first six. The team that gets five points first wins the game. Since we're all of varying levels of proficiency, I would suggest that we switch partners every game."

"That means that we'll each have to keep track of how many points we have individually," Claire interrupted.

"I would suggest we keep a book to keep track of points, but yes, we would each get five points for a game won," Christianne agreed. "And however many points you receive in the individual hand—one point per trick."

"But what are we wagering? What are we playing for?" Mrs. Aldridge asked.

"Well, most commonly one wagers a penny or a ha'penny a point," Christianne said.

"But if we're not going to be playing for money since that would be difficult for some of us..." Miss Hemshawe started to ask. She didn't need to finish her question.

It was quiet for a few minutes while everyone considered this.

The Duchess of Kendell broke the silence with a whisper.

"Secrets."

"What?" Claire said, spinning around to face the duchess.

The lady looked up from her hands clasped tightly in her lap, which had been her focus when she'd spoken. "We all have them. I propose that we wager our secrets—with the understanding that they will not go beyond this group. No gossiping. No spreading of tales. Not a hint to anyone—not even husbands, mothers, or sisters."

"That's a very high price to pay for losing a card game," Miss Sheffield said, her usual smile faltering just a touch.

"It is an extremely high price to pay," Mrs. Aldridge agreed.

"But it won't damage anyone's purse," Miss Hemshawe said, considering it.

"Only your reputation," Claire added. She was one to speak. She was well known for her impeccable reputation. She and Christianne had been friends for years, and yet Christianne had no notion if Claire even had a secret.

"No, not if it doesn't go beyond this group," the duchess explained.

"It could still damage you within the group," Lady Sorell said.

"Yes, that is true," Duchess Kendell agreed.

"It certainly demands a great deal of trust in each other," Lady Moreton commented.

"That's the thing. If we swap partners every game, we will each have an equal chance to win or lose. It balances the play," the duchess began.

"Which means that at some point, if we continue to play for long enough, each one of us will lose at some point," Lady Sorell finished for her.

"Precisely." The duchess nodded.

"And if you don't have a secret to tell?" Miss Hemshawe asked. "What if you've already lost once and have told your secret?"

"I'm certain you have more than one, my dear," Mrs. Aldridge said.

Miss Hemshawe didn't respond.

"I can't say that I like the idea," Christianne objected.

"Nor I," Miss Sheffield agreed, the smile fully slipping from her lips. Christianne thought it was perhaps the first time she'd ever seen the girl without a twinkle in her eye.

"Shall we be democratic and take a vote on this?" Lady Sorrell asked.

"Yes, I think that would be best," the duchess said. Most everyone else around the room nodded as well.

"All right then," Christianne said. "All in favor of wagering for secrets say 'aye'."

There was a round of *ayes* and nods. Miss Hemshawe gave a shrug and raised her hand, saying "aye" along with the others.

"And the *nays*?" Christianne prompted. She herself said "nay" as did Miss Sheffield and Lady Moreton.

"Well, it looks as though the ayes have it," the duchess said with a triumphant note to her voice.

Christianne exchanged a worried look with Miss Sheffield, but there was clearly nothing they could do. They had agreed to vote and now had to stand by and accept the majority decision.

"We'll probably have time to play one, perhaps two games each time we meet. There are three games in a rubber," Christianne said, continuing to explain the way the game would work.

"We should tally points at the end of two rubbers. Whoever has the lowest number of points at that time loses," the duchess continued.

"And reveals their secret," Lady Sorrell said with a nod.

"Agreed." The duchess gave a nod of her head. "As we'll be tallying everything in a book, we are not forced to finish anything more than the hand we are playing."

Everyone looked around at the other ladies to be sure there was consensus.

"Well, it seems as if that's everything," Christianne said finally, wishing she could relax. This idea of sharing secrets made her nervous. She had little choice but to put on a good face, however. She lifted her teacup. "Here's to the Ladies' Wagering Whist Society!"

Everyone copied her, some with a "Hear, hear!" others with "The Ladies' Wagering Whist Society!" There were some giggles, and on the whole, it couldn't be denied that everyone looked pleased.

"We shall begin play next week," Christianne said.

~March 28~

"Now then, Miss Rowan, tell me about yourself," Warwick said, staring across his large mahogany desk at the young woman perched at the edge of the chair across from him. Her hands, neatly folded in her lap, seemed to be clutching on to each other for life.

The girl frowned. "About *myself*? I thought I was here to create a gown for your sister, Your Grace."

"Two gowns actually, but yes, you are. However, I don't let just anyone into her presence."

"You're holding a ball for her with, presumably, hundreds of guests."

"Miss Rowan, do you want this job?" Warwick asked, beginning to feel the slight nag of annoyance.

"I do, but I don't see what my personal life has to do with my abilities to create a gown," she argued.

The nag grew—mainly because she was absolutely right.

"I beg your pardon, Your Grace," she continued, "but I'm not applying to be a housemaid or a tenant on one of your estates. I'm simply going to make a dress. I beg your pardon, *two* dresses."

He frowned. "*Both* dresses are vitally important. And I don't hire the housemaids nor interview prospective tenants. I have people do that for me— my housekeeper and my steward specifically."

"Then why are you interviewing me at all?"

This girl really had some nerve! She was questioning *him*?

"Because I can bloody well interview whomever I want," he snapped. No, now he truly was losing his calm. He never cursed in front of young ladies.

What was wrong with him today?

Ever since this girl with her beautiful face, intensely green eyes, and pert little nose had walked into his office, he'd most definitely not been himself. He'd merely meant to warn her that Margaret would need perhaps a touch more direction or hand-holding than an ordinary client, and then suddenly he was asking her about her life.

She was absolutely correct, it *was* none of his business. She was here to dress his sister and that was all. He hadn't done this with Cousin Sonora's woman. In fact, he hadn't interacted with her at all— and she'd been a dismal failure. This time he was determined to get a jump on things before they fell apart as they had with the last modiste.

Judging by the way she dressed herself, Margaret certainly could not go wrong working with Miss Rowan. Her delicate figure was well accented by her modest, but well-designed, gown. She wasn't above average height, and yet the flowing nature of the dress' material gave the impression of height and elegance. Clearly, this girl knew her trade despite her young age. If she could do half so well for Margaret, it would be well worth the time he'd spent finding her.

"If you wish, Your Grace, I would be happy to show you some of the designs I drew up for Lady Margaret to consider." The girl offered to open her sketchbook, which had been resting under her hands on her lap.

"No, no." He waved it away. "I know nothing of ladies' fashions. You'll discuss all that with Lady Margaret."

She closed her book again and looked at him, clearly at a loss as to what he wanted.

There seemed to be no way around it, he simply had to come out and tell her the truth. He cleared his throat. "Lady Margaret is, well, that is, she is young and lacking in female guidance. Our cousin is here acting as her chaperone, but she has very little interest in fashion or society. We've already tried one modiste who was rather...well, old. She knew how to make one style of dress, apparently, and was not accommodating. She was also, as I understand it, highly critical of my sister." He sighed, remembering Margaret's valiant attempt to contain her tears when she'd told him about her interview with the other modiste. Thank goodness her maid had had the courage to ask that the woman leave.

"Lady Margaret is sensitive?" Miss Rowan asked.

"Yes, that's it."

"And you'd like me to...guide her?"

"No, not precisely. I don't expect you to know the particulars of society, but you do know what's fashionable, and presumably, you know how a young woman's mind works—a very timid, shy, young woman. And yet one who, as my sister, should command respect."

The woman frowned at him, her forehead creasing. "I'm not entirely certain I understand what you're asking me to do," she admitted.

Warwick ran a hand down his face. He wasn't fully sure he knew himself. "I'd like you—"

"I beg your pardon, Your Grace." Florence, Margaret's maid came in after a brief knock.

"Yes?" he said, grateful for the interruption.

"I heard the new modiste was here. I came to escort her to Lady Margaret, with your permission," she said with a curtsy.

"Yes, yes. That's fine. Just to remind you, Miss Rowen, no expense is to be spared. If Lady Margaret approves of your designs, she is to have only the finest fabric, lace, and"—he waved his hand in the air—"whatever else necessary."

"Yes, Your Grace," Miss Rowan said, standing and looking very relieved. "Thank you, Your Grace." She curtsied and was about to leave when she turned back to him. "I do beg your pardon, Your Grace, but you really shouldn't wear that color."

"*What*?" She was criticizing *his* clothes?

"I said—"

"I heard what you said."

"Oh, well, with your brown hair and brown eyes, wearing a brown coat and tan waistcoat really is, well, too much brown. You need brighter colors and your waistcoat should be—"

"Miss Rowan, I am not hiring you to advise me on my wardrobe. Please go attend to my sister!" He couldn't believe the nerve of this girl!

"Yes, Your Grace." She gave a quick curtsy and darted from the room.

CHAPTER SIX

She walked up the grand staircase, its wooden rail so smooth as if generations of dukes and their families had sanded it with use. Gold and white accents highlighted the entry and stairwell and an enormous golden chandelier hung overhead under a ceiling that had to reach nearly to the roof of the house.

Tina was honestly having a very difficult time not gaping open-mouthed like a green country girl. Honestly, how could someone live like this surrounded by such opulence? It was one thing to have a house full of servants, and "people" who did things like hiring maids and interviewing prospective tenants, but this... This was almost too much.

Lady Margaret's sitting room was much more reasonably decorated. Simple pale green walls, matching upholstery on the sofa and chairs, and a dainty little writing desk off to one side gave the room almost a cozy feel if one could call such a large room cozy. But this was definitely a room Tina could work in. It smelled nice too, thanks to the vase of fresh roses and lavender that sat on a table by the sofa.

The young woman sitting curled up in one over-large chair with a book in her lap was even more reassuring.

"Miss Rowan, my lady," the maid said, announcing her from the doorway.

Tina paused just inside the room to curtsy.

"Thank you so much for coming, Miss Rowan," Lady Margaret said, uncurling her legs and meeting her halfway across the room.

"It's my pleasure, my lady."

"That is very kind of you to say. My brother did mention why we asked you here, did he not?"

"Yes. He said you were in need of a gown for your court presentation and a ball gown for your coming-out ball."

"Yes, that's right."

"Well, I've brought over some sketches, or if you've got something particular in mind, I'm more than happy to work with you on creating that," Tina said, repeating what was quickly becoming a practiced speech.

The woman visibly relaxed, her shoulders dropping just a touch. She gave Tina a small smile. "Oh no, I've got nothing in mind. Although I have been looking through the magazines, and there are some very nice designs there. I'd like to see what you've brought first though."

"Excellent, although now that I see you, I'd like to make some changes to what I have, so that what I make will be more flattering to your lovely figure. We want to make sure that whatever we decide on will show you off to advantage."

"Lovely?" Lady Margaret laughed. "You don't think I'm too slender?"

Tina was confused. She shook her head. "No, not at all. Honestly, I'm looking forward to working with someone as well proportioned as you, if I may be so bold. I've been working with a number of other women and have had to alter a number of designs they'd asked for in order to, er, minimize certain aspects of their form and show off their advantages."

The woman tilted her head just a touch. "Have you spoken with my brother?"

"The duke? Yes. He called me into his study to inform me that I was only to use the best fabrics and no cost was to be spared," Tina said. She certainly wasn't going to tell this sweet girl the truth of what the duke had said to her.

Lady Margaret narrowed her eyes. "Is that all he told you?"

"Yes, my lady, that was all." Tina crossed her fingers underneath her sketchbook where Lady Margaret couldn't see.

"Very well." She gave Tina a slightly disbelieving smile but was clearly willing to move forward. "May I see your designs, then?"

"Of course!" Tina moved to the sofa, placing her sketchbook onto the beautiful wooden inlaid table. "Do you mind?" she asked, indicating the sofa.

"No! Please, sit down," Lady Margaret said, seating herself at Tina's side.

Tina opened up her sketchbook and took a pencil out of her reticule. Quickly, as Lady Margaret watched, she made some adjustments to her designs, so they were more appropriate to one with such a slender figure. It was truly going to be a pleasure dressing this girl. "It's such a shame," Tina said as she worked, "that current court fashions won't allow us to show off your lithe figure. But we'll make up for that with your ball gown." She turned and gave Lady Margaret a smile.

"I know just the sort of dress that would be most flattering," she continued. "Simple lines, perhaps a slight train, but nothing that would get in your way as you danced. Oh yes, I can most definitely create something very elegant."

"You truly think so," Lady Margaret said, clearly still not quite believing her.

"Absolutely." Now Tina understood what the Duke of Warwick had been trying to tell her. It wasn't just that Lady Margaret was sheltered, she was lacking in confidence. She needed a dress and a modiste to show her just how beautiful she truly was. Well, that would be easy. That, in fact, was the part that Tina found easiest and most enjoyable. Finding the beauty in every woman, that was the magic of being a modiste. It was what the amazing Lord Ayres had taught her that day at her mother's fashion party. Truly, she owed the man everything. He had opened her eyes to what was quickly becoming her greatest joy.

At the end of an hour, Tina and Lady Margaret had poured over the preliminary sketches Tina had brought with her and the fashion magazines the girl had on hand. They pulled elements from various dresses and discarded half of what they'd taken. The court gown would be simple without a lot of the flounces some women adopted. It would be magnificent, as befitted the sister of a duke, but as flattering as possible. The ball gown, however, was truly going to be a stunning piece that would allow Lady Margaret to show the world how elegant one could be. Once again, there would be no question in anyone's mind that the woman wearing it was related to a duke. His Grace had said that no expense should be spared, and indeed, none was. Tina could hardly wait to get started making this masterpiece. It was going to take some days to do so and at least one, if not two, more fittings.

~**March 29**~

Claire picked up Christianne in her open barouche at precisely three as her invitation had stated. She could always be counted on to be on time. Christianne liked that about her.

She was also, like her, a no-nonsense sort of person if a little overly precise. Although younger by nearly ten years, she and Claire had quickly become fast friends when Christianne had returned to society four years ago,. It had surprised Christianne that Claire had wanted to be friends with her. She was much better connected than Christianne had ever been and had a reputation as a leader within society. But it turned out that while being well respected was excellent, it didn't mean that one had any true friends. It turned out that Claire was unusually lonely for one who was invited everywhere.

"Is that another one of your Miss Rowan's creations?" Claire asked as Christianne stepped into the carriage.

"Yes, what do you think?" Christianne answered, sitting next to her friend.

"It's a little daring for one your age, but I like it. The girl does have a certain flair to her designs, doesn't she?"

"It's what I like about them. The cut is simple, but there's always something of interest to pull it out of the ordinary."

Claire nodded. "I agree, and I'm beginning to rethink my decision not to get a dress made by her."

"Well, you know where I stand on the matter," Christianne said with a laugh as they passed through the park gates. In truth, all Christianne could do since she'd met with her daughter was think of how else to get that girl more clients.

She still couldn't believe Rowan was blackmailing them. She'd trusted that man with her daughter, with her child. He'd watched her grow up, cared for her—or so Christianne had thought. Now she realized he was just doing it for the money. It hurt to know that her trust had been so misplaced.

She had to set aside her anger, however, and focus on doing all she could to help Tina, and getting her more clients seemed to be the only way.

"You'd like us all to order entire wardrobes from the girl, I imagine," her friend said with a laugh, pulling Christianne from her thoughts.

"Well, I don't know that I'd go quite that far, but yes, I would like to see her become a success." It was such an understatement of the truth, but it was all she could admit to out loud, even to her closest friend.

Claire narrowed her eyes at Christianne. "So tell me the truth, what made you set her up here in London? It couldn't simply be the originality of her dresses. I imagine there are any number of modistes throughout the country creating such things. Was it for your own reputation? To be known as having an eye for fashion?"

"And when have I ever proclaimed to have such a thing?" Christianne asked after a burst of laughter. Even when she was half-terrified for her daughter, Claire could *still* make her laugh.

"Never, which is why it's so curious."

"Oh, do look, there is Lord Vallentyn with his mother. That poor boy, the way she pushes him!" Christianne said, deliberately turning the conversation. She had absolutely no desire to tell

Claire the truth. The fact that her friend suspected there was a truth behind her actions was disturbing enough.

Claire shook her head sadly. "She is determined to not only see him well settled but a politician too. She's constantly pushing him at the daughters of the leaders of Parliament." Claire tsked.

"And he seems to have absolutely no interest," Christianne agreed.

"Well, he is a dutiful son, you have to give him that," Claire said.

A silence fell in the carriage as the two women looked to see who was riding with whom. It helped to keep Christianne's mind distracted from her troubles, and goodness knows she needed that.

Her gaze fell onto the walking path beside Rotten Row. "Oh look, there is Miss Sheffield accompanied by no less than *two* young men," she said with a laugh.

Claire gave a snort of laughter. "That girl. She is like honey to flies."

"And is that another following her?" Christianne asked, craning her neck a little to see properly around the horses.

"Yes, I believe it is Lord Swindon."

"I don't know him."

Claire tsked. "You haven't missed anything. He's not a pleasant person."

"Then I wonder why Miss Sheffield agreed to walk with him?"

"It doesn't precisely look like she did. He is walking behind her and not with her," Claire pointed out.

"Good afternoon, ladies." A deep, smooth voice that Christianne would know anywhere came from her other side. And there was another of her problems. Her heart started to pound in her chest, and she could feel herself grow warm at just the sound of his voice.

"Good afternoon, Lord Ayres," Claire said before Christianne could even catch her breath. What was she going to do about Liam? *Enjoy him!* Her daring mind answered back.

"I had thought it was a fine day for a ride. Now I find it is an absolutely perfect day for one because only on such a perfect day would I find two such beautiful ladies out enjoying the weather as well," he said, his eyes twinkling with good humor.

Christianne giggled—giggled! Her! She *never* giggled. "You are doing it too brown, my lord," she said, reprimanding him with a smile on her lips.

"Me? Never!" he cried, widening his eyes with pretend shock.

Even Claire burst out laughing at that.

"I've been meaning to..." Christianne started.

"You know you've never..." Lord Ayres said at the same time.

They both stopped with a laugh.

"I beg your pardon, ladies first," he said.

"Oh no, it's nothing. I just..." *Have been absolutely wracked with guilt ever since the fashion party and haven't had the nerve to invite you back.* Instead, she curved her lips into a smile. "I've been meaning to invite you over once again. I still feel just awful about that mix up last week."

"No worries. We're all busy now that the season is truly beginning," he said with an understanding look in his eye. It was as if he could see her true feeling on the matter and was telling her that it was all right. Oh yes, *this* is what she'd been missing—someone who understood her.

"I shall, you know," she said.

"I know. And I shall patiently await my summons."

"Or you could just show up. You've been known to do that as well," she said with a teasing smile.

A matching smile grew on his lips as well. "I could, indeed. I wasn't certain what sort of welcome I'd be met with, however." The smile faded from his eyes into something far more serious.

The last time she and Liam actually spent any meaningful time together was twenty years ago—when Tina had been conceived. Christianne had disappeared soon after that without a word and had avoided being alone with him ever since—he was simply too dangerous to her heart and her marriage. But it was time to put an end to that. Her husband was gone, and she was free to do as she liked. Not only that, but she'd lived with her guilt of having hidden his child from him for long enough. Yes, it was time she came clean.

If only she weren't such a frightened ninny!

"I shall send over a note giving you a time when it would be convenient," she said, knowing full well—as did he—that that note might never come.

Why was she so scared? Why couldn't she just face him and tell him the truth? She wanted to. But after hiding it for so long... It was going to be difficult to reveal even to the one to whom it was owed.

And with that thought, the answer to Tina's problem was solved within her own mind.

Of course! How stupid of her! This was something Tina's father would be able to fix. She was sure of it. Liam was a very resourceful man—in more ways than one. He was clever *and,* it had recently been revealed to society not so very long ago, wealthy. Surely, he would be able to think of a way to get Tina out from under Rowan's thumb.

But first, she had to tell Liam that he *had* a daughter. Only after that would he be able to rescue her. Christianne bit her tongue on the curse that hovered there.

"I shall await your missive with bated breath," he said. With a nod he was gone, riding down Rotten Row on his high-stepping gelding, looking better than any man should, especially at his age.

"I don't suppose you'll tell me what that was about either," Claire said with a sniff.

Christianne just gave her a smile before pointing out another young lady, who was riding with her papa looking for all the world as if she'd rather be having a tooth pulled. Christianne absolutely *would* invite Liam over...soon. Very soon. She just had to get up the nerve.

CHAPTER SEVEN

"Eh, Warwick, I think I may have found something," Martin started.

For the past five minutes, Warwick had been sitting and staring at the same line in the report he was supposed to be reading.

"Do you think it went all right?" he asked, voicing what had been going through his mind. Oh, not that the meeting between Margaret and Miss Rowan had been at the top of his mind. No, oddly it had been Miss Rowan herself. Her beautiful, expressive eyes. Her lovely full lips. Her...

"Warwick!" Martin said sharply. "I've found something that I think you should take a look at."

"I'm sure I'll hear about it—I won't be going out to my club this evening, by the way, you might want to tell the chef."

Martin sighed heavily. "I don't know how this could have happened, honestly, Warwick. I've been keeping an eye on these things, but somehow suddenly, there it was."

Yes, there she was, Warwick thought. But she shouldn't be. She shouldn't be on his mind at all. What was wrong with him, thinking about a modiste! A seamstress! Honestly! He shook his head in disgust at himself.

"I know what you're thinking, but in truth, I do check these numbers every month. I would have noticed the irregularity before this if it had been there. I can assure it was not," Martin said.

"I'm sure it was fine. I would have heard if it wasn't, right?" Warwick said, ignoring his secretary. Those eyes were still there in his mind, but now they weren't just staring at him, they were smiling at him. They were beautiful—she was beautiful when she smiled.

"I thought it was fine too. Honestly, I did, but now there's this and it just doesn't add up," Martin agreed.

"Maybe I should speak with her now," Warwick suggested.

"Him. You mean him, and yes, you're right you should. I'll write to him immediately and tell him to get up to London. It'll take him a few days to get here, but that will give me time to go back through the older reports once again." Martin sat back down at his desk and pulled a piece of paper from his desk.

"Him? Him who? What are you talking about?" Warwick asked, finally paying attention to his secretary and realizing they weren't having the same conversation.

Martin turned around at his desk. "Williams. The steward at Finchcomb. What were you talking about?"

"I was talking about Margaret's meeting with Miss Rowan."

"Who's Miss Rowan?"

"The modiste *I* hired because you couldn't find one," Warwick asked his secretary pointedly.

"Oh yes, well... I think you might want to pay attention to this instead. I think Williams has been helping himself to your income."

"What?" Warwick got up to take a look at the ledger that had been pushed to the edge of Martin's desk.

Martin pointed out the discrepancies in rents collected from one month to the next.

"That does not look good. Get Williams up here immediately," Warwick said.

"I'm in the middle of writing the letter!" Martin protested.

"Oh well, good." His mind turned back to Margaret and Miss Rowan. "She'll tell me at dinner, I'm sure she will."

Martin sighed heavily. "Of course she'll tell you at dinner. She's a very forthcoming girl."

"No, she's not. She's actually a very quiet, unassuming girl," Warwick pointed out. Really, Martin should know that about Margaret. The three of them *had* grown up together.

"Well yes, but when she's got something to tell you..."

Someone knocked at the door, and Martin gave him a smug smile. "See? I told you she'd let you know." He got up and opened the door with a flourish.

The butler walked in giving the secretary an odd look.

"Your Grace, the chef would like to know if you'll be joining Lady Margaret for dinner this evening," the man said.

Warwick frowned at Martin. "Yes. Please tell him that I will. Thank you, Archibald."

"Very good, Your Grace, thank you." The man left and Martin closed the door behind him.

"Well, I'm certain you'll hear all about it at dinner."

~*~

Warwick had been certain as well, but Margaret was as quiet as ever that evening. He waited patiently all through drinks before the three of them—Warwick, Margaret, and Cousin Sonora—sat down for dinner. He then listened with growing impatience to their cousin's lecture on the dangers of riding in Hyde Park in the afternoon. When the pudding was placed in front of them, his patience was at an end.

"I do beg your pardon, Cousin Sonora, but I would like to hear from Margaret how her meeting with the new modiste went," he said as politely as he possibly could.

"Modiste? Horrid people!" his cousin said vehemently. "How could you subject your sister to meeting with yet another one? Do you have no care at all for her delicate sensibilities?"

"Actually, Cousin," Margaret said, interjecting quietly, "Tina was wonderful."

"Was she?" Warwick said, giving his sister his full attention.

"Oh yes! You wouldn't believe, Warwick, she actually told me that I have a lovely figure! Can you imagine?"

"She was clearly lying to get you to purchase more gowns from her," their cousin said.

"Well, no. In fact, I had to remind her that I needed two. She would have just made the court gown for me if I hadn't repeat that I need a ball gown as well," Margaret said.

"But she will be making both dresses? And you're happy with her and her designs?" he asked.

"Court gowns are atrocious!" Sonora practically screeched.

"Well yes, they are, and so Tina is going to do the best she can within the confines of what's acceptable. It's going to be very elegant. The skirt will be covered with pearls, the dress itself will be a very pale pink, almost white, and I'll wear the required ostrich feathers in my hair. She said she'd purchase them and dye them to match the color of the dress."

"That sounds very nice," Warwick agreed, nodding.

"Harrumph," Sonora said. She pinched her lips and redirected her gaze somewhere off into the distance.

"And for my ball gown, we'll go with a white gown, naturally, with an overdress of Brussels lace."

"That sounds lovely," her brother said, giving her an encouraging smile.

"The cut is going to be very simple and elegant. She said that with my figure, straight lines would be most flattering and would make me look taller."

"You are not short," Cousin Sonora exclaimed.

"No, she didn't say that I was. In fact, we're the same height, Tina and I, but the dress will be of a more classic, elegant design."

"That sounds perfect," Warwick said. "And you liked her?"

"Oh, very much! She is new to London too, you know. She agreed with me that it was all very overwhelming but was certain we would both feel more comfortable in no time. She thought maybe I should get out more—not to parties, of course, since

I'm not yet presented—but just for rides in the park or walks. She told me of a wonderful bookstore on Bedford Street near Covent Garden and suggested I might enjoy spending some time there as well. Do you know it?"

"What, pray tell, does a modiste know of bookstores?" Cousin Sonora asked.

"Well, she's apparently an avid reader, Cousin. She even recommended a few books to me that sounded wonderful. There's a new novel by Maria Edgeworth, Warwick. Tina said it was marvelous."

"I've heard it is quite enjoyable. I don't know this particular bookstore, however."

"I'm certain it is absolutely scandalous—a novel by a woman! I refuse to allow you to read such garbage!" the cousin said with finality.

"You have been too long out of society, Cousin. Maria Edgeworth is a very respectable authoress. She writes moral tales of which you would certainly approve," Warwick said to Sonora. He then turned to his sister. "The bookstore sounds intriguing. I should very much like to learn more about it. Shall we plan on an outing tomorrow? We can pick up this Edgeworth novel, and I heard there's a book on trade that sounded interesting. And for you, Cousin, there's a book on atonement I've heard about," Warwick said, turning away from Sonora, who was truly beginning to cross the line.

Margaret, who'd been drinking her wine when Warwick said this, choked and starting coughing violently. Warwick reached over and gave her a pat on her back, but she indicated she would be fine.

Their cousin's lips thinned noticeably as she looked across at her charge. But when she turned back to Warwick, she gave him a true smile and said,

"That does sound informative. Just the sort of thing a lady *should* read—not some *novel*."

He gave her a nod.

"Are you certain you have the time to spare?" Margaret asked, now able to speak again.

"For you, I will make the time." He turned to their cousin. "You need not come, Cousin. I'll purchase your book for you. I wouldn't wish for you to feel uncomfortable."

"I... I..." She took in a deep breath and nodded. "I *would* prefer to stay here, thank you, Your Grace." She looked as if she wasn't actually so certain of this but had made up her mind to it lest she appear contradictory.

"Excellent! Shall we say four o'clock tomorrow afternoon? We can go to the bookstore and then drive through the park on our return. Perhaps even stop for ices at Gunter's. What do you say?" Warwick suggested.

This time Margaret clapped her hands like an excited child. "Oh, Warwick, that sounds—r"

"Overindulgent," Sonora interrupted with a frown.

"Perfect," Margaret finished.

"It's settled then," he said, giving his sister a smile.

~March 30~

"What do you know of the Duke of Warwick?" Tina asked her mother as they walked down Bedford Street toward the Wheat & Sons bookshop the following day. It was the oddest thing, but Tina was really enjoying spending time with her mother and found herself doing so much more often. At first, she'd sought her out for help, then guidance, and now companionship. It was both wonderful and made her long for what they could have had.

"Not much. He's a rather aloof man. I've not seen him often at parties even though he's a young man. Why do you ask?" Lady Norman glanced at Tina out of the corner of her eye.

"I've been commissioned to make a court dress and ball gown for his sister, Lady Margaret," Tina said, pausing ever so briefly to look in the window of a haberdashery.

"That's wonderful! Your name is spreading," Lady Norman said, a smile blooming on her face.

"Yes. I believe it was the Duchess of Kendell who recommended me to His Grace," Tina said.

Lady Norman nodded. "That is exactly why I invited her! Oh, not necessarily for her recommendation to the Duke of Warwick but to recommend you to anyone. She is well respected and people to come to her for advice on all matters."

"Then your evil plan is working," Tina said with a laugh.

"Well, I wouldn't consider it evil, but yes, it is working."

The two went into the bookshop and immediately separated, each looking for what interested them. Tina went to the counter.

"Excuse me, but do you have the latest issue of the Ladies' Monthly Museum?" she asked the gentleman there.

"Yes, Miss. We just received a delivery. If you wouldn't mind waiting a moment, I'll get one from the back."

"Thank you," she said, giving him a smile. While she waited for his return, she perused the books on a nearby table. There were titles dealing with agriculture, manufacturing, and business interests.

"Tina!" a familiar voice called out.

She looked up to find the Duke of Warwick and Lady Margaret approaching.

"Oh, Lady Margaret! Your Grace. How lovely to see you both!" she said, giving Margaret a smile and a curtsy. The duke was looking as handsome and yet, at the same time, as boring as he had the first time they'd met. Just like before, he was wearing a drab brown coat. Today, he'd paired it with an even darker plain brown waistcoat. Honestly, what did this man have against color? Even black would have been preferable to brown!

"What a wonderful surprise," Lady Margaret was saying. Tina pulled her eyes away from the duke to smile at her new client. She was in a very pretty, if overly flounced sprigged muslin. The cut of it didn't do anything for her pretty figure, but it didn't detract from her beauty like the duke's clothing.

Warwick gave her a cool nod.

"I'm so pleased you acted on my recommendation," Tina said, turning back to Lady Margaret.

"Of course! And Warwick was so kind to take some time from his work to bring me," Lady Margaret said with a glance at her brother.

"Are you interested in the books on agriculture, or is it the manufacturing that has caught your eye?" His Grace asked with a twinkle of mischief in his eye.

"What?" Tina asked, confused for a second. She followed his line of sight to the books on the table she'd been about to look through and gave a laugh. "Oh, no. I'm just waiting for the clerk—"

"Here you are, Miss. You are the first to get a copy of this month's issue," the shop assistant said, coming up to her just at that moment. He handed her the magazine she'd requested.

"Oh, thank you." She turned and showed it to the duke and his sister. "It's important that I keep up with the latest fashions, naturally."

"Oh, I'd like a copy of that as well," Lady Margaret told the man.

He immediately handed her one from the stack he'd brought with him. "Of course, Miss. And for you, sir?"

The duke looked at the man oddly. "I am not interested in ladys' fashions, thank you."

Lady Margaret burst out laughing. The clerk turned bright pink. "Oh, no! I meant to ask if there was anything in particular I could show you."

"I heard there was a new book on trade," His Grace said, glancing over the books on the table.

"Ah, yes, I know the one you mean. It is this way, if you would follow me." The man led the duke away.

Tina watched the Duke of Warwick go, admiring the breadth of his shoulders and tapering of his waist. The cut of his clothing was exquisite, even if the colors weren't.

CHAPTER EIGHT

"Can you recommend any other novels, Miss Rowan? I've picked up the latest by Mrs. Edgeworth," Lady Margaret said, holding up the book in question.

"I'm afraid not," Tina admitted. "I don't read novels very often, I'm afraid. I usually prefer histories and biography."

"Really?"

Tina nodded. "I've always found other people's lives so fascinating." She laughed.

Lady Margaret smiled. "Well, but novels are all about someone else's life. The characters always have such wonderful adventures, and I'm sure they're more exciting than a dry history."

"Have you read the adventures of Alexander the Great? He traveled all the way to India."

"No! Who is it by?" Lady Margaret asked.

Tina laughed. "Oh, it's not a novel, it's a history. Alexander the Great was an ancient Greek who—"

"Have you found what you wanted?" Tina's mother asked as she approached them, her eyes still focused on a book in her hand.

"Oh, yes. Er, Lady Margaret, may I present Lady Norman? She's my patroness here in London," Tina said quickly.

The two women greeted each other.

"How lovely to meet you, Lady Margaret," Lady Norman said.

"And you, my lady," Margaret responded immediately. "I suppose I should thank you for bringing Miss Rowan to town. She's going to be making a few gowns for me."

"Yes, which I need to get back to. I do beg your pardon," Tina said quickly before things got any more awkward than they were already.

"Indeed," her mother agreed. "I'll just make our purchases." She gave Margaret a nod and then turned to the clerk, who was back behind the counter.

"Well, I do hope you find something wonderful to read, and I'll see you on Wednesday for your fitting."

"Thank you. I'll look forward to it," Lady Margaret said with a smile.

Tina joined her mother at the counter. She started to pull out her purse but was stopped by Lady Norman's hand on her own. "I've already taken care of it."

"Oh! Thank you." Tina felt a little odd having her mother pay for her, but then she had paid for so many things recently as Tina set up her business and settled into London. She supposed she should be used to it by now.

Her mother gave the clerk a nod and started toward the door. Tina kept up with her. "You needn't have..." she started.

"It's nothing."

Tina figured that it probably *was* nothing to her mother, while for her it would mean not having any meat that day or some other economy. If her mother was happy to make such purchases for her, she would accept them—for now.

"If that was Lady Margaret, I think I saw your duke," her mother said as soon as they were outside.

"He's not *my* duke." Tina laughed.

"No, that's not quite what I meant."

"I understand. And yes, he was there too. It was very kind of him to escort Lady Margaret to the book shop. When I met Lady Margaret, she seemed lonely, so I suggested she might try to get out more. Even though she's not yet been presented, I thought it would be good for her to meet some people."

"You are absolutely right, but does she not have a chaperone who will introduce her about?"

"Apparently her chaperone is an older cousin who hasn't been in society for over twenty years and doesn't like going out."

"Oh, no! That won't do at all. The poor girl."

"I know. She is completely dependent on her brother and, naturally, he is very busy."

"Yes, I imagine he is. And yet, he did find the time to take her out this afternoon," her mother pointed out.

"It *was* very good of him." She paused and thought about it. Yes, not only was the duke one of the most handsome men she'd seen since coming to London, he was clearly a thoughtful and kind brother. She'd been shocked and a little flustered when he and Margaret had approached her in the book shop. His greeting couldn't have been haughtier, but the laughter in his eyes when he asked about the books she'd been looking at had somehow immediately put her at her ease. How could a man be both cold and warm at the same time? It must be some talent the gentlemen of the aristocracy had in order to charm a girl with just a wink of an eye.

~*~

"Have you heard of Alexander the Great?" Margaret asked Warwick as they sat in his carriage enjoying their ices after their excursion to the bookstore.

"Who?"

"Apparently he was some ancient Greek?" she said before popping another spoonful of the sweet-tart delicacy into her mouth.

"Oh! That Alexander the Great. Yes, of course I've heard of him. I had to learn about him in school. Why?" Warwick asked, scraping the bottom of his cup and wondering if he wanted to order a second.

"Nothing. Miss Rowan mentioned him to me. I asked her at the book shop what sort of books she liked to read, and she said she liked histories about Alexander the Great and people like that. She said he went on fantastic adventures."

"I don't know. It all seemed rather dry and boring to me, but then the professors at Eton could make even the most exciting topics deadly dull."

Margaret laughed and handed her empty cup to the waiting groom. Reluctantly, Warwick handed his over as well, deciding he probably shouldn't have another.

But whoever heard of a seamstress who read history?

~**April 2**~

After two days of working steadily on Margaret's dress, to the exclusion of all the others she had yet to make—and feeling so guilty for shoving them aside—the court dress was finally ready for a fitting. The ball gown would be much easier because the style was one Tina was familiar with, and it had much more simple lines. But the court dress, honestly, was the most awkward piece of clothing Tina had ever had to create.

She'd done a lot of study to discover exactly what sort of gown Lady Margaret would have to wear. One had to wear panniers and on top of that a voluminous skirt with layers of embroidery, not to mention a train and the feathers one had to have.

Tina had had to take a hackney to the duke's home because of the panniers she was carrying for Lady Margaret to try with the dress. And then there was the dress itself, which was larger and had more material than anything Tina had ever made.

She juggled them all now as she attempted to knock on the door. Finally, to her great relief, the door opened without her having to actually put anything down.

"Oh, thank you!" she said with a sigh as the footman pulled open the door.

"Miss Rowan, isn't it?" he asked.

"Yes. Would you mind very much...?" She indicated the panniers, which were about to fall from her hand as she juggled them, the package with the dress, and her own bag of sewing materials.

"Oh yes, of course!" he said, jumping forward and relieving her of the hoops.

"What are these?" he asked, stepping back so she could enter the house.

"Those are for Lady Margaret to wear under her court dress," Tina explained.

"Oh!" The man almost dropped them as if they were hot coals.

Tina laughed. "It's all right. She hasn't worn them yet."

"Er, no, it's just that... Uh, they're a lady's underthings," he said in a loud whisper.

"Yes, they are," she said trying to hold back her giggles.

"I'll, er, I'll just inform Lady Margaret that you are here." He backed away, still holding the panniers gingerly. "Am I to take these up to her rooms?"

"Please," Tina nodded.

"If you would just wait here a moment," he said then went up the grand stairway.

Tina sighed and settled the other things in her arms more comfortably. She could hear a man's voice somewhere not far off and figured it was the duke speaking to someone in his study, which was just on the other side of the hall.

Her eye was caught by the sparkling of little rainbows on the white marble floor. She turned and saw the sunlight dancing through the fan window above the front door. The rainbows looked so pretty and added some beautiful color to the otherwise stark white and gold of the foyer.

The duke's voice rose louder. She couldn't make out what he was shouting about, but it was obvious he was not happy. A shudder of trepidation slipped down Tina's spine. Her foster father had shouted like that, and you knew when he did so that whoever was on the other side of the argument was most likely to come away with quite a few bruises in addition to a bent ear. Luckily, Tina had learned to keep her own head down. She did her best not to cross the man, but sometimes he would be angered no matter what she did. She was still determined not to upset him.

It reminded Tina of how very grateful she was to the Duchess of Kendell for recommending her for this job. Not only was she being commissioned to make these two gowns, but there would probably be more on top of that, and Lady Margaret was the sweetest girl she could ever hope to work with. Tina was really beginning to like her a great deal. She wasn't certain about her brother though. He was handsome—despite his brown clothes—but she felt on edge when she was around him. He'd been very charming at the bookstore, but she could never allow herself to forget that he was a duke.

The study door opened, allowing the Duke of Warwick's voice to ring out for the whole house to hear. "...dare you attempt to swindle me? Did you honestly think you would get away—"

"Miss Rowan?" A gentle voice next to her made Tina jump.

Lady Margaret was standing there. Tina hadn't even heard her approach.

"Oh, I beg your pardon, Lady Margaret," Tina started.

"It's all right. Goodness, I can't imagine who Warwick is yelling at like that," Lady Margaret said.

"I don't know, but I wouldn't like to be in his shoes," Tina said, trying to give Lady Margaret a smile. She wasn't certain it came across very well though.

"No. Warwick doesn't get angry very often, but when he does, everyone knows it." She gave Tina a sympathetic smile. "He's usually a very kind and gentle person. His anger, while terrifying at its peak, doesn't last very long."

Tina could only nod. So far of what she'd seen of the man, he did seem to be generally kind. He had after all tried to warn Tina about Lady Margaret's need for some emotional support and had taken her out himself just the other day. But, it was more than evident that he was a duke who commanded respect and obedience.

"Shall we go up to my room?" Lady Margaret said, indicating the stair.

"Yes, thank you." Tina gratefully followed her up and away from the shouting.

~April 3~

"Lady Norman, you absolutely must dance this evening. Promise me you will," Miss Bradmore said after she and her parents had welcomed Christianne to her coming out ball.

"Well, of course, should some handsome gentleman ask..." Christianne turned and fluttered her eyelashes at the girl's father.

Lord Bradmore laughed. "I would love to, you know I would, my lady," he began, "but I have been tasked with keeping the non-dancing gentlemen entertained in the card room."

Christianne let out a dramatic sigh. "Well then, I shall simply have to rely on others, I suppose."

"I'm certain you will not lack for partners," Lady Bradmore said with a broad smile. "There are plenty of handsome gentlemen here."

"I believe you, my lady, and if you will excuse me, I shall go and see for myself," Christianne said. She gave them all a nod and then proceeded farther into the ballroom.

She truly wasn't so much worried about getting dance partners as she was on securing one in particular. A quick look around the room was all she needed to locate Liam.

As always, he was surrounded by a bevy of gentlemen most likely all wanting fashion advice, and women of varying ages captivated by whatever charming nonsense he was spouting. There was just something about that man... Christianne shook her head and gave a laugh. He was like a puddle of honey to the flies of society.

"He is handsome," Miss Sheffield said, appearing by Christianne's side along with Miss Hemshawe. "It's almost a shame he's too old for me."

Christianne gave a bark of laughter. "He's old enough to be your father, my dear." The two girls looked lovely. Christianne wondered if the gowns they were wearing were the creations Tina had made for them. Miss Sheffield's peaches and cream complexion was enhanced by her soft white gown, and her green eyes shone with laughter. Miss Hemshawe, always a daring one, was wearing a pale blue gown that showed her strong, petite figure off to advantage and brought out the brilliant blue of her eyes.

"I know," Miss Sheffield said with a giggle.

"I've heard that it's not too unusual for older gentlemen to marry younger ladies," Miss Hemshawe offered.

"It is true," Christianne agreed. "My husband was twenty years my senior, but I'm certain that Miss Sheffield, and you as well, Miss Hemshawe, have plenty of gentlemen much closer to your age just waiting for you to notice them."

Miss Sheffield laughed, and Miss Hemshawe smiled, acknowledging the truth of her words.

"Perhaps that's my problem. There are simply too many. How is a girl ever to decide which gentleman is the right one for her?" Miss Sheffield asked. "One has the most soulful blue eyes, another has a laugh that makes my insides melt, a third can dance like a dream."

"Every gentleman has something that makes him wonderful and special," Miss Hemshawe added.

"I'm sure I'll never find one who I would want to marry above all the others," Miss Sheffield concluded.

Christianne laughed and shook her head. "You'll know when you find the right one. And hopefully, when you do, your fathers will approve as well." Christianne had had to live for too many years with her own father's choice for her despite the fact that another had held her heart. Her eyes settled once more on that other man now.

Chapter Nine

A handsome gentleman with the look of a dandy approached Christianne, and the two young ladies, with Mrs. Aldridge on his arm. On the older lady's other side was her son, who Christianne had met once before. "Dear Lady Norman, Miss Sheffield, Miss Hemshawe, please allow me to introduce to you my nephew, Lord Ainsby," the lady said. "And this is my son." She indicated the other young man with a proud smile on her lips.

The two young ladies curtsied, and Christianne gave the young men a nod as they bowed. The musicians had stopped tuning the instruments, which meant they were about to start the next set.

"It is an honor," Lord Ainsby said. "Miss Sheffield, may I have the pleasure of the next dance, er, if your chaperone doesn't mind?" he asked, looking from Miss Sheffield to Christianne and back again.

"Oh, I'm not her chaperone," Christianne said quickly.

"Lady Norman is the founder of the new Ladies' Wagering Whist Society, of which I am honored to be a member," Mrs. Aldridge explained to her nephew.

"Ah yes! We've heard about this elusive society," her son said with a polite smile. His cousin, Ainsby, raised his eyebrows a touch. "Are you both members as well?" he asked the two younger ladies.

"As a matter of fact, we are," Miss Hemshawe said with a smile.

"Would you mind telling me about it as we dance, Miss Hemshawe?" Mr. Aldridge asked with another bow toward that young lady.

"It would be my pleasure," Miss Hemshawe said.

"And you, Miss Sheffield, would you do me the honor?" Lord Ainsby asked, offering his hand.

"Thank you." The young lady in question put her hand in the gentleman's and allowed him to lead her out onto the floor.

"I'm so glad you saw her off. Now I can beg *you* to join me in the dance," Liam said, as he passed the young couple on his way to Christianne's side. "If you don't mind my stealing her away, madam?" he added to Mrs. Aldridge, who was watching the young couples fondly.

"Oh! By all means, don't let me stop you," the lady said with a start.

"No need to beg, Lord Ayres, I would be most happy to dance with you," Christianne said, beginning to feel downright playful. Oh yes, this *was* going to be a pleasant evening.

After the dance, Liam fetched Christianne a glass of lemonade, then seemed content to merely promenade about the periphery of the room with her, chatting as if they'd never been apart. When they went into supper together, Christianne saw a number of raised eyebrows on faces turned their way.

"I believe we're causing some talk," Liam said quietly, leaning closer to her.

"I've noticed as well," she admitted.

"Do you mind?" he asked, turning toward her, clearly curious to see her response.

She gave a little laugh. "I think I'm old enough I can do pretty much whatever I want and not bother with the gossips, don't you?"

He gave a laugh. "Oh, my dear, sweet Christianne, I don't think you ever bothered with what others said about you. It's one reason why I like you so much. You are plainspoken and confident enough not to pay others any mind."

Plainspoken, yes, absolutely. Christianne had always known that about herself. But confident enough not to worry about what others said of her? Hardly! Still, it was sweet of him to think so—and even nicer that he called her his "dear, sweet Christianne." Now that was something she did care about—perhaps too much? Never mind. So long as he continued to do so.

After dinner, the Earl of Chester got up the nerve to ask Christianne to dance, despite Liam's continued presence at her side.

"An excellent idea, Chester," Liam said, "No sense in continuing to feed the gossips and their wagging tongues any more than necessary." He gave a laugh even as he urged Christianne forward to take Lord Chester's hand.

Christianne gave his lordship a smile and then did take his hand. He was an altogether pleasant gentleman. They'd known each other for years, and she had always been able to count on him to ask her to dance.

"I suppose you're very happy to have Lord Ayres back in town," he remarked as the dance brought them together.

"I am. It has been too long since we've seen each other," she answered before moving away from him to take the hand of the lady next to her.

A hop and a turn-about later she said, "Is it very bad of us to spend so much time together this evening?"

They separated, but when they came together again for the simple pousette where he held both of her hands and led her forward and back, he said, "Oh, I don't know, it's certainly given people something to talk and wonder about."

"What are they wondering?" Christianne asked, beginning to get a little worried.

Lord Chester gave an infuriating laugh before moving away with the steps of the dance. It was a full, and very long, two minutes later that they were finally together again. He then had the temerity to change the subject to the weather! Christianne was fuming.

What in the world would people be wondering about? Whether she and Liam would become lovers? Whether they were just friends? If there was a trip to church in their future? It could be absolutely anything!

It saddened her that even she didn't know the answer to any of those questions. Truth be told, she had no idea what her relationship with Liam was or where it might end up. All she knew was that she owed the man the truth about his daughter. And she knew even more firmly that she was absolutely terrified in divulging the truth to him.

What it would do to their budding new relationship she had no idea, but she was almost certain it wouldn't be anything good. She also knew she was enjoying that relationship much too much to put it in jeopardy just yet.

On those disheartening thoughts, her dance with Lord Chester came to an end. She gave him her best smile and thanked him even as her eyes once again scanned the ballroom for Liam.

She didn't see him but was feeling very warm after the dance. A breath of fresh air wouldn't go amiss, she thought.

She was leaning out against the balustrade, enjoying the cool air and wondering if she should fetch someone for her shawl, when Liam's soft voice said, "How have we let so many years pass before we did this again?"

She turned toward him. He was staring out into the darkened garden. "It was you who went away just before I returned to town," she reminded him.

"Ah, yes," he sighed. He shook his head sadly. "Too many responsibilities."

"Which you left unchecked for far too long, I imagine," Christianne said.

He laughed. "You know me too well, my dear."

"You do enjoy your time here in London," she pointed out needlessly.

"And tend to forget all about my estate in Ireland when I do," he agreed. "And I have paid for that by being forced to stay away for so long. I am determined this time to keep an eye on goings on over there even while I am here. I have a new steward who is quite efficient, writing to me weekly."

"That's very good."

"Boring, but yes, it is necessary." He caressed the back of his knuckles down her cheek. "And before I left, it was you who was gone for much too long."

"Yes." She turned and watched through the French windows as the dancers hopped about inside the ballroom. Now, of course, would be the perfect time to tell him the truth. But would she?

Absolutely not! She was enjoying herself far too much.

~April 4~

Warwick stepped from his carriage outside of Powell's Club. He had taken to coming here rather than White's or Brooke's, where he also had a membership, for the quieter, more exclusive atmosphere.

Joshua Powell, the Viscount Wickford, owned the relatively new establishment and had made it into a rather nice club. Only those invited were able to join, and he kept the clientele limited to the upper echelons of society. Despite that, the gaming rooms always had a good crowd, and the reading room was never empty either. Warwick appreciated the quiet of the reading room, and tonight he was particularly looking forward to some good male companionship without a word of dresses, modistes, or any other fripperies enjoyed or required of a female.

He took one step in the door and stopped to inhale the relaxing scent of men, tobacco smoke, and fine liquor.

"Good evening, Your Grace," Lord Wickford greeted him with a pleasant smile. "Are you here to play or relax?"

He turned to his host who, as always, was wearing a well-cut jacket in a deep hue—Warwick couldn't tell in the dim lighting if it was navy or black—and matching breeches. His waistcoat, as well, was of a quiet elegance, soothing to the eye but unmistakably of the highest fashion. The man's straight white teeth and odd gold-colored eyes stood out from his darker complexion.

"Relax. Most definitely to relax. I have had enough of female goings-on for the past week," Warwick said emphatically.

Wickford laughed. "Ah. And the season's barely begun."

Warwick closed his eyes for a moment and took a deep breath. "And quite a season it's going to be, I'm sure."

"Finally looking to jump the broom?" the man asked.

Warwick looked at him curiously. "I'm sorry?"

"Jump the broom. Get hitched. Married," his host clarified.

"Oh! No! Not me. My sister. I'm bringing her out."

"Don't you have a female relative who can do that for you?" Wickford asked.

"Sadly, the only one I have doesn't like society. She's here with us and has promised to do her best, but, well, she's not happy about it. No, I'm afraid it's mostly going to be up to me."

The viscount nodded his head. "That is going to be difficult. My sympathies in advance."

"Thank you."

"Ah! But then perhaps you might be interested to learn that Lord Dartmouth is here. He's the Lord Chamberlain, isn't he? In charge of sending out the invitations for the Queen's Drawing Room," Wickford said, brightening.

"Dartmouth is here? Tonight?" Warwick asked, interested. "But I shouldn't bother him with business at the club. That wouldn't—"

"Oh, I'm sure he wouldn't mind. Come along, I know right where he is."

Warwick followed Wickford with some misgivings. It wasn't right to ambush a fellow at his club. On the other hand, if he could just find out when the next drawing room would be, things might get a lot easier. He'd already sent in Margaret's name, requesting she be on the invitation list, but it couldn't hurt to remind the Lord Chamberlain of this.

"My Lord Chamberlain," Wickford said, approaching the gentleman in question.

Dartmouth had his nose in a glass and his eyes on the newspaper in his lap. He finished swallowing his sip of liquor as he looked up. "Warwick, nice to see you again."

Warwick held out his hand. "Dartmouth. Don't mean to disturb..."

"Oh, not at all. Just reading about this damnable war. Ever going end, do you think?" Dartmouth asked, shaking his hand.

Warwick gave him a smile. "Eventually." He turned to Wickford. "Have a bottle of your finest rum sent over, would you?"

"Absolutely, Your Grace. It'll be my pleasure." With that, he bowed and left the two gentlemen alone.

"The man has excellent rum. Have you tried it? I hear it's from his own plantation in the West Indies," Warwick said, taking the chair next to the Lord Chamberlain.

"Is that so? No, I have to admit I've never much been a rum man. Awfully sweet, isn't it?"

"It is a touch. But the finer stuff is quite good."

A maid came and delivered the bottle and two glasses. Warwick poured them both two fingers of the rich, deep reddish-gold liquid. He handed a glass to Dartmouth. They saluted each other and then drank. The full-bodied liquor tasted of the oak barrel it had been aged in, giving it a wonderful smoky flavor finished off with the pleasant burn of the alcohol.

"Why, that's not bad. Not bad at all," Dartmouth said, looking into his glass from the side.

"Indeed," Warwick agreed.

They drank in silence for a few minutes, each enjoying his own thoughts.

"Your sister ready for the Queen's Drawing Room?" Dartmouth asked.

Warwick sat forward in his chair. "Listen, Dartmouth, I would never bother you about—"

The Lord Chamberlain held up a hand to stop his words. "Quite all right. Happens to me all the time. I'm used to it by now."

He didn't seem to be too upset as he poured himself more rum. He topped up Warwick's glass too. "I've got some very nice drinks and even a meal or two out of it, you know." He laughed.

Warwick gave him an apologetic smile.

"You've already written. I won't forget her when I send out the invitations tomorrow, I assure you. I do believe hers is already prepared, as a matter of fact. They just need to be signed and delivered." He paused to take a sip of his drink. "Oh, and the announcement will be in tomorrow's Gazette."

"I don't know how to thank you," Warwick said. With this invitation, Margaret would be well on her way to establishing herself within society and moving ever closer to finding a husband.

"You already have." He raised his glass once again before emptying it. With a satisfied smack of his lips, he put it down and went back to his newspaper.

Warwick laughed and picked up the paper that had been left on a nearby table. He wasn't finished with his rum just yet, however. There was still a good two-thirds of the bottle left, and he planned to empty at least half of it before he left for the evening. Hopefully, Dartmouth would help him with that, but if he didn't, he was pretty sure he could find someone else who would.

CHAPTER TEN

~April 6~

"Three days? Three days!" Tina repeated to herself staring at the note in her hand. Lady Margaret had sent it over first thing that morning and Tina still couldn't believe it. How was she going to get this court dress, with hundreds of pearls that still needed to be sewn onto the enormous skirt finished within three days?

And not only that, but she was beginning to get inquiries from the other ladies who'd ordered dresses from her. They weren't done because Tina had been working on getting Lady Margaret's court gown finished and her ball gown started. She'd also had to go back and forth with a few ladies on their designs and the material they wanted. Luckily, Lady Margaret's ball gown wouldn't take too much time thanks to its simpler lines, but still, it needed to be done, as did all of the other dresses she was making. So far she'd only finished two of the four that had been commissioned most recently.

For a moment, she just sat there pulling at her hair.

Why had she ever thought she could make it as a London modiste? How could she have come to the conclusion that she could do this? She shook her head. She'd had no choice. With her foster-father's threat hanging over her head, she'd had to come up with something. This was the best she could do at that moment.

But just because she'd designed and made a gown for her mother, clearly didn't mean that she could do the same thing ten times over. Designing dresses for the women of her village and the surrounding area wasn't the same as dressing the ladies of London society. Well, she supposed she could but not at the speed with which the dresses were expected. Somehow the ladies of the ton just didn't understand the time necessary to create a dress from scratch. Between tweaking each design for the individual lady, to the actual cutting and sewing of the dress, and all of its details of lace, hand embroidery and so on, making a dress could take days. And then there were the fittings, which because Tina didn't actually have a shop of her own, required a good deal of travel. It was too much!

She couldn't do it. She just couldn't do it!

She was going to have to slink back to her village a failure unable to make it in the big city. She was going to have to marry Caleb and somehow figure out how to calm his temper and live with his volatility or simply get used to being bruised and battered. Tina ached at the thought.

And somehow she was going to have to figure out how to reimburse her mother for the money she'd already lent Tina to buy the fabric to make these gowns she couldn't finish—because naturally none of these women had given her even a farthing for all the materials she'd needed. No, they would pay her afterward—maybe!

Tina stopped pulling at her hair and just dropped her head onto her knees. She was dizzy and her eyes burned with unshed tears. She would not cry. She *would* not!

But what *could* she do?

She was a coward and didn't have the nerve to marry Caleb. She didn't know if she would have the strength to deal with the pitying looks of other women when they saw her bruises.

But did she have the courage to stay here and try to finish the job? Did she have the wherewithal to actually succeed as a business woman, a modiste, and seamstress?

Her mind drifted back to all the nights she'd sat sketching dresses, copying the drawings she'd seen in the fashion magazines, and then making up her own versions of the same gowns. She'd made and remade clothing, working on getting the fit just right for each woman, taking in a tuck here, letting out an inch there until the fit was just right and as flattering as could be. She'd worked hard on her craft. Was she really ready to let all of that go?

Tina slapped away the tears beginning to escape the corners of her eyes.

No. She wasn't. She *could* do this! She had to!

Tina straightened her back. She was an excellent modiste. She'd proven that to herself and to so many others. Just as she had worked at learning how to draw and design dresses, she would learn to be a business woman. What she wasn't terribly good—or quick at—was the actual stitching.

That was what she needed! She shouldn't quit. No, absolutely not! She simply needed some help. She needed a seamstress. It was the only answer. She could design and cut the dresses, she just needed someone to do the actual stitching.

In a minute, she was on her feet with her hand gripping the handle of her front door. But there she stopped. It was all well and good to decide she needed help, and she even knew where she could get it, but how was she going to pay for it? Every single penny she earned had to go to her foster-father. All that her mother paid him every month, plus fifteen percent! And then there was the fact she didn't have any cash at hand because she hadn't received even a down payment from any of the ladies for whom she was making a gown.

But that was exactly what she needed. A down payment. An advance.

She turned around and went back into her front room. She pulled out a piece of paper from a small side table and dipped her pen in ink, then stopped. Who could she write to? Who could she ask for money?

She couldn't ask her mother, who'd already done enough, no, more than enough. There were even a few women whose dresses she'd actually finished but who hadn't paid her yet. But truly, it was Lady Margaret's dresses which had really cost the most both in terms of materials and time, and it was her court dress which had to get finished today. The duke it was!

She quickly wrote out a note and then reread it. It was polite but to the point. She needed a small advance on the cost of the dress in order to finish it on time, she'd written, and she asked that money be sent over that afternoon at the latest. She didn't specify how much. To be honest, she hadn't yet decided how much she was going to charge for the court dress. She would worry about that later. For now, she just needed enough to pay a seamstress to get the dress finished.

Within minutes, she was running down the stairs and to the fabric store just next door. She paused and grabbed a hold of the boy who was always hanging about trying to snitch purses from unsuspecting passers by. She gave him her note and the duke's address and promised him a ha'penny when he returned with an answer. The boy took off like a shot.

"Mr. Carpenter," Tina called out to the owner of the fabric shop. He was standing behind bolts of muslin counting something. "Mr. Carpenter, you don't happen to know of any journeywomen or seamstresses looking for work, do you?"

The gentleman looked up, his eyes wide. "Why, Miss Rowan, how do you do?"

"Very well, thank you, sir. And you?" she answered, giving him a quick curtsy. How embarrassing to have been reminded of her manners in this way. But truly, she hardly had time for such niceties.

"I am doing just fine, thank you. Now, what was it that you asked, my dear?"

"Seamstresses. You don't happen—" Tina started.

"Yes, yes, as a matter of fact, I know of a number of them who are always looking for work. Can you pay daily?" he asked, giving her a kind smile.

"Yes, naturally," Tina said, praying the boy would actually deliver her note and the duke would act on it by that evening. It was a great leap of faith, she knew, but she had no other choice.

"Excellent. I shall send someone up to your rooms in about a quarter of an hour."

Tina nearly sagged with relief. "Thank you, sir. Truly, I cannot thank you enough." She turned and trudged back up to her room.

Tina had just finished cutting out the pieces of Lady Sorell's ball gown when there was a knock on her door.

"Excuse me, but you wouldn't 'appen to be Miss Roman, would you? I was told she needed a seamstress?" The girl on the other side of the door asked.

"It's Rowan, and yes, I do," Tina said, giving the young woman a broad smile.

"Oh, well, today's yer lucky day! I'm Jane and I'm the best seamstress in Covent Garden," the girl said with a bright smile, puffing out her chest.

Tina swallowed her laughter and, instead, invited her in. "Excellent! Come right this way, Jane, and I'll put you to work."

She set Jane down in front of a window with the skirt from Lady Margaret's court dress and the box of pearls that needed to be sewn on to it. "Stitch on a pearl wherever you see a mark on the skirt. There's a pattern to it."

The girl nodded and began to work. Tina then sat herself in front of the other window and started to piece together the dress she'd just cut. When she looked up again about half an hour later, she noticed that the box of pearls looked to be more than half empty, and yet the skirt had very few pearls sewn onto it.

She closed her eyes and bit back a scream. It wasn't the girl's fault, it was her own. How could someone who worked as a journeywoman not be enticed by a box filled with expensive pearls?

Tina paused to think about how to handle the situation. How would Mrs. Britsworth, who she'd apprenticed with, have dealt with such a situation? She was a very clever woman, Tina knew, so she would have to be clever as well.

She stood up and set aside the dress she'd been working on. "Jane, I'm leaving the room for a moment. When I return, either that skirt will have a lot more pearls attached to it, or that box is going to have a great many more pearls in it. And then we'll switch and you can begin sewing this yellow gown, and I will finish with the pearls."

She didn't even wait for the girl to exclaim or deny anything but simply turned and walked away. It took a number of calming breaths out in the hallway to stop her hands from shaking. She could no more afford to lose those pearls to a desperate seamstress than that girl could afford to lose this job.

When she returned to the room, Jane was sitting in the chair Tina had been occupying, sewing together Lady Margaret's ballgown and the box was once again nearly full of pearls.

"Thank you," Tina said, taking up the court gown and settling herself in the other chair.

The girl just kept her head down and continued to sew.

A short time later, the urchin came knocking at her door. He handed her a note and she, in return, gave him the money she'd promised him. She started back to her front room when there was a second knock on the door. My goodness! Never had she had so many visitors!

"Yes?" she asked after finding a liveried footman standing on the other side.

He handed over a small leather pouch. "From His Grace, the Duke of Warwick." He then bowed and left her standing there, watching his retreating back.

"Well, that was fast!" she said to no one. She weighed the pouch in her hand. It was a lot heavier than she'd expected, but she certainly wasn't going to argue. She would have enough to pay Jane, and perhaps even Mr. Carpenter for some of the materials she'd purchased on credit from him. Silently, she thanked the duke. It was truly good of him to do as she'd asked so quickly.

She tucked the pouch inside a hidden pocket of her skirt and went back to work.

~April 7~

Warwick had never been so happy to see a day arrive since he'd been a boy waiting for Christmas. Although to some, only allowing three days between receiving the invitation for the Queen's Drawing Room and the event itself would probably be impossibly short, for him it had been three days of living hell. His sister had jumped and panicked at every little thing. She asked constantly if he thought Miss Rowan would make it on time with the dress. Their cousin had done nothing but wander the house muttering to herself. Finally, he'd simply had to leave to get any work done for the constant interruptions and overall tension seeping through the entire house. Even the staff was on edge, falling into squabbles amongst themselves.

That morning Warwick strode into the breakfast room ready to enjoy a hearty meal.

"What in the world could make you smile so brightly on this God-awful day?" Martin greeted him.

Warwick stopped. "It's not an awful day, it's a wonderful day. Today is the day we can all stop waiting and act. Today is the day of the drawing room, and by three o'clock this afternoon Margaret and Cousin Sonora are going to be at the palace meeting the queen, and I am *not* going to be there or have to do anything more than listen to how magical it all was at dinner tonight. Or perhaps I'll go out for dinner to celebrate—by myself. What do you think? Would that be too awful of me?"

Martin laughed. "Yes, I do think it would. Your presence will either be required to celebrate with your sister or console her for whatever might have conceivably gone wrong, or what she thinks *might* have gone wrong."

"Damn! I'm certain you're right." Warwick sighed. "Very well. I'll be here."

Chapter Eleven

"Is she here yet?" Margaret asked, appearing in the room like a ghost.

"Not as far as I know," Warwick answered, not even looking up from his current occupation of filling his plate with eggs, a ham steak, and potatoes.

"Oh, goodness," she said, probably wringing her hands if Warwick knew his sister, and he did. "Perhaps we should send a note asking her when she'll be arriving?"

He finally turned to her. She looked pale and drawn. "Did you get any sleep last night?" he asked.

"No, why, do I look as if I haven't slept?" she asked, a panicked note to her voice.

"No! No. You look radiant," he said.

"I do not! You are a horrid liar, Warwick," his sister said but smiled at him nonetheless.

He flicked a finger across her cheek as he passed her on his way to his seat at the head of the table. "Well, I'm certain you will look radiant once you are dressed. Have you considered wearing a touch of rouge?"

"Oh dear, is it that bad?" Margaret put her hands to her cheeks.

"No... Well, as I said, I'm sure you'll be fine later. And no, I don't think you should send a note to Miss Rowan. It is only just after eight and you don't actually have to get dressed until closer to two this afternoon."

"What? I've got to be there at 2:30!"

"All right, then you don't have to get dressed until one."

Margaret sighed. "Yes, I'm sure you're right. She probably won't be here until noon or so." His sister's shoulders sagged with disappointment for a moment, but she straightened them quickly.

"Are you going to eat?" he asked.

"Goodness, no! I couldn't stomach a thing!" And with that, she turned and left him to his peace and quiet. It was short-lived however as Miss Rowan showed up merely an hour later.

Warwick was in his office trying to concentrate on his work when a commotion in the foyer had him up and out of his chair to see what all the fuss was about. The floor was riddled with pins, spools of thread, odd bits of lace, and material.

"My sincere apologies, Miss Rowan!" a footman said, chasing after a tin that was rolling away with a clatter.

"It's all right, just so long as that box doesn't open. It's got pearls in it and if we lose them, it'll be a *real* problem," Miss Rowan said.

"What is going on here?" Warwick asked, his voice coming out much more sternly than he'd meant.

"I beg your pardon, Your Grace, it was my fault. I bumped into Miss Rowan as she was coming in the door," the footman said hurriedly.

"Don't listen to him, the fault was mine. I was just carrying too many things," Miss Rowan said.

"I don't care whose fault it is, get all of this picked up. Miss Rowan, Lady Margaret has been waiting anxiously for you all morning," Warwick said, frowning at both of them.

Miss Rowan's eyes widened, and she looked almost as if he'd hit her. Immediately he regretted his harsh tone of voice. He hadn't meant to upset her, he was just... Oh hell, he didn't know what he was doing when he was around this woman. All he knew for sure was that he wasn't himself, and he didn't like it. She was such a gentle, sensitive thing, certainly not much older than his sister, and here he was yelling at her. She clearly didn't deserve such treatment, and yet it was the way he'd been taught to treat the lower classes.

Yes, that was it. He needed to remind himself of their respective status and not think twice about how he treated her. Goodness, what was he doing worrying about the sensibilities of a seamstress?

"Oh, no!" Margaret said, coming on the scene. She immediately bent down to help pick up all the pins and bits and bobs.

"Lady Margaret, you shouldn't be doing that. I'll get all this picked up in a trice," Miss Rowan said, slipping a worried glance at Warwick. It felt like a stab to his chest seeing that fear in her eyes.

No, he couldn't deal with this any further. "Margaret, I'm sure that it will go faster if you let Miss Rowan and the footman take care of it."

"Perhaps," Margaret said, standing up again.

"Yes, indeed, His Grace is right. I'll be with you in just a moment, my lady," Tina said, her voice beginning to sound strained.

"I am certainly glad to see that you came early, Tina," Margaret said, clutching her hands together in front of her.

"Of course! We have a lot to do to get you ready for this afternoon!" Miss Rowan said from the floor, putting the last of her pins into her bag. She started to rise, but Warwick quickly stepped forward and held out a hand to help the woman onto her feet.

Her bright green eyes stared up at him as she gently placed her hand in his. She was so small and delicate compared to him, but he was surprised to discover that her hands were toughened like a man's. It was a rude reminder that she worked for her living and it saddened him. Such a beautiful, delicate woman should have soft hands to go with the rest of her gentle femininity.

Even her scent was delicate and alluring, he couldn't help but notice as it washed over him. She smelled of lavender and fresh cotton. He'd noticed it before but couldn't put a name to the smell, and now it bathed him like the warmth of a summer's day when the maids put the laundry out to dry in the sun. It was that which she smelled of, sunshine.

Once on her feet, she quickly pulled her gaze away. "Thank you, Your Grace." She turned and collected the rest of her things from the footman.

"Is that it? Is that my dress?" Margaret said coming closer and staring at a package wrapped in brown paper.

Miss Rowan smiled broadly. "Yes, it is! May we go up to your room? You should try it on so I can make the last-minute adjustments."

"Oh yes, please!" Margaret said. Warwick had never seen his sister so happy and excited. She was actually bouncing on her toes!

He quickly wiped the smile from his face before saying, "Well, I'll leave you ladies to it, then." He gave them a nod of his head and started to return to his office. He couldn't help but look back before entering the room. Miss Rowan was staring after him with a thoughtful expression on her face. He wondered what she was thinking.

~April 8~

Tina followed Lady Margaret up to her room. From the moment the duke had come out of his office, she'd worried he'd be angry, and indeed, he seemed to have been. It was odd, though, for a moment after he'd yelled, it had seemed as if his eyes had softened, and he'd almost looked as if he was about to apologize for his harsh words. But then his expression had changed again. Tina wished she'd been able to tell what he'd been thinking. Was he sorry he'd yelled or not? One moment he was treating her like a member of his staff and the next like a lady, helping her to stand. She had no idea what he was doing and wondered if he did.

Tina wasn't sure about him. In truth, he scared her a bit. It was especially noticeable because Lady Margaret so warm and friendly, but there was no reason her brother should be. He was a duke after all.

Tina shook off her odd thoughts and focused back on Margaret, where her attention *should* be. She helped Lady Margaret carefully into her new gown, saying "I'll replace the last of the pins with stitching once we're sure that it fits just the way it should."

"Oh, it's so lovely! All the pearls look so beautiful."

"I'm so happy you like them. Do you see, they're organized to form leaves in the same shape as the embroidery around the edges."

"Oh! Yes! How clever!" Lady Margaret stood in front of her mirror turning this way and that in order to see. Tina almost hated to cut short her admiration, but she had to fix the bodice and set the sleeves just right, and she needed Lady Margaret to stand still for that.

Once all the pins were in just the right place, they carefully removed the dress, and she helped Lady Margaret into her day dress again. Tina then sat down to stitch everything together once and for all.

Lady Margaret stood watching, which made Tina feel awkward. She smiled up at Lady Margaret and said, "So is your cousin's dress is all finished? Is she ready to go?"

Lady Margaret's eyes went wide. "I don't know. I haven't seen her all day. I do know that a package was delivered for her yesterday. I assume that was her dress, but I haven't seen it."

"Perhaps it would be good for you to check in on her, then?" Tina suggested gently.

"Yes! I'll go and do that."

Lady Margaret returned just minutes later. Tina, in the sitting room, could hear the door slam next door, punctuated by a few sobs.

She got up and tested a door she suspected led to Lady Margaret's bedroom. It did and as she feared, the girl was lying across her bed crying for all she was worth.

Tina rushed over to her. "Lady Margaret, what's wrong?"

She sat on the edge of the bed, stroking the girl's back as she cried, but all Tina could make out through her hiccoughs was "Cousin Sonora."

Not knowing anything about the lady, Tina had no idea what she might have done to cause Margaret to break down like this, but she was definitely going to find out.

She left Lady Margaret's room and went exploring the hall. There were just two more rooms on this floor and the door to one of them was open. Tina peeked in.

At first, she thought the room was empty. A small single bed was pressed up against the far wall, and there was little else in the large room aside from a dressing table and an armoire. Tina was about to turn and leave when she caught sight of a woman's back.

She was sitting on the floor facing the corner, rocking back and forth. Her brown hair, streaked liberally with gray, hung loose to her waist. She was wearing a simple brown calico dress and had her knees tucked up under her chin. Tina inched closer.

"Er, Lady Sonora?" Tina asked quietly. "My lady?" she asked again when she received no response. Nothing. The woman either didn't hear her or just wasn't going to respond.

Oh, dear. If this was Lady Margaret's cousin then, indeed, there was a serious problem.

Tina walked as quickly as she could down to the duke's study and knocked.

A man she hadn't seen before answered the door. "Yes?"

"I'm Tina Rowan, Lady Margaret's modiste. Is the duke here?" she asked.

The man took a step back so that she could enter the room. His Grace was sitting at his desk, pen in hand, frowning down at the piece of paper in front of him.

"I beg your pardon, Your Grace," she said quietly, loathe to disturb his concentration.

He didn't move.

"Warwick, you have a visitor," the man who answered the door said more loudly.

"Hmm?" the duke looked up, startled.

Tina came forward. "I'm sorry, Your Grace, but I think we have, er, a problem."

"Is there something wrong with Margaret? With her dress?"

"Actually, it's with Lady Sonora—the lady with graying hair in the bedroom across from Lady Margaret's?"

"Yes." The duke drew his eyebrows down over his intensely blue eyes.

"She, er, looks like she might be incapable of escorting your sister to the drawing room this afternoon. And Lady Margaret is now crying hysterically in her room."

The man was on his feet and walking out the door faster than Tina had expected.

She followed him back upstairs. He went first to Lady Sonora's room but stopped just inside the doorway. He clearly knew just where to look and swore softly as soon as he saw his cousin sitting on the floor.

He turned back to the hallway where Tina was standing.

"She's not going to be getting up any time soon, is she?" Tina asked.

He pursed his lips together. "No." He brushed past her, heading to Lady Margaret's room. With one hand on the door handle, he stopped. Lady Margaret could still be heard sobbing inside.

Turning toward Tina, he suddenly looked completely lost. His eyes softened and turned worried. His mouth opened, but he didn't say anything.

"Is there anyone else who can take her? You?" Tina asked.

He sighed and shook his head. "Gentlemen are not invited to the Queen's Drawing Room. A girl *must* be presented by another lady." He faced the door, put his hand on the door handle, but didn't open it. "I don't know what to do. She's been wanting this, and then not wanting this. Maybe it *would* be best..." he said as if speaking to the door.

"No! She was so excited to meet the queen and be presented. Terrified, yes, but that's natural. And her ball is already scheduled and the invitations sent out. She needs to be presented before then, doesn't she?" Tina asked.

"She *should* be, yes. But this is not something I can do for her," the duke answered still staring straight ahead.

"Is there *no one* else you can call on to ask if they can present her?"

At that, he turned toward her. "But *who*?"

Tina thought quickly. Who could present the sister of a duke to the queen? She ran through all of the ladies she'd met since she'd arrived in London.

Of course! A duchess! "What about the Duchess of Kendell?"

CHAPTER TWELVE

"**Y**es!"

Tina suddenly found her upper arms grabbed by two strong hands.

He bent down putting his face at the same level as her own. "You are brilliant, Miss Rowan."

For a moment, she thought he might pull her into an embrace, but instead, he simply let go of her and went striding down the hall, screaming for his horse to be brought around to the front of the house.

He paused at the top of the stairs and turned around. "Take care of Margaret. Get her dressed and ready to go. I'll be back as quickly as possible."

Tina sighed. She certainly had her work cut out for her now!

~*~

Warwick pounded on the door of the Kendell House, not caring one whit whether the neighbors heard or not. It was immediately opened by a very startled looking footman—one that Warwick hadn't seen before. "May I help you, sir?"

Warwick tried to push past the man, but he proved to be an immovable force. He supposed this was a good thing. He would expect the same of his own footman should a crazy man try to gain entry into his own home.

Warwick stopped. "I'm the Duke of Warwick, I need to speak to your mistress immediately, it's an emergency." He patted his pockets searching for his card case, but he didn't have it on him. Finally, he just threw up his hands into the air. "Please tell Her Grace that Warwick is here. I'll wait outside if I need to."

The footman bowed. "Just one moment, if you please." He closed the door in Warwick's face.

It seemed like hours later, but couldn't have been above ten minutes, when the door reopened.

"Warwick? What's going on?" It was the duchess herself staring at him as if he'd lost his mind. He wasn't certain that he hadn't.

"Your Grace, I am so sorry to disturb you in this way, but we have a serious problem, and I was wondering if you could assist us."

"Of course! Come in," she said. She proceeded toward her private drawing room, pausing only to have a word with the footman. "When someone tells you that he is a duke, put him in the formal drawing room. Do *not* make him wait outside!" she said quietly but vehemently.

The young man blanched. "Yes, Your Grace."

"Dear Warwick, please come up. I am agog with curiosity as to how I can help you."

"You are too good, Your Grace."

She sat at the edge of one of well-built chairs by the fireplace and waited for him to begin.

He followed suit even though he could hardly sit still, he was so anxious. He forced himself to take a deep breath and relax. "I'm afraid it is my cousin. She is unwell and, therefore, unable to present my sister at the Queen's Drawing Room this afternoon. I know it is a great imposition, but might you?"

"Oh my! The poor girl! Dear, sensitive Margaret—she must be going out of her mind with worry," the duchess said with a sad shake of her head. "But I have no invitation to the Queen's Drawing Room. I don't know how I could possibly present her."

"I'm sure that if the situation were explained to the Lord Chamberlain, an exception might be made? You are, after all, a duchess. Surely you can attend the Drawing Room?"

The woman shook her head. "It would be highly unusual..." She thought about it for a moment turning to stare into the small fire that burned in the grate no matter the time of year. "Perhaps she can be shown that this is an opportunity?"

Warwick shook his head, not understanding. "An opportunity for what, Your Grace?"

"Well, for her to take her time with her debut. Perhaps return to Warwick and make her curtsy to the queen next year when she's a little more mature?"

Warwick's blood ran cold. "I'm afraid that's not possible."

The lady sat back. "What do you mean?"

Warwick sighed. He hated sharing with others the malice with which his father had treated Margaret. It was embarrassing, like having a madwoman in the attic. His father had nearly been unhinged when it came to how he treated his daughter. Warwick had never understood it.

"I'm afraid my father stipulated in his will that Margaret had to marry by the time she was twenty or else lose her dowry," he admitted.

"But surely you can replace it?" the duchess said.

"No. He accounted for that as well. If I even try to give her anything of the sort, I will lose control over all my properties aside from Warwick, which is entailed." He frowned. "My father made sure that Margaret either marry by twenty or be left destitute. So, you see, we have no choice. She must be brought out this year."

The woman looked at him with such sadness in her eyes, Warwick couldn't even stand to look directly at her. He turned his gaze to the fire blazing next to her. "Is there *no* way you could possibly chaperone her to the Queen's Drawing Room this afternoon? No way at all?" He hated begging even more than he hated airing his family's dirty laundry, but for Margaret he would do anything.

"Well, I *am* friendly with a few of the courtiers... I wonder if I might be able to..." She stood, forcing Warwick to do the same. "I shall get dressed and have a note sent over to the palace. Tell Margaret I will pick her up at two."

Warwick let out a sigh of relief. "Thank you, Your Grace! Thank you!" He took her hands in his. "I *cannot* thank you enough. Margaret will be so relieved."

She smiled at him. "I have always liked that girl." For a moment, her smile flickered. "It is such a shame that your parents couldn't see the joy in having a daughter, but you have done very well by her."

Warwick gave a little shrug. "She's my sister. I have always loved her, from the moment she was born and my parents...."

The memory of his parents—both of them—rejecting their newborn child was still seared into his memory. He was only eight, but he'd been so affected, especially when his father had picked up the baby and thrust her into his arms saying, "If you care for the girl so much, you can have her!" Warwick had considered Margaret as his own ever since—he'd even named her. Her happiness then and now was all he cared about.

The Duchess of Kendell shook her head again. "You're a good man. And now, I believe I will finally have an opportunity to wear that court dress I purchased last year. I thought I would go to the Queen's Drawing Room, but..."

"With the passing of Kendell, you couldn't," Warwick finished for her.

She blinked rapidly for a moment but still managed to keep the slight smile on her face. "You, however, have given me a happy opportunity."

Warwick rode as fast as he could back to his house. Bolting through the front door, he called out to anyone who could hear, "Get Lady Margaret ready, she's going to the Queen's Drawing Room!" He said it three more times as he ran up the stairs to her room, throwing open the door as he said it for the third time.

He stopped on the threshold almost unable to believe his eyes. Miss Rowan was sitting on Margaret's bed, his sister's head resting in her lap as she gently stroked her fingers through her hair. For a second, jealousy flashed through him. How ridiculous!

Miss Rowan sat up. "You did it?"

"I did it. The duchess is going to pull some wires, call in some favors, and get a last minute invitation to the drawing room. She'll be here at two to pick you up, Margaret."

His sister, her eyes only slightly red from crying, sat up as well. "Truly? Honestly, Warwick? You wouldn't tease me with this, would you?"

"Never!" he said, affronted that she would even think such a thing.

"Well then, we'd better start getting you dressed!" Miss Rowan said, hopping off the bed with a broad smile.

Margaret turned to her, a slightly frightened but very enthusiastic expression on her face. "Yes!"

~*~

Tina marveled at all the duke had done for his sister. It was obvious he cared for her a great deal—much more so than anything she'd ever witnessed in her life. Her own foster siblings had fought constantly throughout their childhood and even as adults didn't seem to like each other very much. Seeing a man—a powerful duke—going out of his way to do anything and everything to make his sister happy was just incredible.

Tina, with the help of Lady Margaret's maid, got her dressed in her court finery. Broad skirts of the palest pink covered in pearls, mimicking the shape of the deep green leaves of the embroidery, emphasized Lady Margaret's décolletage. It was as elegant as Tina could make it while still adhering to the dictates of a court dress.

As she carefully arranged the skirts over Margaret's panniers, she looked up to see the girl just staring at herself in the mirror. "This is just...well, beautiful, Tina!" Lady Margaret breathed.

Tina laughed. "Well, if the style weren't so awkward, I'm sure it would be."

Even in her nerves, Lady Margaret managed a smile. "It is a strange style with the hoops and the waist just below the bosom, but you've done an amazing job."

"I hope it's not too simple," Tina said, looking over the dress.

"Oh no, it's elegant. Truly beautiful."

She was grateful that Lady Margaret was happy. "Have a seat, if you would, my lady, so that your maid can finish your hair."

Most of the elaborate coiffure had been done already, and now there only needed the finishing touches of the ostrich feathers, a bit of rouge on her lips and cheeks, and powder to cover up the touch of redness that still lingered around her eyes.

Less than a quarter of an hour later, she was ready. Both Tina and Margaret were thrilled with the entire effect—the nearly pink dress, white pearls, and the feathers which Tina had died the same color of the dress with green edges bleeding into the pink to match the embroidery.

"Wait until Warwick sees," Lady Margaret giggled, finally beginning to relax a little.

Indeed, the duke's response was a sight to behold, and Tina was surprised to find a little lump growing in her own throat at the expression of pride on his face. She *knew* that man had a softer side.

"My God, look at my little sister," he said, with a smile growing on his face.

Lady Margaret just reached up and gave him a hug. "And it's all thanks to you, dear brother."

He gave her a quick squeeze. "I don't want to mess up your hair," he said with a laugh. "I'm sure your maid or Miss Rowan would kill me if I did anything to disturb your coiffure or your dress."

"Oh, no! They spent so much time on me. I probably shouldn't even breath." Lady Margaret's eyes grew wide. She looked over at Tina.

"Goodness! You can breathe! Nothing will happen to your dress if you hug your brother," Tina laughed.

There was a brief knock on the door before the footman came over and announced that the Duchess of Kendell's carriage was waiting.

"Oh." Lady Margaret's expression turned from sheer happiness to fear in a moment.

Tina grabbed her hands. "You look beautiful, and I'm sure you've practiced your curtesy and know exactly how to behave and what to do. You have nothing to be frightened of. Just let yourself relax and trust in your training."

Lady Margaret gave a slow nod.

"And Duchess Kendell will be there with you if you begin to falter. You know her, and you know that she will help in any way," the duke added.

Lady Margaret took a deep breath. "Yes. You're both right." With a nod of determination, she headed out the door.

Tina followed her, standing in the doorway. She watched as the footman helped Margaret into the carriage, and then waved as they drove off. Only after the carriage was gone did she realize that the duke was standing directly behind her, watching as well. His proximity made her suddenly very aware of herself—and him.

"Miss Rowan, you have performed a miracle here today," he said, looking down at her.

She gave a bark of a laugh. "Oh no, Your Grace, I think that was you. You managed to save the day by convincing the duchess to present Lady Margaret."

"After you suggested it!"

Tina gave a nod of acceptance. She was suddenly overcome with such a sensation of relief, she wondered that her knees didn't buckle under her.

As if the duke could read her like a book, he said, "Come, I think we both deserve a drink." He turned and led the way up the stairs to the drawing room, not even looking back to see if Tina followed. She clearly had no choice but to do so.

Chapter Thirteen

As Warwick walked up the stairs to the drawing room with Miss Rowan following, his mind flew back and forth between desperately wanting to be alone with her and wondering what in the world he was going to say to her. How should he behave?

It was the oddest thing. Never in his life had he been in such a quandary. He'd always known how to behave. He was a duke! And before then, he'd been heir to one. He took the lead. He was, usually, the highest-ranking person in the room. Everyone always deferred to him.

This strange woman didn't seem to realize this, and he wasn't certain he wanted her to. He enjoyed her honesty. The forthright way she treated him most of the time—as a man, not a duke.

Not only that, but he wanted to get to know her. How could he do that if she were deferring to him? If she were treating him like a duke? For some very strange reason, right now, he wanted to be merely a man and nothing more. And he desperately wished that she were merely a woman.

But she was his sister's modiste!

And he shouldn't be inviting such people upstairs for a drink! His father would be horrified.

He'd always adhered to his father's dictates that he was better than everyone else. He knew that others owed deference to him as the duke but this time? Today...with Miss Rowan...

He wanted nothing more than to forget that she was not of his class. She was simply too sweet, too beautiful, and too intelligent to be nothing more than a member of the staff.

No, he wanted to get to know her. He wanted to spend time with her. And damn it, if that's what he wanted, that was what he was going to do no matter how inappropriate it was! For just a short time, he wanted to forget that he was a duke and she nothing more than a seamstress—if only he could.

With a sigh, Warwick headed straight to the side table in the drawing room where the drinks were laid out. "Brandy or Madeira?" he asked Miss Rowan, picking up a clean glass.

"Oh no, I'm sure I shouldn't..." she started.

"Of course you should! You've worked very hard today." And he needed a drink more than he would care to admit.

He turned back to the bottles with determination. Would the world end if he were nice to this young woman? He was pretty certain it wouldn't. "Brandy it is," he said, deciding for her.

He poured for both of them, then handed one of the glasses to her.

She raised it saying, "To Lady Margaret."

"To Margaret." He took a sip, appreciating the fine liquor and relaxing a touch as it hit his stomach.

He indicated one of the chairs. "Please, sit down."

"Thank you." She lowered herself gingerly onto the seat as if it might reach up and attack her if she sat too quickly.

"So, tell me, Miss Rowan..."

She looked up at him, her bright green eyes widening. He couldn't help but smile. She looked both curious and slightly terrified at the same time. It was adorable.

"Yes, Your Grace?" she asked when he hadn't continued right away.

Ah, there, she had to remind him, didn't she? "How is your business going?" he asked, unable to think of anything else.

He actually had very little interest in her business. He'd much rather learn about her. He wondered for a moment why he hadn't asked her anything more personal. He *was* curious. Where did she come from? How long had she been in London? What did she think of the metropolis? But no, he'd taken the easy route, keeping things polite and in line with what their current relationship dictated. How boring!

"It's going very well, actually. Almost too well." She started to put down her half-finished drink. "I should probably be getting back to it."

"Absolutely not!" he said. He had to stop her or else she'd leave and that would be even worse. He kicked himself for asking about her work. He wanted to spend time with her, not run her off! "You deserve a break," he said a bit more gently when her head snapped up at his initial command.

"I've just got so much work to do. I'm afraid it's piling up faster than I can keep up with," she admitted.

"Well, I understand how that can be! I swear, for every report I read and respond to, I get five more on my desk," he said.

She gave a little laugh. "Yes, it does feel like that. I finish making one dress, and there are three more waiting to be started. I don't mean to complain, though. I'm grateful that I've got so much business..."

"But it's difficult. Sometimes you just feel as if you're drowning," he finished for her.

Her mouth opened a touch in surprise. "Yes! Yes, that's it precisely!"

He nodded. "Which is why it is all the more important that you take the time now, while I'm forcing you to do so," he said, giving a little laugh.

She giggled, a sound that warmed him from the inside out. "Very well, Your Grace. I certainly wouldn't want to alienate one of my best clients."

"No, absolutely not. You mustn't. So you'll sit here for just a few minutes more, have your drink and allow me, once again, to thank you for being so very wonderful to my sister. Honestly, you have gone beyond what I'd hoped for her. You've given her the confidence she needed. Truly, what you've done is quite extraordinary. Do you do this for all your clients, Miss Rowan?"

She flushed prettily, looking down at the glass in her hand. She took a sip and then said, "Well, I do try to make all of my clients look beautiful. That is part of being a modiste. It's important for them to be happy with the way they look in the dresses I make for them and for the dress to make them look beautiful. Does that make sense?"

He frowned for a moment. "So you ensure that the woman not only looks her best but *feels* that she does so."

"Yes, that's it exactly. And I try to make dresses that flatter the woman, that bring out her best qualities. I would do my best to dissuade someone from wearing a color that would make them look sallow or a design that would hide their figure instead of showing off their good points."

Warwick nodded, understanding. "Clearly, this is why you have so much work you can hardly keep up. A modiste who truly cares about making her clients look good is one that must be quite highly valued."

"Well, I hope so. I'm still developing my reputation. But with enough happy customers like Lady Margaret, I'm hoping that I'll attract more clients and be able to build my business."

"Even though you're already drowning in work? It sounds as if you're well on your way."

"I am. I do need to learn to delegate the more simple tasks to a seamstress while I take care of the more creative aspect. I'm beginning to do so, happily."

"Ah, hirelings. Yes, they are what allow you to keep your head above water. I don't know what I'd do without my secretary, Martin."

"Precisely! I'm sure he makes it so you can keep on top of all that you need to do."

"Yes, he does. So you need someone like that as well?"

"I do. I'm still in the process of trying out people, but I'm sure I'll find someone I can work with soon. Then if I have enough work, I'll be able to hire her on a more permanent basis."

"It sounds as if you've got it all figured out."

He was confused when she lost her smile. "I don't know about that," she admitted, "but I'm trying."

"I'm sure you'll do very well."

She swallowed the last of her drink. "Thank you, Your Grace." She stood. "And thank you for forcing me to take a moment of rest. I think I sorely needed it. You were right."

He stood as well, putting his own empty glass on the table by his side. "Of course. It was a pleasure sitting and chatting with you. I hope we have a chance to do this again sometime."

She gave him a smile. "I don't know if that would be appropriate, but it was kind of you to say it anyway. And now, I really must be going. I'll return with Lady Margaret's ball gown in a few days."

She needed to pass him to get to the door. For a moment, he had the oddest desire to stop her, to step *into* her way instead of out of it. And what would he do then, he dared to ask himself. *Kiss her, obviously!*

With a sigh that was a little too loud, he stepped aside but still inhaled that sweet, clean scent of hers as she neared him. It was even more intoxicating than the brandy he'd just imbibed.

She paused only for the slightest moment as she passed next to him. Her eyes looked up directly into his as if asking for that kiss before she dropped into a proper curtsy then took her leave.

~April 9~

Two days later Tina delivered Lady Sorrell's newly finished ball gown to her home.

"Her ladyship isn't at home," the footman said after he answered the door.

"Oh, I'm very sorry I missed her. I have her gown."

"You can leave it with me, and I'll see that she gets it," he offered.

"Yes, I can do that, although it would have been nice to have her try it one last time to be sure it is exactly right," Tina said, reluctantly handing it over.

"Today is her Whist Society meeting, so she will be gone for a few hours."

"Oh, of course, it's Wednesday! I'd completely forgotten." Tina frowned. "But don't they meet at three?"

The footman raised his eyebrows in surprise that she was so well informed. "I believe she was going to be making a few stops before going to Lady Norman's home," he offered.

Tina thanked the man, leaving the gown with him.

She turned and started down the street. She paused, however, and turned around. There was no reason why she couldn't go to her mother's house to inform Lady Sorrell that she had delivered her dress. She strode purposefully over to her mother's house, merely a quarter of a mile away.

"Tina!" Lady Norman said, with joy lacing the word. "I didn't expect to see you today."

"I stopped by to deliver Lady Sorrell's new gown to her home and was reminded that today was your Whist Society meeting. She wasn't home, so I thought I'd meet her here to tell her the dress has been delivered," Tina said, coming into the gold and blue drawing room. It always made her smile because her mother seemed like the least fussy person and yet she had this magnificent, imposing room.

"Lady Sorrell isn't here yet. I do expect her in about half an hour, though, with the other ladies.

Would you mind waiting?" Lady Norman said, indicating that they sit down.

"I was hoping you would have a few minutes to sit and talk. I've been so busy, I don't think I've seen you for over a week," Tina said, sitting on the sofa.

Her mother looked so happy—probably because Tina wanted to sit and chat. Tina could see that Lady Norman was doing her best to not be overbearing but was still trying to be motherly toward her. It was a difficult balance to achieve, and so far, she had been doing a wonderful job of it. Tina had someone nearby on whom she could rely for help but wasn't being smothered with motherly affection from one who'd only seen her once a year throughout her childhood.

"I'm glad to hear you've got plenty of work," her mother said.

"Oh, yes! Well, you know I was making a court dress and ball gown for the sister of the Duke of Warwick."

"Yes! How did that turn out? The court dress?"

"I think it came out well. Lady Margaret and the duke were certainly happy with it—and really, that's all that matters, right?"

"Absolutely," Lady Norman nodded. "The Drawing Room was yesterday, wasn't it? I remember seeing the announcement in the paper, but I haven't had a chance to read a reporting of it."

"It was yesterday. I delivered Lady Margaret's gown in the morning, well in advance because I knew she'd be anxious," Tina started.

"That was good of you."

"Well, it turned out it was a very good thing because her chaperone—a cousin, I believe—was unable to take Lady Margaret to the drawing room.

The duke had to go and beg the Duchess of Kendell to introduce her instead."

"No!" Lady Norman sat forward on her chair.

"Luckily, the duchess very kindly agreed to do so," Tina said.

"And she had an appropriate gown to wear?"

Tina shrugged. "I suppose so."

"I'll have to ask her about that," Lady Norman said.

"What was odd was what happened after Lady Margaret left for the drawing room," Tina said, a little more quietly. She wasn't entirely certain her mother was the right person to discuss this with, but if she didn't speak of it with her, who *would* she talk to?

Her mother tilted her head a touch to the side. "What do you mean? What happened?"

"The duke invited me up to the drawing room for a drink. Is that normal?"

Her mother's eyes widened. "No! He *gave* you a drink or had a drink with you?"

"He had a drink *with* me. We sat and had a very pleasant talk."

If Lady Norman's eyes could have widened even more, they would have. "He had a drink *with* you? With his sister's modiste?" Her mouth dropped opened and she gave a little gasp. "Does he know..."

"That we're related? I don't think so. I mean, he didn't mention you at all."

"Then what did you talk about?"

Tina gave another little shrug. "Work. He asked me how my business was going, and I told him that I was extremely busy. It was the oddest thing... He completely understood what I meant and said that he sometimes felt as if he were drowning in work too!"

"Really?"

"Yes! It was the nicest thing! And well, I'd never really thought about it much before, but I guess a duke really is very busy. He's got so many estates he has to look after and manage."

"And he's a member of the House of Lords, so he has to keep up on what's happening in the government and have a hand in it. Noblemen—and dukes especially—are extremely busy men."

"The Duchess of Kendell," the footman announced just at that moment.

CHAPTER FOURTEEN

"And speaking of dukes," Lady Norman said with a laugh as she stood up to greet her friend.

"Who is speaking of dukes?" the duchess asked with a smile as she came into the room.

"We were," Lady Norman said.

"We were saying how very busy they were," Tina explained.

"Ugh! Too busy! My poor dear Kendell was constantly working. It's what sent him to his early grave," the duchess said as she sat down on the chair next to where Lady Norman had been sitting.

"And yet the Duke of Warwick still manages to find time to spend with his sister," Tina commented, not sure if she should sit back down. She could no longer act like a guest or a friend in her mother's house now that the duchess was there.

The duchess gave a warm smile to no one in particular. "Warwick is a very special young man and his relationship with Lady Margaret couldn't be closer. There's a story to tell!"

"Oh?" Tina asked, suddenly intensely curious.

The duchess frowned at her for a moment before saying, "But it is not my story, it is his. Are you here to deliver another dress to Lady Norman, Miss Rowan?"

"Oh! Er, no. Simply to inform Lady Sorrell of the delivery of her gown, Your Grace," Tina said.

"Hmm. This is an unusual place to deliver a gown, is it not?" the duchess asked.

"Yes, Your Grace, it would be. I left it at her home. I simply wanted to inform her of this."

Tina noticed some other ladies come into the room as she spoke with the duchess. She supposed she should finish up here quickly and go before the whist game began.

While she had the duchess's attention, she added, "I, er, I also wanted to thank you for stepping in yesterday to present Lady Margaret at the Queen's Drawing Room. That was extremely kind of you."

The duchess just raised her eyebrows, and Tina suddenly realized that it wasn't her place to thank the duchess for doing such a thing. She was simply the young lady's modiste, not her friend or guardian.

"How *was* the Drawing Room?" Miss Sheffield asked. Tina hadn't even seen the young woman approach, but she was very relieved because she redirected the duchess's regard away from her.

"It went quite well, actually. Her Majesty was very understanding when I explained Lady Margaret's chaperone was unwell and allowed me to present Margaret in her place," the duchess answered, ignoring Tina and her remark.

"It truly was very kind of you to do so," Lady Norman said, also joining them. "And you had an appropriate gown to wear?"

"Yes. I had one I meant to wear before Kendell... But then I couldn't attend, so there it was, unworn," the duchess said. She seemed to find her own hands quite fascinating for a moment, and Tina thought she saw the duchess blink rapidly a few times.

"I am so sorry. How very distressing to be forced to recall such an unpleasant time," Lady Norman said. "I'd quite forgotten how fond you were of your husband."

The duchess found this to be amusing and gave a little laugh. "Yes. Kendell and I actually got along very well. I was quite saddened with his passing."

"I am sorry, Your Grace. I hope attending the drawing room didn't bring out painful memories," Miss Sheffield said.

The duchess took in a deep breath. "No. Not at all. Lady Margaret is such a sweet, gentle girl. I completely understand why Warwick would do anything for the child."

The footman entered the room once again and announced more women including Lady Sorrell.

Tina curtsied to them all, then approached her client as the ladies greeted each other. "I beg your pardon, Lady Sorrell, I just wanted to let you know that I've delivered your gown."

"Oh! How very kind of you to let me know," the lady said with a smile.

"If could you try it at your convenience and then drop me a note if you need any further adjustments..."

"Yes, yes, of course. I would be happy to," the lady said. "Thank you, Miss Rowan."

"Thank you, my lady." Tina turned and tried to catch her mother's eye, but she was too busy with her guests so she just slipped out. She did notice a narrowed glance from the duchess as she did so and wondered what she was thinking.

As she was walking out the door, Miss Hemshawe came barreling in, wearing a smart navy blue riding habit. "Oh! I beg your pardon," she said, after nearly colliding with Tina.

"It's quite all right," Tina laughed. "You're clearly in a rush."

"Yes. My race ran a little later than I had expected. I do hope I will be forgiven for coming in my filth."

The girl did smell very strongly of horse, but Tina didn't say so. "I'm sure they'll be happy you're here."

Miss Hemshawe gave her a hopeful smile and then entered the drawing room to join the other ladies.

Tina decided to walk back home. It was a bit far but certainly nothing too taxing for a girl used to living in the countryside. As she walked, though, she did wonder what had gotten into her to thank the duchess for helping Margaret.

Tina had no official ties to Margaret, aside from being in her—or, she supposed, the duke's—employ. And being a girl's modiste certainly did not make her responsible for her. If she were, then yes, she could certainly thank the duchess. But since she wasn't—and not only that, was merely a hired laborer—she most definitely didn't have the right to thank the duchess, no matter how grateful she was for stepping in to help Margaret.

Honestly, Tina shook her head, she was beginning to give herself airs. With a laugh, she hopped across the street and headed through the park to cut short her journey home.

~*~

Everyone was taking their seats in the card room for their game of whist when Miss Hemshawe came in.

"I do beg your pardon for being late," she said.

"Were you riding?" Lady Sorrell asked.

"Yes, and I'm afraid I didn't have a chance to change. You will, I hope, forgive me?" the younger woman asked, looking around at everyone.

The duchess scrunched up her nose at the obvious smell of horse, but Mrs. Aldridge said kindly, "Of course, my dear. It's better to be here as you are than not at all."

"Oh, thank you for understanding!" Miss Hemshawe said, taking a seat next to the older woman.

"Yes, clearly Mrs. Aldridge doesn't mind, but I do, so I shall sit here," the duchess said, deliberately taking a seat at the other table.

Christianne didn't mind the smell so much but still found herself facing the duchess. She wasn't quite sure how that had happened. In fact, she was thinking that she'd rather avoid the woman just at the moment until she could figure out what in the world her daughter had been thinking to thank the woman on Lady Margaret's behalf.

Christianne avoided the duchess's eyes as she dealt the cards around the table. Seated to her right was Miss Sheffield and partnering her this week was Lady Moreton. Both of them were sweet young women, although quite the opposite in temperament. Miss Sheffield was still very much like a child with her exuberant energy, while Lady Moreton, although only a year or two older, was more quiet and introspective. It wasn't surprising as the lady had lost her husband on the battlefield only two years earlier after probably the shortest marriage in history. Christianne had heard that she and Lord Moreton had grown up in each other's pockets and had had a spur-of-the-moment wedding the night before he left to join the war effort. It was beyond sad that he'd been killed in his very first battle.

Christianne gave the two younger ladies an encouraging smile and did her best to put Tina's bewildering behavior out of her mind. She dealt the last card, a four of spades, face up in the center of the table "There is your trump suit, ladies," she said, before turning expectantly to Lady Moreton to play her first card.

She played the jack with a small frown. Christianne couldn't remember how much experience Lady Moreton had playing the game. It was her first time playing with the young woman.

"Rather presumptuous of Miss Rowan to thank me for taking Lady Margaret to the Queen's Drawing Room, don't you think?" the duchess asked, putting down the ace and looking Christianne in the eye.

Christianne worked to keep the contact and not immediately drop her eyes to the table in embarrassment. She didn't have anything to do with Tina's behavior, but still, as her mother, she felt responsible for it nonetheless. The problem was that no one knew she was Tina's mother, and she *had* to keep it that way.

"Oh, my goodness, yes!" Miss Sheffield said enthusiastically, much to Christianne's relief as it took the duchess's glare off her. "Why it was almost as if Miss Rowan felt responsible for Lady Margaret." She laughed at the ridiculousness of such a thing.

"On the other hand, it *was* exceedingly kind of you to step in as you did, Your Grace," Lady Moreton said. As the story had been reported in the morning's gazette, everyone knew of the duchess's magnanimous behavior.

"But what gives that mantua-maker the *right* to thank me?" the duchess asked, snapping up the trick she'd just won. She tapped the edges of the cards against the table as she straightened them, and then glared at Christianne as if it were her fault Tina had behaved improperly. The duchess placed the ten of diamonds into the center of the table.

She couldn't possibly know. The terrifying thought raced through Christianne's mind. No. The duchess was merely directing the criticism to her because it was she who was sponsoring Tina.

Christianne opened her mouth to defend her daughter, although for the life of her she had no idea what she might say when Lady Moreton forestalled her. "I have a feeling she's become quite attached to Lady Margaret. What else could explain such behavior?"

Christianne followed Miss Sheffield's three of diamonds with the king. "I'm sure you're right, Lady Moreton. I haven't met Lady Margaret myself, but from what you said earlier, Your Grace, she is an extremely sweet girl. You can hardly blame Miss Rowan for feeling some sort of affection, and therefore, responsibility for her."

Lady Moreton set down the ace and took the trick, nodding her agreement as she did so.

The duchess softened a touch. "Margaret *is* a dear, sweet girl. Not only that, she is such an innocent that she does tend to bring out the motherly instinct in all of us." She watched as Lady Moreton led with the queen of diamonds.

"Well, in that case, Miss Rowan's behavior is quite understandable," Miss Sheffield said, putting a two of diamonds on top of the duchess' six.

Christianne was so relieved that the duchess was beginning to calm down. She put a king down on top of the pile, then started to pick them up.

"I believe the trick goes to Lady Moreton, Lady Norman," the duchess said with a lift of one eyebrow.

"What? I put down the king," Christianne said, looking down at the cards.

"Of hearts. The suit was diamonds," Lady Moreton said gently.

"Oh! I do beg your pardon. I wasn't watching as closely as I should have."

"Is your mind wandering from the game, Lady Norman?" Claire's voice called from the other table. She gave a deep, throaty laugh. "I bet I know what is distracting you, and it isn't your modiste."

Christianne turned around to face her accuser and friend.

"What do you think it is, my lady?" Miss Sheffield said, leaning around Christianne.

"Oh, just a certain gentleman who we happened to meet the other day while out driving in the park," Claire said, her eyes twinkling with mischief.

"Ooh, you don't mean the very same one who was practically sitting in her pocket all evening at Lady Bradmore's ball, do you?" Mrs. Aldridge asked, joining in the conversation while carefully placing a card down on the table in front of her.

"Why yes, the very same," Lady Blakemore said innocently but with a crafty smile on her face.

Well, she hadn't been thinking of Liam, Christianne thought, but she was now. She kept her mouth shut and placed a card on the table.

"Please, Lady Norman, watch what you are playing!" the duchess scolded her.

Christianne looked at the card she'd just put down. It was the ace of clubs, but the suit in play was hearts. "Oh! I do beg your pardon." She picked up the card and put it back into her hand and this time played a spade winning her first trick of the afternoon. She didn't imagine there were going to be many more of these today, so she might as well enjoy the feeling of having won this one for as long as she could.

CHAPTER FIFTEEN

Tina was working on a walking dress for Lady Fareham when there was a knock on her door. With a scowl and then a sigh, she put her work aside to answer it. Oddly enough, she hoped it wasn't a lady come to buy a gown from her. She already had too much to do in too little time.

She fully expected her mother to be on the other side of the door. She was sure she would be by to question her about thanking the duchess the day before. The more Tina thought about it, the more she was certain that it was not only inappropriate behavior but quite possibly horrifically rude. She sincerely hoped her mother hadn't had to defend her all afternoon.

Tina was surprised by the presence of a footman in the now familiar livery of the Duke of Warwick. "Miss Rowan?" the man asked.

"Yes."

He handed over a note, then turned to leave.

"Is there a reply needed?" she called after him.

"No, miss. I was not told to wait for one," he said, turning back to speak to her before continuing down the stairs.

"Huh!" Tina closed the door and broke open the duke's seal. The handwriting was strong and spare.

You will wait on Lady Margaret on twelfth April from 3:00 o'clock. In addition, your presence will be required at the ball that evening.

W

Tina read the short note through three times. There was no salutation. No closing. No thanks. Nothing but commands.

A haze of anger formed in front of her vision.

"How dare he?" she said to no one. "How dare he!"

The fact that she'd already planned on seeing to Lady Margaret the afternoon of her ball was completely beside the point. And she hadn't counted on staying through the ball.

What in the world was she going to do there? She couldn't attend as a guest, she knew that much, so why was she required to go? She had no idea, but she did not appreciate this high-handed approach...

...and so she would tell him!

After being so friendly the day of the Queen's Drawing Room, this note, and more significantly its tone, was completely unexpected. She didn't expect to the best of friends with the duke, but she certainly wasn't his servant who he could command and order about.

They'd had a drink together! They'd sat and talked and commiserated over having too much work. She'd even begun to think of him as something more than just a duke. She'd begun to think of him...

As a man.

A very handsome, intelligent man. A kind man.

Oh certainly, he was a duke, no one could ever forget that for even a moment. But he'd condescended to speaking with her. He'd smiled, and for a moment, he'd been like anyone else. Kind. Caring.

He had eyes she could just sit and stare into. Hair that made her wonder if it was as soft as it looked. It had taken all her will power to walk past him and not reach out and touch him.

And now she received this! She scowled at the note still in her hand. How dare he!

She turned away from the door to fetch her pelisse and hat. She was not going to stand for this. They'd connected. He had no right to order her in this way.

She'd only taken a few steps away from the door when there was another knock.

Ha! That must be him coming to apologize for his high-handedness., Sadly, in her heart, she knew full well that he would probably never in his life do so.

"Lady Norman!" Tina said as she opened the door to her mother. Her mother's expression wasn't exactly as bright and friendly as it usually was when Tina opened the door to her.

"Miss Rowan, do you have a few minutes?" her mother said, keeping up the pretense just in case there was anyone within hearing distance.

"I was just about to go out, but do come in," she said, stepping back.

"Oh! Do you need to meet a client?"

"No, well yes, but it's not for a fitting. Anyway, come in, please," Tina said, forcing herself to be polite.

"Thank you. I just..." Lady Norman paused until they had sat down in the drawing room. Then she continued, "I just wanted... Whatever made you thank the Duchess of Kendell yesterday? She was extremely perturbed by your behavior. It was completely inappropriate coming from you. You do realize this, don't you?"

"I am not so ignorant that I don't know it was wrong," Tina admitted.

"Then why did you?" her mother asked again.

Tina's gaze dropped for a moment and landed on the note still clutched in her hand. Fury once again filled her chest.

Why *had* she thanked the duchess? Because she'd mistakenly thought she had some sort of relationship with Lady Margaret—and possibly even her brother—beyond that of employer and employee. Because she liked Lady Margaret and her happiness was important to her. Because she'd witnessed just how important Lady Margaret's happiness was to the duke and the thought of him being happy... Well, it made her happy.

But she was wrong. She was nothing to him. No one... just like she'd been nothing and no one of any importance to her own mother from the day she was born. She was of so little importance, in fact, that Lady Norman hadn't even kept her to raise as her own. No, she'd gotten rid of her, tried to forget her horrid mistake. She paid off Rowan every single month to keep her hidden.

How many times had Tina's foster parents *told* her she was nothing? How many times had her foster brother and sisters called her bastard and knocked her down as they did so? How many bruises had she been given by Caleb? The ones from his sisters, although usually not of the black-and-blue variety, had hurt even more. Even to them she was lower than low.

And now her mother was sitting there looking accusingly at her, angry that she'd dared to speak to a duchess. Dared to thank her for a kindness. Lady Norman was as bad as her foster-sisters.

Tina stood up. "I don't think it's any of your business why I thanked her. I honestly don't know why you care. Am I getting too presumptuous? Am I too insolent for the bastard that I am? Oh, believe me, I know I am nothing and no one. You don't need to remind me again. I can assure you the Rowans taught me well just how unworthy I am. And the fact that I'm still beholden to them, that I still have to pay them for my freedom? That is *your* doing."

Lady Norman's jaw dropped.

"Now if you will excuse me, my lady, I have an appointment which I must get to. I do need to earn my keep, you know. I have my foster-father who I need to pay so that I won't be forcibly married to a brute who hits women for fun. And I do hope to someday return all the money you have lent me. So if you will excuse me..." She waited for her mother to leave, feeling the burn of anger in the pit of her stomach.

"You don't need..." Lady Norman started.

"I don't have time to discuss this with you just now, but if you'd like I shall call on you, at your convenience, of course," Tina said coldly.

Her mother didn't say anything. She didn't need to. The pain Tina had inflicted on her showed clearly enough in her eyes before she turned and headed out the door without another word.

Tina followed her out not ten minutes later after she'd retrieved her coat, hat, and gloves.

~April 10~

Nothing. He thought she was nothing. Like a mantra, the words repeated again and again through her mind as she walked to St. James Square.

Well, she *was* nothing. Hadn't she just reminded her own mother of this? Wasn't she well aware of it enough? This note and her mother had to remind her.

It didn't make it hurt any less, though.

Why had she even thought for a moment there was anything more to her or her relationship with the duke than this? She truly should have known better. No, instead she had to be knocked down again and again. Her foster brothers and sisters had done so repeatedly when she was a child; her mother and now the duke were doing so in her adulthood.

Was she so stupid that she could not learn this simple lesson?

Tina closed her eyes as she stood on the street just outside the duke's home. She would not cry in public. She would not humiliate herself even further.

"Tina?" Lady Margaret's voice cut into her thoughts. "Tina, how lovely to see you! Are you coming to visit? We didn't have an appointment for a fitting, I'm sure of that. Oh, *do* say you were coming to visit me!"

Tina took in a deep breath and shoved her emotions down where they couldn't get in her way. "Lady Margaret! I wouldn't dare presume to pay a personal call upon you, but I was in the neighborhood and *was* thinking about you. I have to admit to being so very curious as to how the Queen's Drawing Room went." She even managed to force a touch of a smile onto her lips.

"What do you mean, 'presume to pay a call'? We are friends are we not? I so enjoy our time together. I should hope you would feel comfortable enough to call on me." Lady Margaret looked a little worried and unsure.

"I'm afraid it's not a matter of comfort, my lady, but appropriateness. You see, I too thought we had become friends... Your brother was even kind enough to invite me for a drink after you left for the drawing room the other day," Tina admitted softly, suddenly feeling her throat constrict with tears once again. "But then I received this." She indicated the crumpled note still in her hand.

Lady Margaret took the note from her. Straightening it, she read it and then gasped. Tina hoped it was in outrage, but she couldn't be sure.

"Isn't that just like Warwick," she said, sounding very annoyed. "He has this idea... Well, it's not his fault really, it is simply how he was raised, what he was taught."

Tina couldn't quite figure out what Lady Margaret was trying to say. Her confusion must have shown on her face, because Lady Margaret gave a laugh then said, "But we mustn't stand outside on the street, where are my manners? Come inside and we'll have a cup of tea, and I'll tell you all about it the drawing room."

Tina could have kissed the girl when she tucked her arm through Tina's and walked with her into the house as if they were the closest of friends.

"Oh, Martin," Lady Margaret said as they were heading up the stairs, and the man Tina had seen before in the duke's office was coming down. "Do tell Warwick that I would like a word with him when he has the time."

"I would be very happy to do so, my lady, but I don't believe he is expected home until after dinner." He then looked at Tina and said, "I didn't realize you had a fitting scheduled for today, my lady, is this for your ball gown?"

"I don't have a fitting, Tina is just here for a visit. Please do give Warwick my message, otherwise, I'm sure I wouldn't see him for days," she said, passing him by with hardly a glance.

The gentleman bowed slightly as they passed, but Tina didn't miss the frown he leveled at her.

"I've seen him before in the duke's study. Who is he?" Tina whispered after they'd gained the top of the stairs.

"Oh, that's just Martin Arbeit. He's Warwick's secretary and friend, very much like you and I are friends, I suppose, only Martin grew up with us as his father was our father's secretary. He shared lessons with Warwick when they were young until my brother went to Eton. I was still very little when Warwick went off to school, but Martin stayed home and studied with his father to learn to take his place when the need arose."

"You must be very close to him, then," Tina remarked.

"Oh, yes," Lady Margaret smiled fondly. "He's like a brother to me."

Lady Margaret ordered tea to be brought up. They then settled into the comfortable chairs in her sitting room. Already Tina was beginning to feel so much better. Her anger was gone, and while she still had no idea where she stood with the duke, at least she knew she had a friend in Lady Margaret.

CHAPTER SIXTEEN

Warwick didn't return until close to eleven that evening. He stopped in briefly to his office to pick up the book he'd been reading—the one he'd bought at the bookstore where they'd met Miss Rowan. A note in the center of his desk caught his eye.

"Your sister demands your attendance upon her this evening."

--Martin

Warwick laughed. His sister would never demand anything of him. She probably requested Martin tell him that she wished to speak with him. He tucked the note into his book and headed up to see if his sister was still awake.

She was sitting up in her bed reading when he peeked into her room after a soft knock.

"Oh, Warwick! You're home," she said sitting forward and giving him a welcoming smile.

"Martin left me a note saying that you were *demanding* my presence," he said, coming farther into the room.

"Demanding?" She gave a laugh. "I've never demanded anything in my life."

"I know. I'm sure he meant it as a joke," he said, laughing along with her. "But you did want to see me, didn't you? Or was that him teasing me as well?"

"No, I did. Actually, I'm very angry with you," she said, losing her smile.

Now that was an odd turnabout. "Angry? What have I done?"

"That note you sent to Tina this morning! Really, Warwick! That was the rudest, coldest summons I have ever seen."

"She's a seamstress!" Warwick said, defending himself. "What am I supposed to do, go to her home and beg for her to call upon you?"

"You don't need to beg, but a little civility would have been nice. Just be polite, for goodness' sake. And she isn't *just* a seamstress, she's a very talented dress designer and my friend, so I would appreciate it if you would treat her better."

Warwick started to open his mouth to refute her, but in all honesty, he had nothing to say.

"Oh, don't you dare defend yourself, brother mine. She is too my friend just as Martin is yours," she said before he could say a word. "She was extremely upset by the tone of your note and not just because it was so curt. You apparently enjoyed a drink with her after I left for the Queen's Drawing Room. How could you not tell me about this? It meant a lot to Tina, by the way. She thought that perhaps she was on her way to becoming friends with you as well—and then you sent that horrid note!"

Margaret was truly incensed. Warwick was surprised. She never went on like this.

"Margaret—"

"Don't say Margaret! You owe Tina an apology!"

"She's a seamstress—a modiste, whatever it is. She's in my employ. I can speak to her or send her curt notes as I see fit."

"She's my friend. You would never send such a note to Martin," she argued.

"I not only would, I have," he pointed out.

"Oh, but he's a man, and you see him every day. Tina was truly hurt."

"How do you know?" he asked.

"I found her standing outside of the house practically in tears!" Margaret threw down the book she'd been reading.

That stopped him. She was in tears? He actually *had* hurt her with his note?

"I was on my way back from a walk about the square when I found her there. Naturally, I invited her in and calmed her down. We had a lovely visit, and I told her all about the Drawing Room."

"Why was she outside of the house?"

"I don't know, maybe she was coming to see me, although she said she would never be so presumptuous as to pay a social call. I told her she was ridiculous, and she could do so anytime she wanted."

"Margaret, she's a—"

"Don't you *dare* remind me once more that she's a modiste! She's my friend and the only one I have aside from you!" This time she did shout at him.

Warwick came and sat at the edge of his sister's bed and took her hand in his own. "I'm sorry, Margaret. This has been so difficult for you. You have no proper chaperone. No one to introduce to other young ladies. No way to make friends your own age. You've had to just sit here at home until you could be properly introduced to society." He sighed.

"I had hoped that Cousin Sonora would have been able to do that for you."

"But she can hardly even leave her own room," Margaret said, calming down a little.

"None of us anticipated it would be this difficult for her," he said, stroking the back of her hand. "Even she thought that she would be able to escort you to morning visits and such."

"And now all she can do is sit in the corner of her room. Do you think she'll even make it to the ball?"

Warwick shook his head. "I don't know. But I do know if she can't, I may just send her back to Warwick and try to find another chaperone for you. You cannot be made to suffer because of her."

"I'm not exactly suffering," Margaret admitted.

"No, but you're also not having the season you should be having."

"Maybe it will get better after my ball. Then I'll begin to get invitations. You *will* escort me to parties, won't you?"

"Of course! I'll be honored to do so. If I didn't, who would scare away all of your suitors? I certainly couldn't expect Cousin Sonora to do that even at the best of times," he said, giving her smile.

She laughed and shook her head. After a moment, she sobered again and said, "Warwick, promise me you'll apologize to Tina."

"Apologize?"

"Yes."

"Margaret..."

"Oh, come now, it won't hurt you to climb off that high horse of yours every once in a while. I know you're a duke and she's a modiste, but she's a sweet, intelligent, thoughtful person and I like her a great deal. She's been a good friend to me." She looked at him so earnestly there was nothing he could do but accept defeat.

"Very well, I will say something to her."

"Apologize!"

"Margaret, do not push. I will speak with her," he said again, lowering the tone of his voice to let her know that he'd had enough.

She got the point and gave a nod.

Why did he suddenly feel much lighter? Happier?

It couldn't possibly be the thought of speaking with Miss Rowan again, could it? Of seeing her again and perhaps spending time with her?

No, that was ridiculous. He tolerated the chit. Oh, he was very happy she made Margaret happy, even that they'd become close, but it didn't mean he had to be friends with her. Ha! How could a duke possibly become friends with a seamstress— modiste, whatever she was. A girl.

A woman.

Yes, a beautiful woman, but one more suitable to a liaison than a friendship, surely.

Now that put all sorts of lurid thoughts into his mind. And yet, the idea of simply offering her a carte blanche seemed wrong. No, she was much too sweet, too innocent for anything of the sort. But as sure as he was a man, he couldn't help but imagine her lovely curves and what they might look like without those well-designed dresses covering them.

~April 14~

Tina stood by and watched while Lady Margaret's maid started on the long process of doing her hair. She had come, as summoned, at precisely three o'clock that afternoon with the dress. It had actually been ready the day before, but Tina didn't see why she shouldn't save herself a trip and just bring it when she came to help Lady Margaret get dressed for the ball.

"Are you ready?" Tina asked her friend.

Lady Margaret's eyes widened. "What? No! I need my hair done, and then to get dressed—"

Tina laughed, cutting her off. "No, I meant are you mentally prepared? There are going to be a lot of people there, and I assume your chaperone isn't going to be nearby to help you decide who you should dance with and who you should politely decline."

Lady Margaret laughed. "Do you really think I'll receive so many offers I would have the luxury of choosing some and not others?"

"Of course! Not only is the ball being held in your honor, you are probably going to be the most beautiful young lady there," Tina said.

Lady Margaret scoffed. "I hardly think so. Besides, one cannot decline a dance with a gentleman without sitting out all of the dances. It's not polite. If I dance with one, I have to dance with anyone who asks."

"Oh. I'm afraid I don't know society's rules. But just you wait and see, I'm certain every gentleman there will want to dance with you. You are absolutely lovely when you're not dressed up. I can't wait to see you this evening after Florence is finished with your hair, and you are attired in your new gown."

Lady Margaret smiled at Tina through the mirror. "You are a good friend!" She quickly lost her smile. "You are going to be nearby, aren't you? I know you can't attend—for which I am very sorry— but just knowing that you're near..."

"Of course I'll be nearby. Martin informed me when I came in that I was to wait on the ladies in attendance who need assistance with their gowns—fixing tears and fallen lace and such. I believe I'll be in the lady's withdrawing room the whole time."

"What? But that's a job for a minor seamstress or a maid! You shouldn't be doing such work." Lady Margaret frowned furiously.

"It's all right. It gives me an excuse to be nearby should you need me. And perhaps I'll be able to suggest quick alterations to some lady's gowns to make them more flattering. It could be a good way for me get more clients."

"Oh. Well, in that case..."

"It will be fine, Lady Margaret," Tina reassured her. She didn't know the propriety of trying to get business while at a ball, but she was happy to have an excuse to be nearby should she be needed for any reason. She might as well make the best of it.

"I believe Sally is going to be there to assist you, Tina," Florence commented as she shoved more hair pins into Lady Margaret's hair to ensure it stayed right where she'd put it.

"Oh, that's good. See, I'll have an assistant so it will be obvious that I'm more than just a seamstress," she told Lady Margaret.

"That's all right, then," Lady Margaret said, turning her head this way and that so she could see the beautiful coiffure Florence had created.

"It's lovely," Tina said with a smile to Margaret and a nod for Florence. "Now let's get you into your gown without disturbing all that hard work."

With great delicacy, Tina placed Margaret's white, silk chiffon underdress over her head and then proceeded to tie and pin it into place. The neckline was just low enough to show the slight rise of Lady Margaret's bosom, but she was then decently covered with a lovely white Brussels lace overdress which also provided a slight train in back. Small puffed sleeves of the lace added to the delicacy and elegance of the gown, and Tina had even had a fan of the same material made for her. White satin slippers and just the slightest hint of rouge to brighten up her pale cheeks finished off her toilet.

Tina and Florence stood back, quite pleased with their creation.

Margaret stood in front of her mirror admiring herself. "Oh, you both have done such a beautiful job. I look like a fairytale princess," she breathed.

The clock struck seven making Tina jump. "I believe that it's time for you to go down for dinner, my lady. And for you to knock your brother right off his feet," she added with a laugh.

Margaret smiled, then gave both women a light hug. "Thank you both!"

They followed her to the top of the stairs and watched as she floated down to the foyer where the duke waited with his mouth hanging open just a touch.

"My God, but you're lovely! Like an angel come down from heaven," he told her with a smile as he held out an arm to escort her into the drawing room. He glanced up to Tina and gave her and Florence a slight acknowledgment. It was enough to make them both proud of the work they'd done in preparing Lady Margaret for her big night.

"Your Grace," Tina called to him before they disappeared.

He paused and turned back. She'd tried to hold her tongue, honestly, but she couldn't! She'd thought about it the entire time she'd followed Lady

Margaret down the stairs and watched her brother greet her, but she simply could not stay quiet.

"Brown, Your Grace? Even tonight you're going to wear brown?" Tina asked despairingly. It was true that at least he had worn a slightly nicer waistcoat with his usual brown wool coat. This one was beige shot with gold, but it was still in the same color family. Even the man's cravat was brown!

He just gave her a tolerant smile before turning and continuing into the drawing room, closing the door firmly behind him. No, she supposed, that was not the best way to win his friendship or respect, but honestly! Wearing brown to a ball!

CHAPTER SEVENTEEN

$\mathcal{W}$arwick stood proudly next to his sister, greeting guests as they came into the ball. The dinner he had hosted beforehand had gone well. He'd been careful to invite people Margaret had met before and felt comfortable with, including the Duchess of Kendell. Still, he was keeping his fingers crossed and relying on Margaret's lifelong training to get her through the rest of the evening.

They had been standing welcoming guests for perhaps three-quarters of an hour when a footman slid in behind him and said very quietly, "Your Grace, the prince has arrived."

Margaret swung around, her eyes wide. "The *prince*?" she whispered. She turned and looked at Warwick. "Did you invite the prince?"

Warwick could only shake his head. "No, but we're certainly not going to turn him away."

"Oh, my God, Warwick, I can't meet the prince!" she said, luckily still keeping her voice low.

"Why ever not? You met his mother last week."

"That was different. She was up on a dais well away from me and everyone else. And all I did was curtsy to her and answer a question before backing away."

"Well, now you get to meet a royal in a much more personal fashion," Warwick said, giving her a reassuring smile. "Perhaps he'll ask you to dance. Wouldn't that be a coup for your come-out?"

The panicked look in her eyes made Warwick begin to worry.

"It'll all right, Margaret. You know how to behave. You'll be fine."

"No, no, I won't!" she said just as the butler announced, "His Royal Highness, the Prince of Wales, and Mr. Brummel."

"Warwick is the room spinning? I think the room is spinning," Margaret whispered, clutching on to his arm.

"Pull yourself together, Margaret, and curtsy to the prince," Warwick said fiercely as he, himself, bowed at the waist.

He heard his sister take in a deep breath and saw her lower herself in a proper curtsy. When he straightened, the prince stood in front of him looking Margaret over as if she were a piece of horseflesh he was considering purchasing. "Warwick," he said, giving a nod.

"Your Royal Highness, what a wonderful surprise," Warwick said. "May I present my sister, Lady Margaret?"

She curtsied once more, keeping her eyes lowered. "Your Majesty," she said softly.

"How very…" the prince paused and looked to his friend.

"Charming," Mr. Brummel supplied with a slight smile, as he lifted his eyeglass to one eye.

"Indeed, charming," the prince mimicked.

"Thank you, Your Highness," Margaret murmured.

"Has the dancing begun?" the prince asked.

"Not yet, Your Majesty. We were going to open the ball officially in just a few minutes," Warwick said.

"In that case, we will honor your sister with the first dance," His Majesty said, giving Margaret another look.

"You are too good, Your Majesty," Margaret said.

"Yes." And with that, he sauntered off to greet some friends.

Warwick immediately grabbed Margaret's arm, just in case she should decide to swoon. He turned to the footman, who was still standing nearby, and said quietly, "Fetch Miss Rowan immediately."

The man went running.

Warwick managed to lead Margaret from the room without too much fuss. They just had about ten minutes before she would be expected to stand up with the prince for the first dance. She had to be well fortified and stable by then.

Miss Rowan met them in the hallway with a glass of wine in her hand just moments later.

"That is exactly what she needs," Warwick said with a sigh when he saw her.

"Luckily I passed a footman bringing out a tray of them on my way here," she said, handing the glass to Margaret. "I figured if you needed to call me, she would be needing this. Is it true that the prince is here?"

"Yes, and he wishes to have the first dance with Margaret," Warwick said.

Her beautiful lips parted in surprise for a moment. She turned with a smile to his sister. "What an honor, Lady Margaret! Your season will be made!

Why, it probably already has been just by his attendance. No hostess will fail to invite you for any gathering now." She laced her voice with just the right balance of awe, excitement, and a touch of calm.

"He called me charming," Margaret said, still in a bit of a daze.

"Well, Brummel did so, and the prince parroted him," Warwick said with a laugh.

"Because you are! You look stunning, and I'm sure you behaved properly. What is not charming about that?" Miss Rowan said.

"But now I have to dance with him, Tina! That means I'm going to need to speak with him! What does one say to the prince?" Margaret's eyes went slightly wild once more.

Miss Rowan looked stunned for a moment and then shook her head and said, "I imagine the same thing you would say to any gentleman. Oh, and fashion! He loves fashion, doesn't he? And what else?" She looked to Warwick for help.

"The theatre," he quickly filled in. "The arts." He turned to his sister. "We went to that excellent art exhibition a few weeks ago when we first arrived, do you remember?"

Margaret clearly had to think back, but then slowly she nodded her head. "Yes, yes. That's right."

"And you can ask him for recommendations as to what play to see. I'm sure he'll be more than happy to tell you," Miss Rowan suggested.

"Excellent idea!" Warwick approved.

"Lady Margaret, you look beautiful, you are quick and clever, and most of all, the prince already thinks you charming, so no matter what you say he will be pleased. Just ask him his opinion on this or that, and he'll be very happy to share his thoughts with you. I have yet to meet a man who didn't like to tell you exactly what you should do and what is best," Miss Rowan said with a little laugh.

His sister actually smiled back. Warwick couldn't believe it. Thank God for Miss Rowan. Honestly, this girl had more common sense than almost anyone he'd ever met. Who would ever believe a modiste would be able to advise the daughter and sister of a duke on what to say to a prince?

"We should return and instruct the musicians to begin the first dance," Warwick said.

"Lady Margaret," Miss Rowan said, stopping his sister for just a moment. She looked her in the eye and smiled. "Enjoy yourself and know that you are equal to anyone. Oh, and once you've danced with the prince, everything else will easy."

Margaret gave her friend a quick hug, then took Warwick's arm as they headed back into the ballroom. He noticed she'd managed to drink more than half of the wine in that short period of time they'd been talking. He hoped this was a good thing.

~*~

"She truly is quite stunning, you know," a man's voice interrupted Warwick's thoughts. He stood watching his sister giggle and look shyly at the prince as he walked her around in a circle as the dance prescribed.

He turned and found the Viscount Wickford standing next to him. "Well, this *is* an evening of miracles. You know, I don't believe I've ever seen you outside of your club," Warwick remarked.

The man gave a laugh. "It happens every so often. You know, I've got to keep up with the latest gossip, and what better way to do so than be present when it happens."

"I'm certain you'll be hearing all about this tomorrow," Warwick said, nodding his head toward his sister.

"Tomorrow? Tonight, Your Grace," he said with a scoff.

Warwick sighed and nodded. He was probably right, but right now Warwick really didn't care. He was just happy to see his sister having a good time. That it was all thanks to a modiste, he wasn't going to mention to his gossiping friend.

~*~

Christianne watched, along with nearly every other guest at the Duke of Warwick's ball, as Lady Margaret opened the dancing with none other than the prince himself. There was no doubt that tongues would be wagging the following day, wondering how the duke had managed such a coup for his sweet, young sister. The prince almost never attended coming out balls and even more rarely did he dance with the young lady in question.

Christianne spied Miss Sheffield among the dancers, giggling away with some handsome young man. That one would never lack for a partner, she thought to herself. Good for her! Christianne gave a decisive nod.

She approved of strong-minded young women who didn't try to hide their emotions behind a fluttering fan. Miss Sheffield was just such a girl. She laughed when she found something funny, and... Well, she almost always found something funny. And she was always making others laugh right along with her, Christianne noted with a smile as the gentleman she was with burst out with a loud guffaw.

Across the room, beyond the dancers, Miss Hemshawe stood talking with the Duchess of Kendell. The girl cleaned up well. It was a shame she didn't do so more often. It was rare that Christianne saw her at a party. She was much too involved in her horses and the races her father took her to. It wasn't right and Christianne wasn't sure that it didn't hurt the girl's marriage options. Who would want to marry a woman who knew more about horses than nearly anyone and could beat you were you to be so stupid as to race against her?

It looked like poor Mrs. Aldridge was trying to be a part of that conversation, but the duchess had so far managed to keep her at arm's length. It was such a shame. Mrs. Aldridge tried so hard to fit in but always went for the top instead of being happy with befriending less exalted peers. At least she didn't have that dog with her this evening. Duchess was adorable, but she tended to get into everything and command the attention of everyone around her. The little pup certainly did have an appropriate name, Christianne thought with a laugh.

"And what is tickling your fancy this evening, Lady Norman?" a smooth, deep voice said from just behind her, sending chills of happiness racing up her spine. Liam's familiar scent of sandalwood and soap assailed her welcoming senses.

Christianne popped open her fan and tried to cool her cheeks, which she was certain had flushed the moment she'd heard her friend's voice. How ridiculous she was being, behaving like a young girl! For goodness' sake, she'd known this man for over twenty years—and intimately—which only just reminded her that she had to tell him about the product of that intimacy soon.

She still stung from Tina's brash words the other day, but sadly, everything her daughter had said was true. It *was* her fault Tina had had to grow up in such a horrid situation. And it *was* her fault she would probably be paying for her freedom until... Well, until she could tell Liam and get him to put a stop to it.

But not tonight. She just couldn't face up to such harsh realities tonight. For just one night, she wanted to laugh and forget all of her troubles. Was it too much to ask?

She looked up into Liam's smiling green eyes. He'd changed so little in the intervening years. Oh yes, there were now lines like starbursts streaking out from the corners of his eyes, but that only showed how much the man smiled, and indeed, the lines around his mouth bespoke of so many years of laughter. But other than that, he was still the man she'd fallen in love with so very long ago.

"Oh nothing, just my own silly thoughts," she admitted, giving him a welcoming smile.

"You? Having silly thoughts? Is it possible?" he asked, teasing her.

She rapped his arm with her fan, but that only made him laugh. "And where is your bevy of admirers?" she asked.

He looked at her curiously.

"At Lady Bradmore's ball you were surrounded by young men," she prompted.

"Oh, them. Yes, well..." He frowned for a moment. "They weren't actually wanting to know the name of my tailor or to learn about the latest fashion. In fact, they are the ones who now set that fashion, not me."

"What? You cannot convince me that you are not still a leader among the most fashionable gentlemen," she said laughing.

He gave her a wistful smile. "I have had my day and it is past. Those young men wanted advice on how to be a leader of society and fashion from an old hand who is no longer quite in that role."

"Oh, I am so sorry," she said, sobering. "How awful it is getting old."

"Indeed! But I refuse to give in! Come, let us dance!" He grabbed her arm and started to pull her toward the floor.

"What? It's the middle of the set, we can't just—" But he'd already pulled her onto the floor. There was nothing for it but to join in and stop complaining.

"I must warn you, my lord..." Christianne said once the movements of the dance brought them close enough together so that they could talk.

"Yes?" He wiggled his shoulder at her as they went round each other so close their shoulders almost touched.

She couldn't help but giggle at his antics. "We are not to have such behavior as we did at Lady Bradmore's party," she said, completing her thought.

"Oh no? But I thought you enjoyed yourself that evening."

"I did, but our behavior was completely inappropriate," Christianne said, trying to maintain at least a façade of decorum.

"Ah yes, but old people can be forgiven so much," he said before moving away from her with the steps of the dance.

"You are incorrigible, sir," she said, once they were together again.

He sighed heavily but with a broad smile on lips. He didn't have time to say anything further as the dance moved them apart once more.

The next time they were together, he completely changed the topic by making funny observations about their fellow party-goers. He had her giggling throughout the rest of the dance—so much for proper behavior, she thought with a laugh.

CHAPTER EIGHTEEN

After the dance, Christianne did manage to convince him to pay attention to other ladies, but he was back by her side a mere twenty minutes later. "Come outside with me. The evening is cool and it is much too stuffy in here," he said, commandeering her hand and tucking it into the crook of his arm.

She pulled back. "And what if I don't want to go outside with you, my lord?" she said, raising an eyebrow at him.

He mimicked her but said nothing.

"Oh, very well," she conceded.

He gave a laugh and drew her outside into the garden.

"It is a lovely night," she agreed, taking in a deep breath of fresh air.

"And these garden paths are absolutely perfect," he said, leading her away from the house.

The moon was nearly full and quite bright, which was a good thing, otherwise it would have been too easy to get lost in such a large garden. On the other hand, Christianne supposed there were a number of couples only too happy to do just that.

They walked slowly, but even then they managed to get far enough away from the house that the strains of the music and the incessant chatter of so many people could hardly be heard.

"My goodness," Christianne said, "just how big is this garden?"

"I honestly don't know, but considering the size of the house and that it is owned by the Duke of Warwick, I imagine it could be much larger than what you'd expect in town," Liam commented.

"Yes, I believe you're right."

"I don't mind. It allows me to have some time alone with you," he said, pausing and turning toward her. He ran the back of his hand down her cheek. "Do you know how much I've missed you?"

She gave an awkward little laugh. "It couldn't have been too much. You were always a popular one. I may have been in the countryside, but I still read the London papers, and they were filled with stories of your conquests."

"I never had any conquests!" he said immediately. He calmed his voice and continued, "On the contrary, my popularity within society only emphasized the fact that you weren't there."

Warmth filled Christianne's heart. "You did always know just the right thing to say, my lord."

"My lord? What happened to Liam?"

Christianne just smiled up at him. "You've always been Liam in my heart."

"Your heart is a very good place for my name, but I'd like it on your lips as well."

She gave a nod but didn't have a chance to say anything as he bent toward her and touched his lips to hers. At first it was just the lightest kiss, but it quickly grew into something a great deal more passionate. His arms wrapped around her waist, pulling her close. She opened her mouth to his and reached out tentatively with her tongue. She was well rewarded for her bravery as he responded likewise. Soon their tongues were dancing together as his hands shifted lower, grasping her buttocks and pulling her tightly against his growing admiration.

"Oh, Liam, I have missed you," she whispered into his shoulder when they separated in order to catch their breath.

"And I you, my sweet Christianne."

She closed her eyes and rested her head on his chest but didn't dare leave it for long for fear of messing up her hair. She didn't want the entire world knowing what they'd been up to.

"Do you think we can stop playing the silly courtship games of the young and just be together?" he asked, looked down into her eyes.

"I would like that but..." But how could she be with this man and not tell him the truth? She owed it to him. He deserved to know he had a daughter. But if she told him... how much would he hate her for keeping it from him all these years? No, she couldn't risk it, and yet...

"But what? What's going through that busy mind of yours? Are you worried about what people would say?"

"No."

"About your sons? Would they mind, do you think? You are a grown woman and a widow," he pointed out.

"Yes, of course. No, I don't think Henry or Francis would mind at all, honestly. They only want me to be happy."

"Then what is it, Christianne? What's stopping you?"

She pulled away from him. "I..." She couldn't do it. She couldn't tell him just yet, but she couldn't be with him until she had. "I think we should return to the party and leave serious discussions for another time," she said finally.

She was such a coward!

~*~

Tina was enjoying a lull in the flow of ladies needing assistance with their gowns. She had made a small recommendation to one young lady, whose gown was simply hanging off her shoulders, to make it sit better and be more flattering. A few pins later and the young woman's jaw dropped when she saw the result.

Immediately following that, a stream of ladies, young and old, had come in to ask Tina to work her magic on their dresses. She had been able to help a number of them, although not all. And she had made appointments to pay calls on a number of ladies to make new gowns for them. In all, it was turning out to be a very profitable evening. Surprisingly, Lady Margaret had been right, Tina thought with a little smile.

It seemed as if just thinking of her made the young lady appear from nowhere. "I'm so glad to see you smile," Lady Margaret said, coming up to her little corner of the ladies' withdrawing room.

"I was just thinking how right you were that this would be a good way to get new clients. I've made appointments with no fewer than four ladies so far this evening."

"Oh, I am so happy!" Lady Margaret clasped her hands together and gave Tina a bright smile.

"And how are things going for you? How was your dance with the prince?"

"You were right about that too! It was a lot easier to manage once I began to think of him as merely another self-centered gentleman." Lady Margaret laughed. "I've danced with two more gentlemen since."

"Excellent! I'm so happy for you. Are you enjoying yourself?"

"I didn't think I would, but yes, I am!"

"That is wonderful, Lady Margaret," Tina said, relieved that things were working out well for her friend.

"I have to admit, I didn't come here to tell you how the party was going but to ask you to come out to the garden. I believe my brother wanted to have a word with you," Lady Margaret said, a bright smile growing on her face.

Tina was immediately suspicious. Why would the duke want to have a word with her? She wondered if Martin had said something to him earlier about her visiting with Lady Margaret. But surely he wouldn't choose the middle of his sister's ball to reprimand her for presuming to be friends with his sister.

She even debated whether she really wanted to speak with the duke just now. She was still sore from his commanding note the other day, although Margaret had done a great deal to make her feel better.

Well, she didn't really had a choice. He was employing her, so she couldn't very well refuse to speak to him.

She gave Lady Margaret a small smile and stood. "Of course."

She followed her friend down the hall, through the kitchen—a madhouse of activity as the cook and her assistants prepared for supper—and then, oddly enough, out the servant's door that led to the back gardens.

"I'm sorry for the circuitous route, but I don't think I could have taken you out through the ball itself," Lady Margaret said, turning slightly to speak to her.

"Oh, of course," Tina said. "He wanted to meet in the garden?"

"Yes. It's so much cooler and quieter here."

Tina did have to agree, and it was pleasant to get a breath of fresh air. It wasn't too dark thanks to a nearly full moon.

She was led to a broad oak close to the small kitchen garden. This part of the garden was hardly more than a patch, just big enough to grow a few herbs, but it was still quite a luxury for being in the middle of London. Tina hadn't seen the rest of the garden, but it seemed to be of a good size, at least from where she stood.

"If you would just wait," Lady Margaret said, "I'll inform Warwick that you're here."

Before Tina could say a word, Lady Margaret had disappeared.

~*~

Warwick was wondering if he could possibly avoid the pointed looks from Lady Shipton. She was well known to enjoy the comforts of another man's bed while her husband was warming his mistress's sheets.

"Warwick," his sister's voice startled him.

"Margaret, what are you doing sneaking up on people," he said with a little too much pique in his voice.

She laughed. "I didn't sneak up on you, I walked straight up to you. You simply weren't watching." She craned her head to the right.

"Who were you looking at?"

"No one. What did you need?" he asked in a much more moderate tone.

"Oh, Tina is waiting for you outside in the garden, by the oak tree," she informed him.

"What? Why?"

"You said you would apologize to her," Margaret reminded him.

"I said I would speak to her," he corrected.

"Well, she's in the garden. Go speak to her."

"Not in the middle of your ball! Don't be ridiculous. I'll speak to her tomorrow or the day after," he said.

"Oh, I see what it is. You would much rather dance attendance on Lady Shipley. Is that it? Do you know, I heard the most shocking—"

"How have you heard anything about Lady Shipley?" he asked, cutting her off.

"I danced with the prince. That man gossips like you wouldn't believe! He told me—"

"I don't think I want to hear all that he told you," he said, interrupting her once more. My God, he might be a prince, but surely the man would know better than to fill an innocent girl's ears with lurid gossip! "It is very inappropriate that he even mentioned such things to you."

"He felt I should know something about the members of society since my chaperone has been indisposed," Margaret said, coming to the prince's defense.

Warwick sighed. He would have a word with the man if he thought it would do any good, but the prince didn't listen to anyone but his bosom beau, Brummel. Well, it looked like he was caught. He saw his sister's smirk. Yes, she knew it too.

"Very well, I will speak with Miss Rowan. Where did you say she was?"

"By the oak tree in the garden. The one by the kitchen entrance. I thought that was a more appropriate place for her to wait for you."

Warwick shook his head and headed out to the garden. Only his sister would think that meeting in a romantic garden at night was an appropriate place for him to meet with her friend rather than in his office. Granted, it would have been the following day but still...

On the other hand, it was a *romantic* garden. One might get ideas meeting out there.

On the other hand, Miss Rowan was a *modiste*. In his *employ*. He had no right to be thinking anything romantic about her. He should *not*, he sternly reminded himself.

On the other hand, he had had a very pleasant drink with her the week before. He'd truly wanted to get to know her better, to spend some time with her. Nothing had changed since then.

On the other hand, what was the point of getting to know her? It wasn't as if he could give her a carte blanche. He respected and admired her much too much to do that. Yes, she was beautiful with spectacular green eyes, a luscious figure, and a mouth that looked... No! He would not allow his mind to wander into that labyrinth.

Warwick paused and took in a deep breath of the cool night air. It was very refreshing and did wonders to clear his head, which was a good thing because with the way his thoughts were going right now, he had more hands than one of those Indian gods he'd seen in the museum.

Miss Rowan was standing, looking a trifle awkward by the oak tree just as Margaret had said.

He walked up to her. "Good evening, Miss Rowan."

CHAPTER NINETEEN

"**G**ood evening, Your Grace," Miss Rowan said with a curtsy. "Lady Margaret said you wished to have a word with me? I hope I haven't done anything... Has someone complained about the service I'm providing here this evening? You aren't still bothered that I said something about the color of your coat?"

He gave a laugh. "I can't say that I'm happy to receive such criticism just when I'm about to host a ball, but I suppose you simply can't help yourself when it comes to fashion—be it women's or men's. And no, I have heard no complaints about your work. In fact, I believe I overheard a few women talking about how talented you were with your needle and pins. Did you do something to someone's dress?" He tried to remember exactly what it was he'd overheard. As soon as he'd realized they were discussing feminine things, he'd turned away and sought a dancing partner elsewhere.

"I did fix the dresses of a few women. There was one poor girl whose dress was so ill-fitting as to be almost indecent," Miss Rowan admitted.

"Well, whatever it is, you're certainly gaining an excellent reputation."

"That's very good. Then, er, what did you wish to speak to me about?"

"Ah! Yes, well..." This was a lot more awkward than he'd thought it would be. "I, er, that is Margaret felt I should apologize for the note I sent you the other day asking you to be here this evening."

"*Margaret* felt you should apologize?" she asked with a boldness that probably shouldn't surprise him. She was a brave woman. Very few people had the nerve to question a duke. Perhaps she just didn't know the proper way to behave.

And if that were the case, he secretly wished she never learned. Having someone stand up to him—aside from Martin—was refreshing.

"She asked me to do so," he acknowledged.

"But *you* don't feel that you should?"

"I am a duke, Miss Rowan, I don't apologize to anyone and—"

"Certainly not to people who you pay to work for you," she finished for him.

"Precisely."

"And do you always invite the people who work for you into your drawing room for a drink?" she asked.

She had him there.

"No, of course not. That was an exception."

"Lady Margaret told me that you and your secretary are good friends and have always been so."

"Yes. We grew up together," Warwick said.

"And you pay him, don't you?"

"I pay him a great deal of money."

"And you're still friends with him," she said, pressing her point.

"I am, but I don't want to be friends with you," he said, finally tiring of her relentless attack.

"I beg your pardon?"

What was wrong with him, Warwick wondered. He hadn't even had all that much to drink, and here he was wanting nothing more than to kiss this beautiful woman. He shouldn't! He couldn't... Well, he could, but it would be very wrong. But he couldn't stop looking at her lips. It was positively distracting!

"I'm sorry, that came out wrong. I, er, I do want to be friends with you, but it's..."

"Awkward? Wrong because you're a duke and I'm a seamstress?" she filled in as he faltered for something appropriate to say.

"Beautiful," he said finally, voicing what was in his heart. "Attractive. And much, much too sweet and innocent."

He took a step back, suddenly realizing he was standing so close they were practically touching. He also noted that she hadn't retreated. He could feel the heat emanating off her body. That was nice. Very nice. But he still couldn't kiss her. It would be wrong.

"How do you know I'm so innocent?" she asked, taking a small step toward him.

"I can see it in your eyes," he said, shifting backward just a half step.

She took another step forward and looked up at him, a small smile playing her immensely kissable lips. Her scent of lavender and cotton played havoc with his senses. "Are you certain? It's quite dark out here."

"You are playing with fire, Miss Rowan," he warned her.

"I know, and if anyone were to ask me why just now, I honestly would not be able to answer them."

She took a step back and shook her head. "You are a duke, and I am no one."

"You're *not* no one. You are an incredibly intelligent, beautiful woman who has done more for my sister than anyone ever has."

Miss Rowan's lips hitched up into a one-sided little smile. "Lady Margaret."

"She means more to me than anything, and the fact that you've been kind to her and have helped her... If you had helped me personally, it wouldn't have meant nearly as much."

Her gaze moved back to his. "She just needed a friend."

"And you were there."

She nodded.

"And now you're here," he added, giving in to the overwhelming urge. He took that last step that separated them and pressed his lips to hers. She tasted as sweet as he thought she would. Clean and fresh and delicious.

He deepened the kiss, pulling her even closer so their bodies fit together like two pieces of a puzzle. She pulled away with a gasp. "Just as I thought," he said with a smile. "A complete innocent."

"You're a horrid man, Your Grace! Did you do that just to tease me? Just to prove your point?" She started to turn away, but he grabbed her arm.

"I would never do such a thing." His anger was on the rise. "I would never touch a woman who didn't want to be touched, and I would never harm an innocent."

She stopped trying to pull away. "Then?" she asked.

"Then what?"

"Why did you kiss me?"

"I think I already told you that. You're a beautiful woman."

"Ah, so you think that because I'm nobody—"

"Stop saying that you're nobody! You *are* somebody. You're somebody wonderful and important, and you do excellent work of which you should be proud! I kissed you because I'm attracted to you. I would like to do so again, but I won't because I respect you." He calmed his voice. "I allowed my feelings to cloud my judgment. I apologize."

She let out a deep breath. "Thank you."

"For losing control?" he asked with a little laugh.

"No. For being honest with me...and for respecting me. Many men wouldn't. They would see someone in my position as fair game."

Warwick nodded. "There are men like that. I am not one of them."

"I appreciate that."

He gave her a slight nod. The sound of music died away, and suddenly he was recalled to his duties. It was probably time for supper, and he had to escort Miss Sheffield. "I must go..."

"Of course. I'm sure I'm needed back in the lady's retiring room."

Neither one made a move to leave for a moment, they just stood there looking at each other. Warwick, strangely enough, felt as if he could stare at her all night. But he couldn't.

With a short bow, he turned and went back into the ball.

Tina could only stand there for a moment. She needed to pull herself together and go back to work, but when she raised her hand, her fingers were shaking.

~April 15~

Tina couldn't put it off any longer, she had to apologize to her mother. She'd seen her the night before at the ball but hadn't said anything. She wasn't certain whether Lady Norman had seen her sitting in a corner of the withdrawing room. In any case, she had been remiss in not going to her immediately. She was going to remedy that today.

The footman at her mother's home no longer even blinked an eye when she came asking for Lady Norman. He simply showed her directly into her private drawing room where her mother was sitting at a small writing desk.

"Tina, did we have an appointment today?" she asked, giving the footman a nod. "Bring some tea," she instructed him.

He bowed and left.

Tina curtsied and held it for slightly longer than usual. "I've come to apologize for my horrendous behavior the other day...and for taking so long to actually come say this."

Lady Norman gave a little shake of her head. "It's never easy facing someone after words have been exchanged." She indicated that Tina sit on the sofa, then took the seat across from her.

"No, but I should have done so sooner in any case." She paused and then added, "I was angry that day, and I had no right taking it out on you. I'm afraid I do that. I know it's wrong, but somehow I just can't help myself."

"I think you were angry with me as well and rightfully so. What I did to you... Well, at the time I thought it was a good solution. The Rowans were a good, upstanding family in the village. They already had children, so I knew you would have playmates. I never thought they would treat you as anything other than their own."

Tina had to laugh or else she would cry. "No, they certainly never treated me as their own, unless you count the beatings which they gave regardless."

"Beatings?" Her mother sat up.

"Not enough to permanently mark me, but certainly something to make sure I behaved," Tina corrected.

"Oh. Yes well, even Norman used a cane on his sons every so often. I never approved, but there was nothing I could do to stop him."

"Was he a good man, Baron Norman?" Tina asked. She assumed he wasn't her father, otherwise she wouldn't have needed to be gotten rid of, but still, she was curious.

Her mother looked toward the fireplace, but Tina could tell she wasn't actually looking at it, but rather seemed to be lost in thought. After a moment, Lady Norman shook her head. "He wasn't what one would call a kind or thoughtful man, but he never did take his switch—or a fist—to me. He tolerated me only a little more than I tolerated him." She sighed. "He needed heirs. I was young and could provide them. That was the extent of our relationship. Once he had his two boys, he let me seek my pleasures elsewhere." She turned back and smiled at Tina. "Which is how you came about."

"But you couldn't tell him about me?" she asked.

Her mother's face paled slightly. "No! My goodness, no. If he, or anyone else for that matter, ever found out..." She shook her head. "No, when he brought me back to London it was with the express instructions that no one was to know we had such an arrangement. He even insisted on escorting me to some parties and doting on me in public just to maintain the illusion that we had a happy marriage. When I discovered I was expecting..." She bowed her head, studying her fingers as she spoke. "I panicked. I disappeared. I told no one but my maid and hid myself away in the dower house at the abbey. I'd had no problems giving birth to my boys, so I assumed I would have none with you, and thank goodness I didn't because I didn't even have a midwife with me when you came."

"My goodness! You bore me entirely by yourself with no one there but your maid?" Tina was shocked.

"I was too terrified of someone telling Norman. I couldn't risk it." She looked up and met Tina's gaze. "Absolutely no one knew I was carrying a child, and no one knew I bore one. No one but the Rowans have ever known we have any sort of connection, and I've paid them well to keep that secret since the day I left you with them."

Tina could only laugh, but there was no amusement in it. "Yes, you paid them well, and so shall I for the rest of my life."

"No! No, you won't. I'm going to fix that. I promise you, Tina, I will see this situation corrected."

"I can't imagine how," Tina admitted.

"I... I have a plan. I just need some time to get it started."

Tina nodded. What else could she do? She had to accept what Lady Norman said and hoped this plan of hers would work. But she also couldn't forget she was here to apologize. "I suppose it's not really your fault, what my foster-father is doing. You did what you could in a difficult situation and tried to do what you thought was right."

"It's not that I didn't want you, Tina," her mother said. "It's that I feared what would happen should anyone find out. I'd heard tales... Women being thrown out of their homes, never allowed to see their own children. Having to go to work houses along with the bastard children they bore. I knew my parents would never accept me back if they found out. I had no one I could trust." Her mother's eyes grew glassy with unshed tears. "I'm so sorry. I didn't mean for you to have a hard life. If I could have done something, *anything* more for you, you know I would have. I'd hoped that Norman would die quickly. He was much older than me. I was certain he would die before too long. But that man... He lived to the age of eighty! A bitter, angry old man."

"He only died, what, a year and a half ago?"

Lady Norman nodded. "Much too late for me to do anything more for you than what I'd been doing."

Her mother got up and moved to the sofa, enveloping Tina in a long hug. "I'm sorry. I'm so sorry, Tina. I wanted to do so much more for you. I wanted so much to take care of my little girl. To raise you as my own but... I just couldn't!"

Tina accepted her mother's hug, and her own eyes stung with tears. She too had wanted her mother to do more. To be there for her. The woman she'd called mother had been nothing of the sort, and Tina had always longed for a little, just a little love.

They stayed that way for a few minutes before Tina pulled back and asked, "What about my father? Did he know? Was there anything he could have done?"

Lady Norman pressed a finger to the corners of her eyes to dispel the tears. "No. He still doesn't know. But I'm determined to make things right and tell him. It's he who I think will be able to solve our problem with your foster-father."

Tina nearly jumped. "What? Do you really think... And you haven't told him? You haven't spoken to him?"

Her mother grasped her hands in hers. "I will do so soon, very soon, I promise. And then, once he knows, I'm certain he'll do everything he can to get out of this horrid situation."

"Why haven't you told him before now?"

"I...I'm afraid. I don't know what he'll say. What he'll do."

"Do you think he won't take it well?"

Her mother shook her head. "I have no idea. Absolutely none, I'm sorry. But I will tell him."

Tina nodded. She had no other choice but to accept this.

CHAPTER TWENTY

Lady Norman sat back and looked at Tina. "How is your life here in London going—aside from your business? Have you met anyone? Made friends with other young people?"

Tina couldn't help the laugh that burst out of her mouth. She cleared her throat. "I have been doing nothing but working, my lady. When and where would I have a chance to meet people?"

Her mother smiled sadly. "I don't know. I'd just hoped..." She let her voice trail off with some expectation.

"No. The only friendship I've made is with Lady Margaret."

"That's a very good friend to have—the sister to a duke!"

"Yes, and she has been quite wonderful. You know she asked me to work at her ball last night so I could gain more clients," Tina mentioned.

"And did you?"

"Yes, as a matter of fact, I did. I have four new clients who I have to pay calls upon."

"Excellent!" Her mother was quiet for a moment. "I would have been very happy to hear that you'd had some male admirers as well," she said with a suggestive smile.

Tina debated telling her about the duke but thought it best not to name any names, so she gave a little shrug of her shoulders and said, "Well, there is one gentleman who has been rather particular in his interest."

"Oh? A gentleman?"

"Yes. The relation of one of my clients," Tina explained.

Lady Norman's expression grew wary. "You do know—"

"That he might think I'm a light-skirt?"

"Yes," Lady Norman admitted.

"I know, and I've been very careful to keep him from getting that idea."

"It could ruin not only your business but your life here in London. Tina, beware of such gentlemen," her mother said, clearly becoming worried.

"Have no fear, I've been absolutely straightforward with him. There has been nothing beyond a little light flirtation, and even then I told him there would be absolutely nothing further. He said he respects me and wouldn't dream of pursuing anything further. Neither one of us has any fantasies this could go beyond what it is."

"And you trust him?"

"Yes," Tina said, thinking about. "Yes, I do. He's a man of his word." Her mother seemed satisfied with this so Tina gave her a little nudge and asked, "Might I turn the question around and ask about you?"

Her mother actually flushed slightly. "Well, there is a gentleman I am quite enamored of and who, I believe, feels the same about me. Sadly, I don't believe it will go much further than that."

Tina gave a little laugh. "Well then, it looks like we're in the same boat of failed romances."

~*~

Warwick was at work in his study when a footman came in. "There's a gentleman caller, Your Grace, for Lady Margaret. Shall I inform him that she is not at home?"

"Ah, and so it begins," Martin said with a laugh.

Warwick glared at him just long enough to understand his comment was not appreciated. He then turned to the footman. "No, Marcus. Show him into the drawing room and inform my sister." This was a good thing, Warwick reminded himself. Gentlemanly interest in his sister would move her one step closer to finding a man she could love and marry.

But one thing was certain, he was not going to allow her to marry just anyone. No, the man his sister eventually married was going to care for her as he did, if not more. He was going to be intelligent, wealthy, and a man of integrity. Warwick would accept nothing but the best for his little sister.

The footman bowed and left to do his bidding.

"I suppose I'll have to go and chaperone. My cousin hasn't been seen or heard from in days," Warwick said, popping his pen back into its stand and straightening his papers.

Martin sniggered but wisely said nothing.

The gentleman in question was some sort of fop who clearly had too much time and money to spend on his wardrobe. He was wearing a brilliant peacock blue coat with large silver buttons. His matching waistcoat was embroidered with silver birds— peacocks to match the color of his coat, Warwick assumed. Thank goodness, his lower half was covered by standard buff-colored knee britches and boots so gleaming they had to have taken hours to polish. He was staring out the window when Warwick entered the room.

Did this fop really think he was good enough for the sister of a duke? For Margaret? Warwick nearly scoffed out loud. He supposed, however, he should give the fellow the benefit of the doubt and allow him to prove his worthiness, despite the initial impression the man made.

The man noticeably paled when he saw who had come in. "Your... Your Grace," he stammered as he bowed. "I, er—"

"You came to see my sister," Warwick interrupted him. "Yes, of course, as you should. My apologies she hasn't set a particular day when she is at-home to callers. I shall remind her to rectify that. But for now, please, have a seat. I'll see to it that tea is served." He popped back out of the room feeling like a fool. Domestic chores were not something he was used to performing—even something as mundane as remembering to order tea for guests.

Happily, Margaret was already having a word with a maid just outside the door when he closed it behind him. "Oh good, you remembered. I walked in and realized I'd forgotten to ask for refreshments to be served," he said to his sister when she turned toward him.

She smiled up at him. "I would have been extremely surprised if you *had* remembered." She turned back to the maid, "And do see if Cook has made more of the lemon cake the duke likes so much."

Margaret turned back to Warwick. "Who's come?" she asked.

"I haven't the foggiest, some fop. The footman merely told me that a gentleman caller was here to see you. I wasn't in the room long enough for him to introduce himself." He took her hands in his. "Margaret, I know you're under a great deal of pressure to find a husband, but please remember you don't need to accept the first man who asks for your hand. I want you to be happy. You need to choose the right man for you, preferably someone…"

She squeezed his hands, then said with a laugh, "Warwick, no one is going to propose to me today. They are just coming to call to get to know me better, and so I can get to know them. Don't worry. I will take my time and find the right person, I promise."

He nodded and let go. "You are too smart for me, my girl." He started to turn back to the drawing room but remembered the other thing he'd meant to tell her. "Oh, and you need to decide which days you will be at-home to callers."

Margaret gave a nod of acknowledgment. But before she had time to respond, there was another knock on the door.

"That must be another one," Warwick said.

Margaret agreed and then went into the room before the next gentleman could be announced.

The first young man jumped up from the sofa when she entered. "Lady Margaret, so good of you to see me," he said, bowing to her.

"Oh, Lord Ainsby, how very kind of you to come visit," Margaret said as she curtsied in return. "I should have known it was you who had come when my brother told me that a gentleman of taste had come to call."

Warwick lifted an eyebrow at Margaret. She had managed to turn his description of the fellow into something much more polite.

"I, er, brought a posy of flowers for you," he said, whipping them out from behind his back. Warwick nearly burst out laughing. The fellow had managed to hide them the first time Warwick came into the room. Clearly, he'd wanted to make a show of giving them to Margaret.

She smiled and took the flowers. "Oh, they're beautiful, thank you."

The footman came in at that moment to announce the next gentleman. "Lord Roseberry."

Roseberry came in with a flourish, holding out a bouquet of roses. "My dear Lady Margaret," he said. He came to a dead halt when he saw Warwick standing there as well. "Er, and Your Grace. How good it is to see you as well," he added stiffly.

Warwick nodded in the gentleman's direction.

"Are those for me?" Margaret asked, indicating the flowers still in the slightly stunned gentleman's hand.

"Oh, yes! Yes, beautiful roses for a, er, beautiful lady," he said, keeping a wary eye on the duke.

Warwick tried his best not to laugh but clearly didn't completely succeed as he was given a stern look of warning from his sister. He cleared his throat and went to sit down.

The maid came in, pushing a trolley filled with tea and enough cakes to feed an army. How many people did they think were going to call?

It turned out, quite a lot! Not forty minutes later, although Lord Ainsby and Lord Roseberry had left after the prescribed quarter of an hour, a steady stream of gentlemen and lady callers had crossed their threshold.

Warwick was having a great time watching Margaret's admirers blanch when they caught sight of him. Their easy, well-rehearsed speeches came out haltingly as they kept one eye on him and the other on Margaret.

"Miss Sheffield and Lady Moreton," the footman announced to the crowded room.

Warwick had escorted Miss Sheffield into dinner the night before in a strange quirk of fate. He hadn't intended to escort her, but due to something she'd said, he'd found himself doing so. He'd actually enjoyed himself immensely in her company. She was a bubbly girl, always giggling about something. Lady Moreton, however, he'd not met before but was happy to see more ladies join their little party. So far, the gentlemen had greatly outnumbered the females.

About ten minutes after they'd arrived, Miss Sheffield came over to Warwick where he was sitting right in the middle of things. She gave him a bright smile as he stood. "Your Grace, I have heard that your gardens are absolutely spectacular during the day. Since I was only able to glance at them last night in the dark, I was wondering if you wouldn't mind showing them to me now?"

"I don't know that I would call them spectacular, Miss Sheffield. I would be more than happy to show them to you another time. I'm afraid my duty is here just at the moment, however."

"I would be more than happy to take over chaperoning your sister," Lady Moreton offered.

"That's very good of you, but—"

"Then it's settled," Miss Sheffield said before he could truly object. She took his arm and nearly dragged him from the room.

"I really don't know that this is a good idea, Miss Sheffield," Warwick said, trying to slow her down.

"No, you're right, Your Grace, it's not a good idea. It's a wonderful one," she said with a laugh.

"But Margaret—"

"Will do very well without you there, I assure you," she said. "In fact," she added as they stepped out into the garden, "she will do a great deal better *without* you than she was doing *with* you."

"What do you mean? She seemed to be doing quite well…"

"I beg your pardon, yes, Lady Margaret is doing well," she said, correcting herself. "The gentlemen are the ones who will do so much better without you there, alternatively glaring and laughing at them. It's difficult enough for a young man to pay a call on a lady, but to do so under the watchful eye of her older brother—and a duke, no less! Why, it's a miracle they managed to hold any sort of conversation at all." She started to laugh again. "You might not realize it, Your Grace, but your mere presence can be quite intimidating."

"Oh no, I am very well aware of what I'm doing, I can assure you," he said, giving a little laugh of his own.

"Hmm… Well then, it's even more important you are removed from the room. How do you ever expect your sister to make a match when you are there? And I do assume that is why you had her presented to society, is it not?"

He gave a little sigh of defeat. "Yes, yes it is. I stand corrected, Miss Sheffield. It's not easy for me, though."

"I'm sure it's not, but I'm certain you want to see your sister happily married."

"I do."

He couldn't admit that scaring off potential suitors was not the true reason he'd been behaving the way he had. In truth, it was the only way he could think of to entertain himself.

He'd always found such social gatherings to be deadly dull. With the only acceptable topics of conversation being the weather or who was seen with whom, he honestly could think of at least three dozen other things that he'd rather be doing—although he did stop short at having a tooth pulled.

"Then do, please, show me these beautiful gardens of yours," she said, giving him a bright smile.

CHAPTER TWENTY-ONE

*M*iss Sheffield was a very pretty girl and a great deal more forward than most young ladies of his acquaintance, but he couldn't help thinking she still wasn't nearly as appealing as Miss Rowan. Why was that, he wondered.

Perhaps it was Miss Rowan's lovely blonde hair that curled just so around her sweet face as compared to Miss Sheffield's pretty sable locks. Or maybe it was her brilliant green eyes, which held such intelligence rather than merely good humor as in Miss Sheffield's eyes. He rather suspected Miss Sheffield's non-stop giggles would drive a man to distraction after a while. Yes, Miss Sheffield was a very agreeable young lady, but no, she couldn't hold a candle to Miss Rowan.

When they returned to the drawing room a quarter of an hour later, Lady Moreton had been joined in her chaperone duties by the Duchess of Kendell.

"Ah, Warwick, I was wondering when you were going to show and scare away all these gentlemen," the older lady said with a chuckle.

"Miss Sheffield requested a tour of the garden precisely so I *wouldn't* do that," he responded with a smile of his own.

"Smart girl," the duchess said with a nod of approval to the young lady in question.

"Have I missed all of the gossip over who wore what and who was seen with whom?" Miss Sheffield asked with a twinkle of laughter in her eye.

"My God, I thought we'd already covered all that," Warwick said, suppressing a shudder.

"You may have with others, but we have yet to broach the topic," the duchess said, giving Miss Sheffield a conspiratorial wink. She turned back to Warwick. "You did very well hiring Miss Rowan to make Margaret's gowns. She did an excellent job on her court dress. I expected no less from her for Margaret's ball gown."

"I thought you didn't approve of Miss Rowan, Your Grace," Miss Sheffield said.

The woman leaned away from the young lady. "Didn't approve? What gave you that idea?"

"Oh, just how angry you got when she spoke to you at the beginning of the last Society meeting," she said, with a slightly worried look in her eyes.

"Did she say something inappropriate?" Warwick asked, curious beyond reason.

"Well, in a sense, yes," the duchess answered. "She thanked me for stepping in and presenting Margaret to the queen."

"I'm certain she only did so because she's my friend," Margaret said, joining in their conversation.

"You are friends with your modiste?" the duchess asked, sounding surprised.

"Yes. She's more than just a modiste to me. She's been so kind, so encouraging and helpful in so many ways. Even Warwick, who likes so few people you know, likes her."

Margaret gave him such a happy smile, it would have been horribly rude to contradict her. The fact that it was true wasn't necessarily something he was ready to admit publicly, though. He kept quiet even when the duchess raised an imperial eyebrow in his direction.

"Well, then," the duchess said, "perhaps I need to rethink my opinion of the girl. If she is as wonderful as you say..."

"She is," Margaret gushed.

"I have to say, I've always found her to be very kind and thoughtful," Miss Sheffield added.

The duchess nodded. "I will forgive her, then, for her presumption. She was clearly acting as a friend, in that case."

"I'm certain she meant no disrespect," Warwick added quietly.

As if that confirmed her opinion, the duchess nodded.

Talk turned to the next big social event, and Warwick knew for certain he was in for a very long season, indeed.

~April 23~

The following Wednesday, Christianne was happy to welcome the ladies of the Wagering Whist Society for another game of cards. She needed the diversion it would provide her. She'd been doing little else but worrying over what and when to tell Liam. It had to be soon, she knew that, for Tina's sake if not her own.

She was so grateful she and Tina had had their talk. It meant the world to her to be able to be open and honest with her daughter. Truly, it was the way she preferred to be with everyone. Yes, it had gained her a reputation for being a little too blunt, but no one could ever accuse her of bending the truth.

That was why it was so very difficult meeting Liam as she was—for she had met him just the day before at Lady Wasting's soirée. She'd flirted and tried to behave normally, but her heart just wasn't in it, and Liam could tell. He was being so very patient with her. Truly, she could not ask a man to be any more wonderful, which only made her feel even guiltier for not being able to tell him the truth.

But she did so love how their relationship had grown once more. He'd hinted once again that he wanted more, but she couldn't. She just couldn't until she'd told him the truth and then... She was certain he would be furious with her, and rightly so. But again, for Tina...

She was in such a quandary! She went back and forth in her mind—she *should* tell him, but she knew for certain now that she loved him, and she didn't want to lose him. She *needed* to tell him so that he could help Tina, but how furious was he going to be that she'd kept this from him for twenty years?

After playing a hand of whist, the duchess called for everyone's attention. "Ladies, ladies," she called out over the chatter. The ladies at the other table clearly hadn't heard her and continued to talk and laugh.

"Ladies!" the duchess called, clapping her hands.

"Duchess, I think you're going to have to be a little louder than that," Mrs. Aldridge said with a laugh. She had partnered with Christianne this time, which had been a very sad pairing since neither one had played well.

Duchess, Mrs. Aldridge's little dog, gave a number of sharp barks, which managed to catch the attention of the other four women, who all turned around to look to see what the commotion was about.

The dog was clearly thrilled with the attention her barks had received and ran over to Miss Hemshawe, who was sitting at the other table. Jumping onto her hind legs, Duchess gave a few more barks before resting her forelegs on Miss Hemshawe's knees.

The girl clearly loved dogs nearly as much as she loved horses. She clapped and laughed before scratching behind the dog's long, floppy black ears. "Oh, you are adorable and you know it, don't you, you sweet little thing," she said, bending toward the dog.

"Normally I would reprimand you for your dog's awful behavior, but in this case, I appreciate she got everyone's attention," the duchess said to Mrs. Aldridge.

The woman just gave a little snort of laughter. "Good girl, Duchess, good girl," she said to the puppy. Knowing this usually meant she was about to get a treat, the dog abandoned Miss Hemshawe to run to her mistress. She sat at her feet, her tail wagging so fiercely her whole bottom wiggled.

No one could hold back their laughter at the dog's antics.

Mrs. Aldridge dutifully rewarded her pet with the last bite of her cake.

While the dog was enjoying her treat, the Duchess of Kendell took advantage of having everyone's attention and said grandly, "Ladies, I believe it is time for us to tally the points."

"Have we completed the game?" Miss Sheffield asked.

"Yes, indeed we have. Now, who has the book with the points?" the duchess asked.

Christianne stood up. "I do. I'll include the points from the hands we just played, and then I'll add everything together."

She did so and was dismayed to find that she, herself, had the fewest number of points! She looked up to find everyone watching her.

She gave a little laugh. "Well, it looks as if I am our first loser."

She handed the book over to Lady Blakemore to check her calculations.

"Yes, I'm afraid you're right, Christianne," her friend said, handing the book back.

"Well then, Lady Norman, your deepest darkest secret," Mrs. Aldridge said with a bit too much anticipation in her voice.

Christianne froze. She absolutely froze. And she began wondering what had ever enticed her into agreeing to these terms. But wait, she hadn't agreed. She had been one of those who'd voted against them.

"Surely, for those of us who didn't agree to these terms..." she began.

"We voted, Baroness," the duchess reminded her. "And it was agreed by a majority of our members as to what the forfeit would be if one lost."

"But truly..."

"Lady Norman, whatever your secret is, know that it shall never leave this room," Lady Sorrell said earnestly.

"No, never!" Lady Moreton agreed. Many of the other women nodded as well.

"No one will breathe a word of it outside of this group. No one will tell their husband or any other member of their family. Remember, Lady Norman may be the one with the least points today, but in a few weeks, it could be you." And with those ominous words, the duchess turned back to Christianne.

Well, it wasn't as if she didn't have a secret to tell, Christianne thought sadly. It was one she'd been grappling with for the past few weeks. So, maybe this was a good thing. She could tell these women as a sort of practice for telling Liam. Surely once she'd faced the scrutiny and disgust these women would display, whatever response Liam had couldn't be any worse, could it?

"Very well," she said finally. "But once again, I must remind you that what we say here is to be held in the strictest confidence. No telling anyone—and I mean anyone—what you hear. Is that agreed?"

Everyone nodded. Miss Sheffield even held up her right hand and swore she would not tell a soul.

Christianne cleared her throat and took a deep breath. She sagged for a moment and then straightened her spine. She could do this! "All right, I'm ready for the social condemnation." She gave them all a slight smile. "Miss Rowan, Tina, is my natural born daughter. I was not careful when having an affair after my sons were born and... Well, I fostered her as soon as she was born and never told a soul about her. My husband never knew, my sons don't know, even her own father doesn't know of her existence."

"Her own father doesn't know?" Lady Moreton exclaimed. "Oh, I feel so sad for him. She's such a sweet person!"

"And so talented. I would definitely want to know I had such a lovely and talented daughter," Lady Blakemore said.

"Indeed," the duchess agreed. "I do not blame you for keeping her a secret, but her father should know of her existence."

"Does she know who her father is?" Miss Hemshawe asked.

"No. I couldn't tell her without telling him first," Christianne explained.

"But then you must tell him!"

"Yes, indeed." Everyone chimed in their complete agreement.

Christianne noted that no one said anything about the fact she'd had a child from a man other than her husband. Where was the shock, the outrage, the name-calling she'd always expected? Perhaps it would happen behind her back when she wasn't in the room. Yes, that must be it. Oh, but she hated the thought of people talking about her!

"You are not shocked?" she asked hesitantly. "I would rather you say so to my face than behind my back. I value straightforward speaking, as you all know."

"I'm not shocked," Mrs. Aldridge said. "I'm rather surprised when such things do *not* happen considering the morals displayed by so many of the *ton*."

"I agree completely," the duchess said.

"It is a sad fact, but there are enough children born outside of the confines of marriage that... Well, I'm sorry, Christianne, but your secret, while terrible and shocking to you, is rather ordinary and not so surprising to us," Lady Blakemore said.

"It *is* a sad reflection on our society," Lady Moreton agreed. "But no, we don't condemn you at all."

"It was a stupid mistake," Christianne admitted. "Not to be careful."

"Yes, for certain, but these things happen more often than anyone will admit," Lady Sorrell said.

Christianne blinked back her tears of gratitude, of relief. "Then you think... You think perhaps her father won't condemn me for not telling him? I'm terrified of doing so, but I know I must."

"May I ask a terribly personal and possibly inappropriate question?" Miss Sheffield asked.

Christianne had to laugh at that. "As if this entire conversation were not personal? Yes, of course, go ahead."

Everyone gave an embarrassed laugh but then turned to Miss Sheffield.

"Indeed, we couldn't get more personal, and yet I'm about to do so. But is the father, perhaps, Lord Ayres? Now that I know Miss Rowan is your daughter, I remember seeing the two of them together at your fashion party where you introduced her to us and remarking that they looked..."

Christianne felt her face blanch. "Is it that obvious?"

"They do look alike," Lady Blakemore agreed, "but you wouldn't know it unless they stood right next to each other."

"As they did that afternoon," Miss Sheffield agreed.

"And you have been rather close of late with Lord Ayres," Miss Sheffield pointed out.

"Yes," Christianne had to admit, but not without a warmth growing inside of her. "I believe we might have rekindled what we once had."

"But that's wonderful," Lady Moreton said, a smile growing on her face.

"It would be if I weren't so worried about telling him about Tina. I just..."

"Are you afraid he'll be angry?" Mrs. Aldridge asked.

"Furious, more like," Christianne said, nodding. "And I worry he won't be able to forgive me for not telling him twenty years ago when I should have."

There was silence in the room for a good minute.

"It wouldn't be overly surprising." Lady Sorell said out loud what they were probably all thinking.

"I just... I don't know what I would do if he were to reject me. I... I'm afraid I've quite fallen in love with the man—again," Christianne said, blinking furiously.

Claire came over and put her arm around Christianne's shoulders. "He won't reject you."

"Well, he might," the duchess said. She received some glares from the other women.

"And he would do so rightfully," Christianne agreed.

"But on the other hand, he might not," Miss Sheffield said. "He might be very happy to learn he has a daughter, no matter what her age."

"In any case, you *must* tell him," Lady Moreton said. "It would be wrong if you didn't."

Christianne sighed. "Yes, I know." Christianne could only hope he was as understanding as these ladies were.

Chapter Twenty-Two

"Margaret, I've been waiting for half an hour," Warwick called out, knocking on his sister's bedroom door.

"I'm sorry," she said, opening it. She seemed to be dressed, thank goodness. "I don't have Tina here to help me get dressed, and I couldn't decide what to wear."

"Why didn't you choose a dress this afternoon?"

"I did, but then I changed my mind...and then changed it again. But I think I've settled on this one. What do you think?" She twirled around, sending her pretty white dress with lavender ribbons flying around her.

"Very pretty. Now can we leave?"

"Yes. Let me just get my fan and my reticule," she said, looking around for the articles.

Warwick spied them on a chair by the window and retrieved them for her.

"Oh, thank you," she said with a sigh of relief.

Warwick held back a sigh of his own and ushered his sister out the door.

"I am so glad we're going to a party. I feel as if my season has finally begun. And you'll be able to meet young ladies as well."

"I'm not interested in getting married just yet. First I have to see you settled, then I'll begin to look around for a suitable wife for myself," he said, hoping she wouldn't suddenly get it into her head to play matchmaker for him.

"Yes, I know that's what we agreed, but still, it couldn't hurt for you to meet people and dance a few times with some promising young ladies. I'm sure there will be plenty for you to choose from."

She wasn't at all wrong. In fact, the moment they walked into the soirée, Warwick was openly stared at by both young ladies and their hopeful mamas.

They seemed hesitant to approach him, but once one daring mother had breached the fortified wall of his coldest look, he was suddenly swarmed. So much so, he had a difficult time keeping an eye on his sister. He really needed to work on that haughty look of his. His father was an expert, but Warwick's heart wasn't in it as thoroughly as it should have been. The women could clearly sense this.

"It is very nice to meet you again, my lady, and your lovely daughter, of course, but I do need to stay with my sister, if you wouldn't mind..." Warwick said at least four times within the first ten minutes. These women seemed to have very sharp elbows and were extremely intent on being right by his side. Margaret hardly stood a chance of staying by him.

He'd nearly had to physically move one young lady just so he could keep his sister next to him.

"I say!" she protested when he reached around her and pulled Margaret close.

"This is my sister, Lady Margaret," Warwick said, introducing her to the pouting girl. "I am here as her chaperone so you may go and annoy some other gentleman, thank you very much."

"Well!" The girl trounced off.

"Thank God!" Warwick said, turning to look at Margaret.

She just laughed. "I told you so."

"This is ridiculous. How do I let it be known that I'm not..."

"Oh, Your Grace, how wonderful to see you again!" an older lady said, interrupting him.

"Have I met your daughter? No, I haven't, and I don't particularly care to," he snapped.

"Well good, because I don't have one to introduce to you," the woman said with a laugh.

He looked at her and realized it was Lady Norman. "I do beg your pardon, my lady," he started.

"No need. You seem to have been swarmed as soon as you walked into the room," the lady said.

"I'm afraid I was. And all I want to do is chaperone my sister," he admitted.

"Not an easy task for a handsome, eligible duke," she said, laughing.

"It is much more difficult than I anticipated," he agreed.

"Perhaps if instead of just standing here, you sought out some gentlemen who might be interested in making her acquaintance. It's what chaperones usually do," the woman said, clearly trying not to laugh at him.

"Excellent idea!" He gave her a bright smile then bowed and turned to Margaret. "Shall we?"

She gave a little laugh. "I suppose if we must?"

"Yes, we must." He led her away to where some gentlemen were standing and talking with another young lady and her mother. Happily, he recognized two of the men from those who'd come to pay a call on Margaret after her ball.

It didn't take long, or very much convincing, to see his sister safely onto the dance floor in the company of Lord Roseberry. Sadly, that left him alone to be swarmed once again by those who hadn't already been asked to dance.

"It is so good of you to chaperone your sister," one airy young woman said. She was pretty and didn't seem to walk but float. He wondered how she did that. She also didn't stand still but kept shifting about.

"It is my pleasure. I am determined to see her happily wed before I can begin to think of myself," he said, hoping she would spread the word around so he wouldn't continue to be mobbed.

"How good of you. How very considerate," her mother said, nodding. "Have you taken her to Almack's?"

"No. I must say I'm going to attempt to avoid the place. I know it's all the rage but..."

"Oh yes, I would avoid it myself, only it is exactly where one must go if you want to find a husband for your sister," the woman said.

"I will try by attending private parties first," he said.

"And do you promenade in the park?" the girl asked.

"We have once," he admitted. "Do you enjoy doing so, Miss Holberth?"

"Oh, yes! I love to walk, and there is no better place to do so than along Rotten Row."

"You don't enjoy riding?" he asked.

"Yes, riding is quite pleasant, but walking is more..."

"Riding is excellent exercise," another young woman said, appearing on his other side.

"Indeed," he agreed.

"Do you prefer to ride or walk, Your Grace?" Miss Holberth asked.

"I prefer to ride—"

"So do I!" the second girl exclaimed. "As I said, it is wonderful exercise."

"I don't believe I've ever seen you on a horse, Miss Florent," the first girl said.

She looked down her nose and said, "I ride quite frequently."

"Perhaps you do so in the morning when there aren't so many people out?" Warwick offered, helping the girl out.

She gave him a bright smile. "Yes, that's right. I ride in the morning."

Warwick turned and found that another girl had elbowed her way to his side. He nearly sighed but figured he should probably get used to this. One thing was certain, however, none of the girls he'd seen so far this evening could hold a candle to Miss Rowan. One was too sallow, another too florid, a third had bad breath and crooked teeth. It was wrong to compare them to the modiste, especially since it was from one of these chits that he would have to choose a wife, but somehow he just couldn't stop himself. He had to try harder, he supposed.

"How have you been enjoying the weather, Miss—" he asked, suddenly realizing he didn't even know her name.

"Pendleton," she said with a giggle, although Warwick didn't see what was so funny. "We've met, but perhaps you don't remember," she added.

He smiled. "Yes, of course, I remember, Miss Pendleton. I'm afraid I just had a momentary hiccup. You will excuse me?"

"Oh, of course! It happens to everyone. How are you liking the weather, Your Grace?" she asked, turning the question back on him.

"Very well. I enjoy the warmth of summer and all the greenery," he said.

"I do too. Spring and summer are my favorite seasons," Miss Holberth said.

"Didn't I hear you tell Lord Bradmore that your favorite season was winter?" Miss Pendleton asked.

The girl frowned at her. "I don't recall," she said, narrowing her eyes at Miss Pendleton.

If looks could hurt, this one would certainly have caused some pain, Warwick thought to himself. He didn't want to start anything unpleasant so he said, "The winter is very nice too. Going on sleigh rides when it snows is great fun."

"Yes, indeed it is!" Miss Pendleton said.

"I thought you preferred summer," Miss Holberth said.

"I never said that. His Grace said *he* loved the summer."

"Ladies, I think we can agree that all the seasons have their merits," Warwick said, not wanting to start a fight.

"Oh, yes!" and "Absolutely!" both girls said at once. It suddenly hit him that while they contradicted each other, neither girl had disagreed with him on anything. Just for fun, he pointed outside into the darkness of the evening and said to the girls, "It's so pleasant when the sun doesn't set until late."

"I agree. That is one of the nicest things about spring and summer," Miss Pendleton said.

"Why, it's barely just set now," he added.

"Indeed, it's still nearly light out," the first girl agreed, not even turning to look outside.

Lord Roseberry chose that minute to return Margaret to Warwick's side. "What are you talking about Miss Holberth? It's been full dark for at least an hour if not more," Roseberry said with a laugh.

The girl flushed and turned to look for herself. "Oh, so it is! I have to admit, my lord, I had merely taken His Grace's word for it."

"I'm afraid I was funning with you, Miss Holberth," Warwick admitted.

"Oh." She looked confused.

"Causing trouble, Warwick?" Lord Wickford asked, joining them. He bowed to the ladies and Lord Roseberry before turning back to the girls. "He's a terrible cad, you know. If your mamas knew just how much of one, they certainly would never let you near the man." The man's eyes practically glowed with mischief.

"Oh," Miss Stokes said, forcing out a laugh. "Well then, perhaps I should return to my mother." She gave a curtsy, then fled.

"I believe my father is motioning for me to come to him," Miss Pendleton said, making a quick exit as well.

"I was merely testing a theory," Warwick said, not at all sad to see the backs of both girls.

"And that was?" Margaret asked, with a disapproving lift of her eyebrows, which made her look remarkably like their father.

"I wanted to see if they were simply agreeing with everything I said or actually expressing their own opinions," he admitted.

"And?" Wickford asked with a laugh.

"They were parroting everything I said," Warwick admitted.

"Well, of course they were! How silly you are, brother of mine. They're trying to win your favor," Margaret said.

"Well, *you* should know that's not the way to do it," Warwick laughed.

"Yes, I do. But they're just silly girls—"

"While you, Lady Margaret, are most certainly not," Lord Roseberry interjected. Warwick had nearly forgotten he was there.

"Thank you, my lord," Margaret said, smiling at him. And with that, he'd nearly wished he had stayed quiet. Warwick wasn't so certain he liked seeing that smile of hers directed at this fellow.

On the other, he was here to find her a husband, so he supposed he should put up with such things. Goodness, this was going to be a lot harder than he'd anticipated.

~April 24~

The following day, Christianne was looking through the Lady's Monthly Museum, a copy of which she'd bought with Tina. It was so odd, she'd never been very interested in fashion until her daughter had made it interesting for her.

"Lord Ayres, my lady," Harold, her footman, declared after a brief knock on her sitting room door.

Christianne hid her chagrin. She'd hoped to have a few more days to decide just how she was going to tell him about Tina. Instead, she placed a welcoming smile onto her face as she rose.

"Liam, what a lovely surprise!"

He bowed briefly before coming forward to take her hands. "I've been thinking, Christianne," he began.

She gave a little laugh. "Oh dear. Yes? What about?"

"I've been waiting patiently for you to discuss whatever it is that's been bothering you, but you don't seem able to bring yourself to point. I thought I would help you get there."

To her great shock, he dropped to one knee. "Christianne Norman, will you do me the great honor of becoming my wife?"

"Well now, that's a little drastic, don't you think? Just to get me to spill what's on my mind?" She gave a forced laugh.

He stood. "No, I don't think it is. I love you. I've loved you for years and only now can I truly make you mine. I'm not going to let anything stop me now."

She scoffed. "Just wait until you hear what I've been meaning to talk to you about," she said quietly.

He stood. "Then tell me, but before you do, answer my question."

She looked up into his deep green eyes. They were eyes she'd stared into so many times. Eyes she didn't think she would ever tire of. "I love you, Liam Ayres. I love you with all my heart."

He bent and kissed her lips ever so gently. It was a kiss, not of passion but of true love, and it simply melted her heart.

When he stood straight once again, she dropped down onto the sofa, which was luckily behind her.

He gave a little laugh. "I knew my kisses were good..."

"They turn my knees into water and you know it!" She patted the seat next to her.

He sat. "Are you ready to tell me?"

"Yes. Are you ready to hear it?" She wasn't entirely certain she was ready, but it was now or be alone for the rest of her life, knowing she'd thrown away her once chance at happiness because she was a coward. She wasn't going to do that.

He gave a nod.

CHAPTER TWENTY-THREE

Christianne took in a deep breath. "Tina Rowan, my modiste…"

"The girl who was here that first time I visited after you arrived?" he asked, cutting in.

"Yes."

"What about her?" He frowned, probably wondering why she was suddenly talking about a dressmaker.

Christianne took in a deep breath. "She's your daughter…and mine."

"Wh—" his lips formed the word, but no sound came out.

"You remember our wonderful affair when Norman brought me back to London after my boys were old enough?"

"Of course! It was the most wonderful… You disappeared. You just left without any explanation!"

She looked down at her hands and spoke quickly before she lost the nerve yet again. "I was pregnant and terrified. I was too scared to tell you. I… I didn't know how." Christianne swallowed at the lump in her throat, and then looked up into Liam's eyes.

He was frowning at her. He looked furious.

Before she could say a word, however, he simply stood up and walked out.

Christianne's heart cracked in two. Considering the pain she was feeling, she was certain half of it had just gone out the door with Liam. This time she didn't even attempt to hold back her tears.

~*~

The giggles coming from the drawing room could be heard from the stairway. What Tina couldn't believe when she walked into the drawing room at the duke's home was they were coming equally from Lady Margaret and the duke himself. She had never seen a man giggle!

The two dark heads bent over a table so close they were nearly touching. They were both concentrating intently on a pile of thin sticks while giggling away. It was the funniest thing Tina had ever seen.

"Warwick, you're going to make me move things," Lady Margaret said, clearly trying to hold back her laughter. She delicately held a similar stick between her fingers. "Stop laughing!"

He only laughed harder. "But you're so funny! You're going to move the other sticks, you know you are. You keep going for the most difficult ones."

"I don't! You are merely jealous because I got that last stick, and besides, you are such a coward, you only go for the easiest pieces." She looked up at him and stuck out the tip of her tongue.

He, in turn, touched his finger to the tip of her nose, giving it a light tap. Her tongue popped back into her mouth.

The footman standing behind Tina cleared his throat. "Miss Rowan is here to see you, Lady Margaret."

Brother and sister both sat up and turned toward the door where Tina was doing her best to keep her own giggles from erupting. Never had she seen two people so playful. The fact that it was the very upstanding Duke of Warwick and his sweet and elegant sister, Lady Margaret, only made Tina want to laugh even more.

"Ah, Tina! Come here. You're right in time," Lady Margaret said, not moving.

Her brother, however, stood up and gave her a slight nod of his head. She curtsied as he did so. His curls looked a little more tousled than usual, but other than that, he was wearing his usual brown coat, this one a slightly lighter color brown than others she'd seen. His waistcoat was of a deeper brown but as plain as could be. Not even gold buttons enlivened the dull outfit.

"What are you doing?" Tina asked as she came forward.

"We're playing spillikins," Lady Margaret said as if the answer was obvious.

Tina just shook her head. "I don't know the game."

"You've never played spillikins?" This time it was the duke who sounded amazed.

"No. What is it? What do you do?" Tina looked at the pile of sticks.

"You have to remove all the sticks one by one without upsetting any of the others," Lady Margaret explained.

"Oh. That doesn't sound too difficult," Tina said.

"You try it. Which one would you go for?" Lady Margaret asked.

Tina looked over the pile of sticks. It would be easiest to go for the ones on top, but where would the fun be in that? No, she would go for one that was sticking most of the way out of the pile but had a few other sticks resting on it. She examined it a moment longer, and then reached out and neatly pulled the stick free without upsetting any of the others. She handed it to Margaret. "This one," she said with a smile.

"Ha! I told you!" Lady Margaret said, pointing at the duke.

"Why wouldn't you just go for the one on top?" he asked, his voice a combination of exasperation and laughter.

"Because it would be too easy," Tina explained. "If this is a game, you want to challenge yourself."

"Ha!" Lady Margaret said again.

The duke chuckled and shook his head. "But then you might lose."

"True, but it is only a game after all," Tina pointed out.

"Oh, but the great Duke of Warwick can't possibly lose! He would—what, crumble into dust if he did," Lady Margaret said, clearly laughing at and teasing her brother.

"You don't know I wouldn't, do you? You've never seen me lose a game," he pointed out, his smile not wavering.

"No. No, I haven't," his sister conceded.

"Are you here on a social call or for business, Miss Rowan," the duke asked, turning to her.

"Oh, business. I've brought Lady Margaret's new dress," she said, retrieving the package she'd left on the table by the door.

She opened it and pulled out the beautiful cerulean blue gown she'd made for Margaret's morning calls.

"Ooooh," Lady Margaret breathed. "It's lovely!"

Tina brought it over for her client to touch. "The material is soft and will flow beautifully when you walk into a room," she said with a bright smile. "If this doesn't attract a bevy of suitors, I don't know what will."

"But isn't the color too dark?" her brother asked.

"It is darker than young ladies usually wear, but it will look magnificent with her eyes and coloring." Tina draped the dress over Lady Margaret's shoulder so he could see the effect.

"Oh, my word, yes! That is very flattering," he agreed, giving his sister a smile.

Just for fun, Tina took the dress and put it next to the duke as well. "This color would look good on you too, Your Grace. It even brings out the touch of blue you have in your eyes."

"You're right! I never noticed that before," Lady Margaret exclaimed.

"Many people with brown eyes have green in them. Your brother has some blue in his," Tina explained. "You just never noticed because he always wears brown so it hides the blue."

"Oh, Warwick, you really should get a coat of that color," Lady Margaret said.

The duke laughed. "No, thank you. I'll stay with what I've always worn and am comfortable with."

"But it makes you disappear, it's so dull," Tina argued.

He just smiled at her. "Precisely."

"Oh, you can't mean that, Warwick!" Lady Margaret protested.

"Do I owe you payment for all the dresses you've made?" the duke asked, changing the subject decisively.

"You haven't paid her for them and for the ball?" his sister asked.

The duke's eyebrows rose in his forehead. "No, I haven't. If you would come with me to my study, I'll settle my accounts for that and for this gown as well."

"Thank you, I would appreciate that." Tina gave Lady Margaret a little curtsy then followed the duke to his study.

Martin was at his desk when Warwick came in with Miss Rowan. She paused just inside the door, looking around at the book-lined walls, a small smile playing on her lips. It was odd. He saw these books every day but didn't even notice them. He wondered if it was the sheer number that impressed her or if it was something else.

"Good afternoon, Your Grace," Martin said formally, no doubt for Miss Rowan's benefit.

"It *is* a good afternoon, Martin," Warwick said, coming from behind Miss Rowan, who hadn't moved any farther into the room. "In fact, it is such a nice afternoon, I think you should take the rest of it off."

"Your Grace?" Martin asked, frowning at him.

"Well, it's only fair. I've spent the past hour doing nothing more than playing silly games with my sister. I think you deserve some time off too. Why don't you see if any of your friends are at that pub you like to frequent? I'm sure the walk would do you some good as well."

Martin looked from him to Miss Rowan and then back again.

"She's going to be leaving after I pay her for the work she's done. Isn't that right, Miss Rowan?" he asked the girl who had progressed from simply staring at the books to skimming the titles.

"Hmm? Oh yes, Your Grace. It's three guineas for the dress I delivered today, and I believe I've already sent you the bill for the other dresses and the time I spent working at the ball," she said.

"I would be happy to pay her so you can return to Lady Margaret," Martin offered, frowning at the modiste.

"No, that's all right. I'll take care of it. You run along." Why wouldn't the man just leave already, Warwick wondered. Could he tell Warwick wanted him gone? It was quite likely. Martin had always been uncanny in his ability to read him.

Martin starting putting things away on his desk, which was something he almost never did, Warwick noted. While he did so, Warwick joined Miss Rowan at the bookshelf. "Do you see anything that interests you? I have to admit, it's been a while since I've looked through these titles myself."

She turned a happy face toward him. "There are so many fascinating books here. I don't think I would get a lick of work done in this room. I would always want to read." She gave a little giggle that was utterly adorable.

He couldn't help but smile back at her. "Careful, Miss Rowan, or I might just get the wrong idea about you," he teased. At her raised eyebrows and quick glance at Martin, who was still straightening his desk unnecessarily, Warwick added, "That you were a bluestocking."

"Oh!" She gave a laugh that warmed him.

"Are you certain—" Martin started, as he approached them.

"Absolutely," Warwick said, interrupting him. "You enjoy your afternoon, and I'll see you tomorrow." He couldn't possibly get any clearer than that.

Martin frowned at Miss Rowan again before bowing and heading out the door, which Warwick noticed he left wide open.

The duke didn't hesitate to close it behind him.

"I thought he would never leave," Miss Rowan said, hiding a broad smile behind her hand.

"Neither did I!" Warwick agreed vehemently. He didn't waste another minute but closed the distance between them. "You are so lovely when you laugh, did you know that?" he asked, caressing his fingers down her soft cheek.

She smiled up at him. "As are you, Your Grace." Her eyes held a twinkle of mischief that was utterly charming.

He laughed. "You know, I don't think anyone has ever said I was lovely."

"Clearly you don't spend enough time with people who will speak to you openly."

"And yet you do," he said, tilting his head just a little.

She gave an adorable little shrug. "I'm afraid I never really learned to dissemble."

"Good. I hope you never do learn that. And being obsequious, while useful in some circumstances, is never allowed with me."

She raised her eyebrows at that. "Really? You don't like people bowing and scraping to you?"

"Oh no, I do, and I expect it from everyone—except you."

"And Lady Margaret," she added with a broad smile on her beautiful lips—lips he wanted so much to taste once again.

"Well, my sister has never had any respect for me and my position, no matter how many times I—and my parents—told her she should," he admitted, trying his best to distance himself before he truly did something he might regret later.

"I'm sure you were never very insistent on it," she said.

He gave a little chuckle. "Never."

"She is so lucky to have a brother like you," Miss Rowan said, becoming a little serious.

"Do you have brothers?" Warwick asked, allowing his curiosity to surface.

Chapter Twenty-Four

Tina turned partially away, hiding her face. How was she to answer that?

She wanted so much to tell him the truth. To tell him of her hard life. Of her shameful birth. But if she did, he would turn away from her in disgust. There was no doubt in her mind that he would—and so he should!

It *was* shameful.

She had never been allowed to forget how disgraceful it was to be illegitimate. She knew that her mother, no matter what she said about wanting to keep her, couldn't have done so for the shame of having had a child out of wedlock.

How could she tell this man, this duke, with his perfect, easy, *legitimate* life that she was the product of a florid affair that had sent her mother running into hiding? And yet, there he was smiling benignly at her, not aware in least the anguish she was going through right at this minute.

Well, all right then, duke, do your worst!

Whatever it was that gave Tina the courage to argue with her foster-father reignited within her breast. Tina turned back to him, lifted her chin, straightened her spine, and said, "I have a foster brother and sisters. But they were never what one might call kind."

The smile slipped off his face, just as she expected it to. "Were you not raised by your parents?"

She shook her head. "My mother came to visit me every year on my birthday, but I don't know who my father is. I was born on the wrong side of the blanket, as they say."

There, it was out. She'd said it as gently as she could but had said it nonetheless. She watched his expression closely, but oddly enough, there wasn't the immediate disgust she'd expected.

Oh, he was still frowning ever so slightly, but instead of simply turning away or telling her to get out and stay away from his sister, as she would have expected, he said the most astonishing thing. "That explains how you are so well educated for a seamstress!"

Tina paused and looked up at him. His frown had disappeared, and a slight smile of discovery replaced it.

"I don't think you heard what I said, Your Grace," Tina said.

"Oh no, I heard. You said you were illegitimate, but your mother visited you every year. She's kept in touch. Perhaps she even regrets having given you up, but had no choice in the matter?"

Tina was pretty sure her jaw would have hit the floor if it weren't firmly attached. Did this man have loose stitches in his head? Was his mind unraveling? Didn't he care she was illegitimate? Why wasn't he disgusted as a normal person would be?

Still, Tina nodded. "She's told me as much. And she's done everything she could to make my life easier now that I'm an adult. She probably would have done the same when I was a child if she'd known it wasn't as wonderful as she was led to believe."

He nodded and smiled, but his eyes were still squinting a bit as he was clearly thinking about something. "The Duchess of Kendell, who gave me your name, said you were introduced by a friend of hers," he began.

Tina raised her eyebrows but said nothing.

"Lady Norman, wasn't it? I met her at the ball and then again last night at another party." He stared at her even more intensely. "You could be..."

"You mustn't say any more, Your Grace!" Tina said, quickly before he could finish his thought.

"Ah! So, I am right."

"Your Grace—"

He reached out and cradled her face in his large hands. "Miss Rowan, I swear I will not tell another soul. I am an excellent secret-keeper, I assure you."

Ah, and here it was. Now that he knew her secret, he would think she would just fall under his control and allow him any manner of license with her person. Tears of frustration and anger pricked her eyes.

"I won't do it!" she told him boldly.

His hands dropped back to his side. "Won't do what?"

"I won't allow you to control me now that you know my secret. One man is already blackmailing me with this information. I won't allow another—"

He took a step away from her, the frown returning to his face. "Do you really think I am so low? So cruel and, and...despicable that I would use this to take advantage of you?"

"You...you won't?" she asked hesitantly.

"No, Miss Rowan, I wouldn't. I am not a cad."

She collapsed back against the bookshelf behind her. "No, you're not. I'm sorry. Please accept my apology. I..." She shook her head, unable to finish her thought. She'd been so frightened for a moment there, but truly, a more upstanding man would be hard to find.

The fact he hadn't been disgusted by her illegitimacy was evidence of that. The fact he'd thought first of his sister's well-being and happiness above anything else when she'd first met him told her so as well. A man who played children's games with his sister instead of doing his own work was yet more evidence. He'd been nothing but a gentleman toward her the entire time she'd known him.

"I can't believe I even thought that of you," she said, shaking her head. She took a step toward him. "I have so many reasons to thank you, Your Grace. You have been nothing but wonderful and understanding. I seem to be the one who's the cad." She held his gaze, but it wasn't easy when she was feeling so ashamed of her own behavior.

"Luckily for you, I forgive easily. It was an understandable mistake. Did you say someone was already blackmailing you?"

She nodded sadly. "My foster-father. The only reason he allowed me to come to London, instead of forcing me into marriage with his son, was so I would pay him. He has threatened to put a notice in all the papers making public my parentage if I don't send him money regularly. It's why I am so insistent on being paid on time, I'm afraid."

"That's despicable!" the duke spat, a sneer marring his handsome features.

"It is what I have to live with."

"I am sorry for that. If there's anything I can do..."

"No, thank you." She shrugged, then gave him a little smile. "Being here in London is well worth the price. I love the city, and I've had the opportunity to meet and get to know wonderful people like you and Lady Margaret."

His smile returned. "Of course." His gaze wandered to the books behind her again. "But it seems as if your earlier life wasn't all unpleasant. You *were* taught to read," he pointed out.

She laughed. "Yes, yes I was. My mother insisted the local vicar tutor me. He taught me to read, write, and keep accounts." She turned to the books. "He loved history, and so I learned to love it as well. Reading the adventures of other people allowed me to escape to another time and place." She didn't mention that it also allowed her to physically escape from the Rowans' home as well. When she was at the vicarage, there was nothing her foster family could do to her. She had leave to stay there, reading as long as she wanted, and she'd done so at every opportunity.

"And all of that knowledge gave you the skills you needed to run your business," he pointed out.

"Yes." She gave him a smile. "Which reminds me of the reason we came in to your study in the first place."

"Ah! Yes, I was going to pay you, wasn't I?" He gave a laugh and turned to go to his desk.

~*~

Warwick took a purse of money out of his desk, so incredibly relieved that he and Miss Rowan had gotten back on good footing. When she'd all but accused him of intending to take advantage of her, he'd had a flash of fury like he hadn't felt since his parents had mistreated his sister.

He'd let them know, in no uncertain terms, they would not be doing that again, not if they ever wanted to see him and Margaret again. That he was merely fifteen years old at the time didn't faze any of them. His parents had taken him at his word, which was good because not five minutes later, his anger had faded enough to know he wouldn't have been able to survive without his father's support. He'd regretted his angry words.

Once again, his quickly fading anger had come to his rescue when Miss Rowan understood she'd been mistaken in his intentions. It was with an easy smile that he counted out the amount he owed her, but instead of merely handing it to her and seeing her leave, he left it on his desk and came back around to her side of it.

"I have to admit I wish we could have continued on with the fascinating conversation we had in the garden during the ball," he said. "The memory of it has hardly left my mind."

"Are you referring to the actual conversation or what we shared after we stopped speaking?" she asked quietly.

"I think you know which I mean," he said, coming even closer.

She didn't move away but allowed him to come so close their bodies were practically touching. "Yes, I think I might."

He bent and touched his lips to hers gently at first before allowing his flaring passion to shove aside any thought. She molded herself to him, pressing her soft places against his hard ones. They fit so perfectly and felt so right.

Mine.

The word reverberated through Warwick's very being, shocking him into taking a sudden step back.

"I'm sorry," she started as if *she'd* done something wrong.

"No! I, er, I shouldn't... That is, we shouldn't..."

"No. I believe we'd come to this determination the other night, didn't we? I'm afraid it completely slipped my mind," she said, turning away. "And now with my further revelations today..." she added quietly.

"It's not—"

"It's all right, Your Grace. I will remember my position and...and yours. We'll not let this happen again." She turned to leave.

He should have stopped her. He should have told her how wrong she was in her assumption that it was their respective social positions that made him pull away. But he didn't.

He didn't tell her that it was him, and not her, which made him stop. He didn't tell her that he'd never felt this way about a woman before. That he wasn't sure how one should behave when suddenly overwhelmed by feelings he shouldn't be having.

Immediately, he questioned whether he *shouldn't* be feeling this way. He put a hand to his head. He was too confused. Too off-balance. This wasn't him. He was never unsure of himself. He was a duke, dammit! He was a man who knew his mind.

Except that in this case he didn't.

He turned back to his desk. Her money! It was still sitting where he'd left it.

"Miss Rowan," he called after her.

She'd just walked out the door when he called after her, but she stopped and turned back, looking so damned hopeful it nearly broke his heart. How could he do this to her? How could he let her leave with false assumptions of him, of herself? But he just couldn't say anything. Not yet.

"Your money," he said, coming toward her with it in his hand.

"Oh yes, of course." She didn't meet his eyes but took the money and left quickly.

The moment she was gone, Warwick collapsed into the chair behind his desk and wanted nothing more than to beat his head against the hard wood in front of him. How could he be so stupid? Falling for a beautiful, illegitimate seamstress. Honestly! She couldn't possibly be any more ineligible for him.

She was possibly in every way perfect for him. And in every way the last person he could ever marry.

CHAPTER TWENTY-FIVE

Tina stared at this man who'd introduced himself as her father. Lord Ayres sat across from her in her drawing room and stared back at her as if he were in just as much shock as she.

They'd met once before at Lady Norman's party when Tina had first been introduced to some of her mother's friends. At the time, she had been amazed a man knew as much about fashion as Lord Ayres did. He was not only well dressed but had an excellent eye for what made a gown flatter a woman and had even shared some tips with her. Tips that had made all the difference in her work. She'd be forever grateful to him.

And now she'd learned that he was her father!

What amazed her most was it felt right. Looking at this man, knowing the little she knew about him. Oh yes, she could very easily see he was, in fact, her father—and that just felt so good!

"I can't believe Christianne didn't tell me!" he said for the third time. "For *twenty* years!"

The first two times he'd voiced his disbelief, Tina had let his comment slide by without saying anything. This time he sounded a bit more troubled so she said, "I have to admit I was upset with her as well—for quite a while."

"I can imagine you would have been more than upset," he interrupted.

"All right," she acknowledged. "I was hurt. Very hurt. Not the least because my foster parents told me that she had given me to them because she didn't want me—that no one did."

"*What*? But that's awful! How could anyone tell that to a child? How old were you when they said this?"

Tina shrugged and tried her best to hold back the tears that threatened to fall every time she thought about that horrible time in her life. "It was when I was young. About four or five. I still remember it as if it were yesterday."

Her father's face turned an alarming shade of red. He could only stutter his fury for a moment. Oddly enough, this made Tina feel even better than she already had at having met her true father.

He cared! He'd only just met her, and yet he cared enough to become angry for her.

"The point is, I've spoken with my mother about this—"

"Have you? What did she say?"

"She was horrified and completely understood my anger at her for leaving me with such people. But I'm trying to understand her point of view as well."

"That's very good of you," he admitted.

"She just didn't know what else to do," Tina explained. "She'd had a child who she needed to keep secret."

He nodded reluctantly. "That husband of hers, Norman—he was not a pleasant man. I was rather surprised her parents insisted she marry him. Didn't have the best reputation among the ton. People knew he had a temper."

Tina could only shake her head in disbelief. Before she could ask the obvious question, Lord Ayres said, "Rich as Croesus. I'm sure they came away from that match with a heavy purse."

"But that's awful! How could anyone sell their child like that?" Tina couldn't help but protest.

"How could anyone give away a child to an unloving family?" he countered.

"Indeed."

"But what is truly worrisome is that she didn't tell me," Lord Ayres said. "If she'd told me, I would have taken you."

"Would you? Could you have? A single gentleman raising an illegitimate daughter on his own?" Tina looked at him skeptically.

"Well, I wouldn't have done it on my own, naturally. I would have taken you to my estate in Ireland and gotten you a nanny and a governess."

"And then returned to London, as so many people do. I appreciate the thought, my lord, but at least I had parents and foster-siblings. They didn't love me, but they were there."

"Most children of the nobility are raised by others," he said.

"That doesn't make it any better. And my mother did come to visit me every year and bring me presents. She also made sure I was educated."

"And had an occupation," he added.

"Well no, my foster-father did that. He apprenticed me to the local seamstress when I was twelve."

"Well, it was a good thing he did. You have a real talent, my girl!"

Tina smiled. "I believe I come by it honestly."

Her father looked confused for a moment. "Christianne has no sense of fashion and, from what I know, no artistic talent either."

Tina laughed. "No, but you clearly do!"

"Oh!" He burst out laughing. "Of course! Yes, yes I do. Nothing compared to yours, but I haven't really practiced much. I'm sure that were I to work at it, I could sketch passably well."

They fell into a companionable silence for a moment, which allowed Tina to revel once more in the fact that she had a father! Not only did she now know who he was, but he would have wanted her—and seemed to do so now. He was just sitting there smiling at her, proud of her and her abilities.

This man, who had been nothing more than a stranger half an hour ago, now valued her for who she was and cared for her. Maybe she wasn't a nothing after all.

She'd told the Duke of Warwick a couple of times that she understood he didn't want to be with her because she was a nothing, a nobody. But here was someone who was somebody who *did* want her, who *did* value her. Could it possibly be that the duke might as well?

He did say he respected her. And he had protested when she'd said she was nobody.

This man, her father, had lit a fire under the chunk of ice that encased her feelings of self-worth, and it was melting away.

"Tell me about your life," he said, finally breaking the silence.

Tina shrugged. "I work a lot."

"Do you have, er, anyone courting you, perhaps? Or anyone who you wish would do so?" Lord Ayres gave her a little smile.

She could only laugh and shake her head. "There is one gentleman in whom I'm slightly interested, but he is too far above my touch."

"What? I will have you know that no one is above your touch. You are the daughter of an earl! Granted, an Irish earl, but an earl nonetheless. And not one of those earldoms that is severely impoverished either. I'll have you know my largest estate does quite well. I have two others that don't do as well, but they aren't a drain on my finances either. No, you may tell your gentleman that your father will be very happy to provide you with a nice dowry—a very nice one indeed!"

"My lord, you don't need to do that!" Tina was horrified he might think she wanted money from him.

"I know I needn't, but I want to. You're my daughter! And any fellow who strikes your fancy is good enough for you."

~April 28~

Warwick stared at the man sitting across his desk a few days later. He probably should have invited him to the sitting area closer to the fireplace instead of the more intimidating chair on the other side of his desk, but now he was rather satisfied with his earlier decision. He wanted to be as intimidating as possible when someone dared to ask his permission to address Margaret.

"I, er, find Lady Margaret to be, er, very socially adept," Lord Roseberry said.

Warwick raised an eyebrow. "She is the daughter of a duke, naturally she is properly educated."

"Yes! Yes, of course. I only mean to say I believe she'll make an excellent wife for me. I'm hoping to become more politically active and, er, my wife will naturally need to be able to entertain and, well, be an extension of me and my views," the man said quickly.

"I see." Somehow Warwick couldn't see his sister as a political wife. Naturally, it was hard to see her as a wife at all. He only wished his father had felt that way rather than being so anxious to get rid of her.

It didn't make this any easier for him, though.

"With her easy manner and beauty, I, er, think we'll suit very well," Roseberry continued.

"And what do *you* have to offer into the match?" Warwick asked.

The man's eyes widened for a moment. "I? Well, prestige, naturally. And, er, ten thousand a year."

"She does not lack for prestige at the moment. Actually marrying a mere viscount will be quite a come-down for her," Warwick pointed out.

The man had nothing to say to that.

Warwick sighed. "I will speak with her on the matter and see if she is interested in pursuing this, but I wouldn't get your hopes up, Roseberry. She hasn't said a word to me about you, and when she's excited and happy I can assure you she lets me know."

"You will ask *her* whether *she's* interested in the match?" he asked.

This time both of Warwick's eyebrows went up. "Do you find this to be surprising, my lord?"

"Well, naturally. You are her brother and her guardian. You make the decision regarding who she marries," he said with only slight uncertainty in his voice.

"No, as a matter of fact, she has the final say in the matter. She is the one who will be a part of the marriage, and if she's not happy with it, there is no point now, is there? My primary objective here is to see my sister happy."

"Oh. Er, yes, of course," Roseberry said, agreeing. He reminded Warwick of the girls who would agree with anything he said no matter how ridiculous, and more to the point, whether they agreed or not.

"On the other hand," Warwick continued, "if you believe I should be the sole person to make this decision, then clearly you have made it for both me and Margaret."

"Your Grace? I, er, I don't believe I understand your meaning."

Warwick stood. "If you don't believe my sister is capable or should be consulted on her own marriage, then you are not the right man for her. She is an intelligent woman who should be respected and consulted on all things—especially those having to do with her own life. Clearly, you would not think of doing so, therefore this conversation is at an end. Good day to you, my lord."

"But...but..." Roseberry stammered even as he too rose from his chair.

"Good day," Warwick repeated.

The man clamped his mouth shut, gave Warwick a slight bow, and left the room.

Warwick didn't care if it was only half-past eleven; he poured himself a drink of brandy.

"What an imbecile. I'm glad you didn't accept his suit," Martin said, speaking up for the first time since Roseberry had entered the room.

Warwick was almost surprised he had stayed quiet the entire time, but he'd been good and hadn't drawn any attention to himself at all. Warwick wasn't even certain Roseberry had noticed Martin sitting at his desk in the corner.

"I was almost considering it until he was stupid enough to imply he wouldn't consult Margaret on anything," Warwick conceded. "I just—

"Was that Lord Roseberry who just left?" Margaret asked, bursting into the room without even a knock. "What did he want?"

"Good morning to you, sister," Warwick said, before finishing off his drink and replacing the glass on the table.

"Good morning, Warwick, Martin," Margaret said, giving each man a nod.

"Yes, that was Roseberry. He came to ask for my permission to address you," Warwick said, sitting back down at his desk.

"And what did you say," she asked, coming closer.

"I told him to leave."

"Oh, good! I mean... I like him. He's a very good dancer, but I don't think I'd like to be married to him."

"Good because you won't be."

"Is there a reason you turned him down?" she asked, sitting at the edge of the chair just vacated by his lordship.

"He didn't understand the importance of consulting you regarding your own life. I, therefore, didn't see the importance of even considering his suit," Warwick said with a little smile.

The smile his sister returned to him was much bigger and much happier than his, he was certain. "You are the best of brothers, do you know that Warwick?" she gushed.

He gave a little laugh. "As a matter of fact, I did. Now, unless you have anything else you wish to discuss with me, I have wasted enough time already this morning and really must get back to work."

She stood. "No, that was all. Shall I see you at dinner?"

"No, not tonight. I've an engagement with some friends. I hope you don't mind."

"No, not at all. But do remember we are going to Lady Stokely's soirée later tonight."

"Ah, right! Very well. I promise to return on time."

~April 29~

Tina debated the intelligence of going to see her mother the entire way to her house. She had no idea if Lady Norman knew that Lord Ayres had come to see her. She didn't know if he had discussed it with her first. The only thing Tina knew was that Christianne had finally gotten up the nerve to tell him about her existence at all.

If her father had told Lady Norman that he was going to meet her, Tina wondered how her mother felt about it. She surely had meant for him to meet Tina; she had told him after all. Tina just didn't know if her mother had meant for him to go so quickly—or without her. But still, Tina felt she owed it to her mother to tell her about his visit.

Yes, she definitely should tell her, Tina told herself.

After being let into the house by the now familiar footman, she told him he needn't announce her. She gave the briefest knock on her mother's private drawing room door before going in.

"Oh, Tina!" Lady Norman said in surprise as Tina walked in. From the look of her mother, perhaps it would have been better to have given some advanced warning, after all.

Lady Norman seemed to be wiping her face with a handkerchief as if she'd been crying. There was further evidence in her bloodshot eyes and the fact that she was sniffling. Tina paused.

She almost asked if this was a bad time but then decided if she wanted to have a close relationship with her mother, she wasn't going to run away when it was evident a shoulder to cry on and an ear to listen was needed.

Tina rushed forward, hardly bothering with her curtsy. "Mother, is everything all right? What's happened?" She sat next to Lady Norman, taking her hand in her own.

Lady Norman shook her head and pressed her handkerchief to her nose. When she could speak, she said, "I'm so sorry, Tina, today's not a good day for me. I should have told Harold to say I was not at home to visitors."

"I should hope I'm not just a visitor!" Tina protested. "I'm your daughter! If there's something wrong, I'd like to help if I can. Can you tell me what it is?"

Lady Norman squeezed Tina's fingers. "You are so good! I'm so blessed to have a child like you!"

"What is it that's upsetting you?"

"Of all the ridiculous things! I am crying over a man!" her mother said with a little laugh.

CHAPTER TWENTY-SIX

"That doesn't sound ridiculous to me. It sounds absolutely normal. Who is it and what has he done to make you cry?"

Her mother took a moment to compose herself. "It... Well, it is my own fault, actually. I did something...and when I told him, he was naturally very upset. I was hoping he would not be but, well..."

Tina wondered... "You wouldn't possibly be referring to Lord Ayres, would you?"

Lady Norman dropped her hand from her face and turned toward Tina. "What do you know of Lord Ayres?"

Ah, ha! Her guess was right! She smiled at her mother. "I met him yesterday. He came to see me."

"He did?"

"Yes, and yes, while he is a bit upset with you for not telling him about me, when he left he was beginning to understand why you kept that information from him."

"What did you say to him? What did he say to you?" Her face paled even more.

"He told me everything. Well... He said you had told him that I was his daughter."

"Was he very angry with me?"

"He wasn't happy you hadn't told him until now, but I explained to him what you told me about Lord Norman," Tina said, still stroking her mother's arm.

A hopeful look came to her eyes. "Did he...?"

"Understand? Yes, he did. He recalled hearing that Lord Norman had a tendency to be violent when angered."

Lady Norman nodded. "He did."

"So, as I say, Lord Ayres understood why you'd hidden me away. He just wished you had trusted him with your secret." Tina paused and looked down at her hand resting on her mother's arm. "He said he would have taken me and had raised me on his estate. I don't know if he was just saying that or if he meant it. I also don't know if that would have been any better for me in the end."

"What do you think?" her mother asked quietly.

"I don't know. I wasn't happy with the Rowans, but they did apprentice me to the seamstress and, in so doing, gave me the career I now have. I love sewing, and I love designing dresses. I love making women look beautiful. So in that way, I'm glad I was raised as I was. If I had been raised in Ireland, I probably would never have learned any of this. I wouldn't be where I am now, and strangely enough, I like where I am." She paused again. "And I wouldn't have known you," she added.

"No, you wouldn't."

Tina looked her mother in the eye. "I appreciate the mistakes and the wonderful things. I appreciate *all* you've done for me—. I am who I am because of you."

A few tears began to slip down her mother's cheeks once again. "I don't deserve such a wonderful daughter, not after all I've done, and yet... here you are."

Tina put her arms around her mother, held her, and was held by her. It felt good. It felt right.

When they disengaged, Tina said, "And now you really need to go and speak with Lord Ayres."

Lady Norman laughed and sniffed. "Yes. Yes, I suppose I do."

~*~

Margaret went to bed early the following evening, grateful for an early night with no amusements, but Warwick was feeling restless. Every time he tried to sit down with a book, Tina would invade his thoughts.

He'd gone over and over his last meeting with her. He didn't care that she was illegitimate. As he'd told her, nearly half the members of society had been born in inauspicious circumstances—either outright illegitimate or with parents who wished they had been thanks to the loveless marriages that were common among the *ton*. No, what was bothering Warwick most was his visceral reaction to her.

Mine.

Tina wasn't his. She couldn't be his. She was a modiste, for God's sake! He was duke! There could be nothing between them, no relationship. She understood that. She was a smart girl.

So why couldn't he get her out of his mind? Why did he still have this overwhelming desire to be with her?

Warwick couldn't take this anymore. These thoughts that went round and round in his mind with no resolution possible.

He stormed out of the house and went to the only place where he might get some respite—Powell's.

The gaming house was busy, but that wasn't surprising. It was still early yet, merely ten. It would get a lot more crowded before the night was through.

Warwick wended his way around the gaming tables. Hazard, vingt-et-un, whist, roulette, and other gaming tables filled the large room. Somehow, although he wanted nothing more than something to distract him, Warwick wasn't enticed by any of the games nor the men playing them. He ended up where he always did—in the reading room.

"Warwick, I haven't seen you for some time," Lord Tentley said, giving him a nod.

"Been escorting my sister about," Warwick explained.

"So I've heard. Aren't you the lucky one." The fellow chuckled before burying his nose in his paper once again.

Lord Wickford strolled through, checking to make sure everyone had what he wanted. A footman followed in his wake, refilling glasses and taking orders for what he didn't have right at hand. He stopped directly in front of Warwick.

"Are there no social engagements for Lady Margaret this evening?" he asked as he took the empty seat next to Warwick, a broad smile creasing face.

"No, thank goodness! I needed a night off," Warwick said. He turned to the footman. "Rum, neat."

"I knew I'd make a convert out of you," his host chuckled.

Warwick shook his head, smiling. "I just want the best there is in this hell-hole."

Wickford threw back his head, laughing. "Well then, Michael, fetch the special bottle we opened earlier this evening for Lord Marbury."

The footman went off to do his master's bidding.

"Marbury having troubles?" Warwick asked.

"Oh, you know, the usual—women," Wickford said.

Warwick nodded. "I'm afraid I'm in much the same boat. Can't have the one I want, and yet I can't get her out of my mind."

Wickford narrowed his eyes at the duke. "Lord Marbury couldn't get rid of the one hounding him, but then he shouldn't have married her if he didn't like her company."

Warwick laughed. "I haven't yet made that mistake."

"No..." He paused to fill a glass from the bottle the footman had returned with. "But it sounds as if you're on your way into that trap."

The duke just shook his head. "Couldn't if I wanted to, which is the problem, I suppose."

"How's that? The girl won't have you?"

"Oh no, I'm sure she would. She's just, er, not the sort I should be marrying, if you catch my drift."

Wickford raised his eyebrows. "A lightskirt?"

"No! No. Just not quite up..."

"For a duke, you mean," Wickford finished for him when Warwick hesitated.

"Er, yes."

"But you like her." The club owner paused and then looked more closely at Warwick as he took a large swallow of his drink. "No... It might be even worse than that."

Warwick swallowed hard and fast to be sure not to choke on the burning liquid in his mouth. *Was* it worse than that? Did he feel more for Miss Rowan? Did he... Could he possibly...?

Love wasn't an emotion he'd ever considered. It didn't usually figure in ducal marriages. He was almost certain his parents hadn't loved each other, and they had a perfectly fine marriage.

Did he love Miss Rowan?

"Ah, yes. That is a problem," Wickford said, understanding a great deal more than Warwick himself did. "Have you said anything?"

"Of course not!"

"Might you..."

"I would not. I told you she's not..."

"Up to snuff, yes. Well, then..." The fellow tapped his finger against his chin. "It seems to me you've got two choices—either forget the girl completely or go and show her how you feel. Perhaps if you become, er, demonstrative, it will get her out from under your skin."

"I don't know..." Warwick said from his glass. He didn't know if it would make things better...or worse for him.

"What have you got to lose?"

Warwick put down his glass. "You know, you may be right." Perhaps if he went to see Miss Rowan, he would see it wasn't as serious as he'd thought. Perhaps if he spoke with her, he would realize he didn't actually love her after all.

Wickford gave a little laugh. "I'm always right."

~*~

"Your Grace, what are you doing here? And at this late hour?" Tina said, peering around the door. She'd been roused from her bed when she'd heard pounding on her door. Never had she wished more that she had a footman or a maid to see who was calling. But she didn't, she thought with a sigh as she pulled her wrapper tighter over her nightdress.

"Miss Rowan, Tina, I apologize, but I had to see you," the duke whispered loud enough to be heard if there'd been anyone else in the flat.

"Are you drunk?" she asked, not yet willing to let a man into her home so late, even the Duke of Warwick.

"I am not, although I will admit to having imbibed in some very fine rum," he answered, blinking as if to make sure his vision was clear.

"And whatever it is you need to tell me couldn't wait until morning?"

"No. Absolutely not."

With a small shrug, she opened her door farther and allowed him in. She led the way into her front parlor, lighting the few candles she had.

"This is...cozy," he said, looking around.

"It's small and cramped, but it's both home and shop. Now, what can I do—" she wasn't even given a chance to finish her sentence before she found herself pulled into Warwick's embrace. He crushed her to the wall of his chest, wrapping his arms around her back ensuring she couldn't move an inch.

"This. Just this," he said, his voice muffled against the top of her head. "This is right. Damn Wickford for being correct as always."

"Wickford?" Tina asked. She had no idea what Warwick was talking about. Perhaps he was drunk.

"A friend of mine. Never mind." He rubbed his lips against her hair and began to kiss his way down toward her lips.

Oh. "I thought we'd decided we shouldn't..."

He paused his kisses. "No. *You* decided we shouldn't. *I* thought it was a wonderful idea."

"But you were the one who pulled away..."

"Merely to take a look at you. Merely to attempt to express how I felt," he said. "And then you said we shouldn't, but I never did agree with you, now did I?"

Tina thought about it—indeed, she'd had problems *not* thinking about it. He'd been on her mind ever since their conversation that day. He'd been so sweet and wonderful, accepting her parentage or lack-thereof. And then he'd kissed her, and it had been wonderful until he'd suddenly pulled away. Could he have done so merely to look at her or to say something? She couldn't remember precisely whether it had been she who'd said something first or him. Now that she thought about it, it might very well have been she who jumped to the conclusion that he didn't want to be kissing her.

She looked up into his soft brown eyes, now looking down at her as if she were the most wonderful prize a man could have. "I... I don't know," she admitted. "I don't recall, precisely."

"Then don't. Just let me look at your beautiful face." He traced a finger down her cheek. "And look into your lovely green eyes. And if you don't mind..."

He fitted his delicious lips over hers and kissed her until she was weak in the knees. Thank goodness his arms were still wrapped tightly around her.

Could he have changed his mind? Could he have decided he didn't actually care about their respective social positions? Could it possibly be he cared for her so much he'd be willing to put aside social conventions and marry her? If he truly loved her, wouldn't he do just that?

What would she do if he did? Was *she* able to put aside everything to be with him?

She almost laughed at the ridiculous question—of course she would! She felt... She paused to analyze just what she felt for this man.

Did it matter that he was a duke? No! Not to her. He was a man, not a title. Yes, he was wealthy, but even if he'd been the merest pauper, she'd still love him.

Love him?

My goodness, she thought, yes! She loved him!

She put all of her newly discovered feelings into her kiss and felt them in return. Yes! This was so right.

And then she felt his hand on her breast, feeling its weight, and his thumb rubbing over her most sensitive parts.

Was this love on his part or lust? He hadn't actually said anything about disregarding social standing. Perhaps he'd thought it through and decided since she was illegitimate, perhaps a carte blanche was what he wanted after all. It wasn't as if she had a father who would care, as far as he knew.

But she did have a father who cared. And not only that, she wasn't the sort to lift her skirts for anyone, duke or not.

She disentangled herself from him. "It's late."

She heard him catch his breath, then let it out slowly. "Yes, it is."

"I've got a client coming first thing in the morning."

"Of course." But instead of stepping back, he took another step toward her. "Then I'll say goodnight." He put a finger gently under her chin and ever so gently placed one last kiss on her lips. If she didn't know better, she'd think he was telling her something with that kiss. There was such emotion in that one feather-light touch. But no—she mentally shook her head—he wanted her physically. He was telling her that he'd be patient, at least for now. That was all.

CHAPTER TWENTY-SEVEN

The following morning Warwick paid his biannual visit to his tailor. It was a regular appointment to keep his wardrobe in good condition and up to date. In nearly ten years, he hadn't changed the date nor what he purchased.

"Two new coats for you, Your Grace," the man asked soon after he'd walked in.

"Yes, Mr. Weston, as usual. And three shirts this time. My valet was bemoaning the state of my linen recently," the duke said, without even a glance at the man as he looked through a table covered in different fabrics.

"Can I interest you in a waistcoat or two, as well? I have some very fine—"

"No, no. My waistcoats are perfectly serviceable, thank you." He was fingering a particularly fine blue wool. It was nearly the same color as the dress Miss Rowan had made for Margaret. She'd thought the color would look good on him as well.

"Ah, that is one of our most popular colors at the moment, Your Grace. You've clearly got excellent taste," the tailor said, fawning over him.

"Someone recently told me I would look good in such a color. Bring out the blue in my eyes or some such nonsense," Warwick said, trying to downplay his interest.

"Indeed! Indeed it would. You *do* have blue in your eyes. It's difficult to see with the brown you always wear, but if you wore a coat of that color, it would do wonders to highlight and make the color so much clearer for all to see. Why, it would be quite magnificent," the man said with enthusiasm.

The tailor pulled a standing mirror closer before draping a length of the cloth over Warwick's shoulder so he could see the effect. Tina was absolutely right; it did bring out the blue.

Even as he stood there admiring the color, his father's disapproving voice grew louder in his mind. *"A duke is never showy, never flashy. Have you ever seen a duke who was a dandy? No! You will wear brown, my boy. It's a good, safe, conservative color. If you must, black is acceptable as well. You must maintain the dignity of your station, of your heritage."* And he always had.

Warwick shook his head, as much to say no to the coat as to get his father's voice out of his mind. "No, thank you, Mr. Weston. Show me what you have in brown."

The tailor sighed expressively and returned the blue cloth to the table.

~April 30~

Margaret decided that perhaps spillikins was, in fact, too juvenile a game for her and her brother to play. Instead, she'd set out a chessboard. Warwick was not only happy because it was a more thoughtful game, but also because he knew he could easily beat his sister at this game as opposed to spillikins which she had won handily—twice!

They were deep into their game, but the silence while Margaret considered her next move was overwhelming. He spoke without thinking.

"Have you seen your friend's rooms? I believe her entire flat could fit into our drawing room."

Margaret looked up from her study of the chessboard. "What? Are you referring to Tina?"

"Yes. Are you going to move within this half hour?"

She frowned at him and moved a pawn. "When did you see her rooms?"

Now he was in trouble. That's what he got for trying to fill silence. He should have known it wouldn't go well.

"I, er, was there yesterday, as a matter of fact," he said, making his own move—one he'd planned earlier in the game. "I needed to pay her for your last gown and was in the neighborhood, so I stopped by."

"Oh." She didn't sound very convinced.

"It's your turn," he pointed out.

"I know, but I'm more interested in the fact that you went to Tina's rooms."

"Don't be. It was nothing." Now he was really kicking himself for having said anything. Really, how stupid could he be? "Please make your move—and don't move another pawn."

"I wasn't going to!" she said defensively. She moved a knight directly into the path of his rook. "And how could I not be interested? Tina's my friend and you're my brother. I'm interested in both of you—especially in you both together."

He did not like the suggestive look in her eyes or the little smile hovering on her lips. Yes, he'd as much as told Tina last night that he was in love with her, but he certainly wasn't anywhere near ready to admit it to his sister. Now he needed to distract her, dammit.

He firmly kept his eyes on the board—not to figure out how to win the game but to make his sister's defeat not quite as immediate as it could be. "Well, if you're so interested in Tina and her life, were you aware she's illegitimate?"

Margaret's eyes narrowed, the game temporarily forgotten. "How do you know that?"

"She told me. Please make your move." He indicated the board in between them.

"It's your turn. She told you?" she repeated, clearly not believing him. "How would such a thing come up in conversation? Did she tell you last night when you went to her rooms?"

"No, er, another day when we were talking. She said something along the lines of how wonderful it was that we were so close, so I asked her if she had any siblings." He made his move. "She told me that she had a foster-brother and sisters, but they'd never gotten along." He made a move he hoped would slow his progression to check-mate.

"So she was fostered. That doesn't mean..."

"She then said straight out she was born on the wrong side of the blanket," he continued.

"Oh." She dropped her gaze to the board once more.

There was silence for a few minutes while she studied the pieces in front of her. She placed her hand on a rook, but before moving it, she asked, "Does that bother you?"

The odd thing was his feelings on the matter confused him. "No, it doesn't. I don't quite know why, though. I'm sure that it should. If I were our father, I would have immediately told her to limit her interaction with you to purely business, if not fired her outright and told her never to return to this house."

"But you didn't," his sister said, removing her hand from the piece without moving it.

"No. I stood there like an idiot babbling on about the fact it now made sense that she was so well read. Honestly, I have never met anyone of her station who read history! Even Martin hasn't done so. His education was limited to what he would need to know and understand as my secretary."

"But Tina is well educated and enjoys reading." Margaret nodded, understanding he didn't so much care about her parentage as the fact she was an intelligent, well-educated woman. It was rather incredible, but it was because Margaret completely understood him as no one else did or ever had that made them so close.

"Yes!" He nodded his head. "Why was I so concerned with solving the mystery of her education instead of being horrified at learning she was illegitimate? It just makes no sense to me." He sat back in his chair. Margaret wasn't going to be making her move any time soon anyway. There was no need for him to hunch himself over the board.

His sister smiled at him. She wasn't even looking at their game any longer. She was much more interested in their conversation. It was a funny smile, though, one which made Warwick distinctly uncomfortable.

"I know—" she started to say, but was interrupted by a brief knock on the door. The footman came in and intoned, "Miss Rowan, Your Grace."

The young woman herself followed, stopped to curtsy, and then came farther into the room. "Good afternoon, Your Grace," she said, hardly even looking at Warwick. She then turned to his sister and gave her a true smile. "Lady Margaret, thank you so much for inviting me over. It was too kind of you."

"Oh, no. I am so happy you were able to get away and spend a little time with me this afternoon," Margaret said.

Tina's eyes lit upon the board in between them. "Chess! Now here's a game I know."

"Do you? Then perhaps you can school my sister. She keeps insisting on putting her pieces in harm's way. I've done all I could to draw the game out, but she is determined to lose," Warwick said with a laugh.

"I am not!" Margaret objected.

"What were you about to do with that rook?" he asked, pointing to the piece that she'd put her hand on earlier.

She looked down at it and then said, "I was going to move it there." She pointed to a spot on the board next to Warwick's queen.

"But he would have taken it," Tina exclaimed. She looked more closely at the board. "You should move your knight," she suggested.

Margaret put her hand on the knight on the left side of the board.

"Um, no, the other one. Look more closely and you'll see," Tina said with patience.

Warwick had the hardest time not laughing as his sister studied the board.

"Oh!" she said, finally seeing the move her friend referred to. With it, she could take his rook and put his queen on the defense.

He couldn't help it, he did laugh. It was such an obvious move anyone should have seen it right away.

"Don't laugh at me!" Margaret said in a huff. She tried to hide her own smile but failed miserably.

"I beg your pardon, Your Grace." Martin had appeared from nowhere like a storm cloud on a sunny day. Even Margaret and Tina jumped a little at the sound of his voice. "You are needed in your study," the man finished. He gave Margaret a bow and Miss Rowan a curt nod of his head.

Both women lost their smiles as they properly acknowledged him.

"Of course." Warwick stood. He didn't miss the look shared by the two women. If Warwick read their expressions correctly, they both seemed to be wondering about Martin's obvious distaste for the tableau the three of them had presented. He hated to see their good humor end, however, so he said, "Perhaps, Miss Rowan, your time would be better spent tutoring my sister in chess rather than discussing the latest fashions."

"It's not a bad idea, Your Grace, although I can't imagine anything more important than fashion," Miss Rowan said, a smile returning to light up her face.

He gave a little laugh before nodding to them both and headed off after his secretary.

~*~

Warwick preceded his secretary into the room before turning on him. "Just what was that all about?" he demanded.

"I need your signature—"

"And it couldn't have waited?"

Martin said nothing, nor did he look Warwick in the eye, but instead found the bookshelf behind the duke unusually interesting.

"Well?" Warwick demanded.

The man finally shifted his eyes. "I do not think it proper for Miss Rowan to believe herself an intimate of the family, and yet that is exactly the sort of idea she is coming to thanks to the overly generous treatment from you and Lady Margaret. I am certain that I need not remind you, Your Grace, that she is—"

"*You* are an intimate of the family," Warwick pointed out, cutting off the man. He knew very well who and what Tina was.

"We were raised together!" Martin practically shouted.

"You are my secretary and in my employ," Warwick said. He had no need to raise his voice.

Martin simply stood there staring, so Warwick continued, "Lady Margaret, who never once in her life had a friend of her own, has taken an uncommon liking to Miss Rowan. Am I supposed to simply dismiss her as another tradesman?"

"Yes! That's what she is. And if Lady Margaret needs a friend, she should choose one from among the young ladies of *ton* not her modiste. It is up to you to point her in the right direction not tolerate her whims."

"And is it *your* place to school me on my duties?" Warwick said in a dangerously low voice.

Martin's mouth opened and closed as if he were gasping for air. He then straightened himself and said with all the confidence of man headed to the gallows, "If you don't remember your esteemed status and behave like the duke that you are, then yes, it is my place to remind you. That is the duty of being your secretary."

"I see." Warwick debated how much longer Martin would be holding that position if this was the way he felt.

"It's perfectly fine if you wish to take up a dalliance with Miss Rowan, Your Grace, but to treat her like a familiar, like a friend, is wrong and misleading. She cannot possibly be—"

"I think you've made your point, Mr. Arbeit," Warwick said, his words clipped.

Martin took a step back as if Warwick had just hit him. Indeed, Warwick wasn't certain he had ever called his secretary by his surname before. On the other hand, Martin had never lectured him on proper behavior nor suggested he take a mistress, let alone of someone whom he liked and respected, no matter what the woman's station. He had gone too far, and Warwick made sure he knew it.

CHAPTER TWENTY-EIGHT

Without quite realizing it, Warwick had come to a decision. He turned and walked to his desk. "I believe it is time my cousin, Lady Sonora, return to Warwick. I would like you to escort her there."

He heard Martin gasp behind him. Good. He should know his behavior had gone beyond what was acceptable. To suggest that Tina become his mistress... Just the thought made Warwick's blood boil. Even if his secretary did not hold any respect for Miss Rowan, he certainly did.

His feelings of the previous night roared to the forefront of his mind. He loved Tina. He could admit that to himself now.

In his mind's eye, he saw her laughing with Margaret, guiding her, laughing with him and even exchanging a look of understanding. They connected in a way he never thought he'd connect with anyone beside his sister. Somehow, she understood him. She understood Margaret too. She knew just what his sister needed in terms of respectful, yet honest support. And beyond all that, there was still the overwhelming urge he'd had the last time he'd kissed her.

Mine.

That feeling deep within his being still reverberated. He wanted to hold her and keep her safe. He not only loved her, he wanted to be with her...always.

For a moment, he thought over what Martin had been trying to tell him. It wasn't anything he hadn't thought of himself over the past week or more. She was merely a modiste. On the other hand, she was also born of noble—if unmarried—parents, which made it both better and worse.

But what struck Warwick now was something that Martin had just said—he was a duke. Who was going to gainsay anything he did—aside from his secretary and his sister? And he couldn't imagine Margaret would be against the match.

Society be damned. He didn't care for it anyway. If he wanted to do something, he damn well did it. If he wanted to love an illegitimate modiste, he was going to do so. He didn't give a fig what anyone said or thought. He was duke!

For a moment, his thoughts turned to Margaret. What would happen to her if he married Tina? Would it ruin her chances to find a good husband?

He acknowledged that it might. On the other hand, he hoped whoever she married would be able to overlook Tina's background for the privilege of marrying a duke's sister.

He turned back to his secretary still standing by the door, staring after him with an expression of shock and anger on his face. "While you are at Warwick, I would like you to find my mother's sapphire and diamond ring and return with it."

"You don't mean the one your father gave to your esteemed mother when you were born?"

"Yes, that is precisely the one I mean," Warwick said. His mother had always said he should give that ring to his intended bride and Martin knew it.

Martin opened his mouth to protest, but Warwick cut him off. "If you are even thinking of reminding me of my position once more, I would strongly suggest you not do so, not if you value your current position."

Martin straightened his shoulders and bowed stiffly. "Yes, Your Grace." With a click of his heels, he turned and left the room.

Warwick turned back to his desk. What he was doing was probably madness and he knew it. He knew it too well. His father had made it clear, in both words and by example, exactly how a duke was to behave and how others were to behave toward him. His father believed being a duke was only a small step away from being king, and he'd taught his son the lesson well.

Warwick had always done his best to behave likewise, except when it came to people he cared for—Margaret and Martin. The only people he'd ever allowed to get close to him. Well, now he was going to take that privilege and use it to make himself happy—and, hopefully, Tina as well.

~*~

Christianne wrung her hands yet again. It was silly to be so nervous, it was just Liam. She gave a dry laugh. *Just* Liam, who'd walked out on her when she'd told him he was a father and had been for the past twenty years.

But Tina was right. She was absolutely right, and Christianne knew it. She may not like it, but she knew it. And now...

"Christianne! What's wrong? What's happened?" Liam burst into her private sitting room. "I got your message. I am here." He grasped her hands in the midst of her wringing them once more.

A tear slid down her cheek. It was so stupid of her to cry, especially at this juncture, but he'd come! He clearly dropped whatever it was he'd been doing and rushed to her because she'd told him it was urgent, and she needed to speak with him immediately.

She'd done so merely because she knew if she had to wait even a day, she would have lost her nerve. But he'd come.

"What is it, my love? No, please do not cry. I could not stand it if you did." He brushed his thumb across her cheek, wiping away her tears.

She shook her head and gave a very unladylike sniff. Immediately he was pressing his handkerchief into her hand. She could only laugh at how quick he was with everything that she needed.

"There now, that's better. I've made you laugh. I'm not quite sure how or why, but I so much prefer your laughter to your tears," he said, smiling at her.

"You are so good," she said. "So wonderful! And I have been thoughtless and stupid."

"No! Do not say so!"

"But it's true, and you know it." She pulled him toward the sofa and sat, leaving room for him to sit next to her. She raised her hand when he started to protest again. "You were right to walk out on me the other day. You have every right to be angry, no, furious with me. What I did—keeping Tina a secret— was wrong and I want to apologize. I can only pray you find it somewhere in your heart to forgive me."

His face softened. One moment he was anxious and worried, not knowing why she'd called him to her and simply reacted to her odd behavior, and the next he was relaxed. All of the love she'd always hoped he felt for her shone like a beam of sunshine from his eyes.

"I do forgive you, my sweet Christianne, because I could never stay angry with you for long." He paused, his gaze shifting away from her for a moment. "Tina explained everything to me," he said, looking at her again.

"I'm so glad you went and spoke with her."

He smiled. "So am I. She's a wonderful girl. She's...actually rather amazing. She hasn't had an easy life and yet... She's a strong girl. Sure of herself. Knowledgeable. And... I think, happy."

"I hope she's happy. I've done everything I could to make her so, even though I couldn't keep her next to me as she grew up. I always went to visit her on her birthday. And I tried—"

He took her hands in his. "I know. You had no idea her foster parents weren't treating her the way they should have."

Tears pricked Christianne's eyes once again. She could only shake her head for a moment as she held them back. When she could, she said, "If I had known... But they said everything was fine. They told me what a quick and clever girl she was. How happy she was. She was always a little shy and quiet, but I thought that was just because she didn't know me well."

"You couldn't have known," he agreed.

"I gave her everything I could. She is educated, you know. And then her foster parents apprenticed her to the local seamstress."

"What a wonderful thing that was. She is incredibly talented."

Christianne smiled. "She has your sense for fashion and form. It's quite amazing, is it not?"

He gave a little laugh. "Yes. It's one thing that makes me absolutely certain she's my daughter."

They were quiet for a moment, both lost in their thoughts. Christianne peeked up at Liam. "Then you do forgive me?"

"Of course I do." He caressed a hand gently along her cheek. "And my offer still stands."

Christianne widened her eyes. "You mean...?"

"Yes. I would be honored if you would agree to marry me once and for all, Christianne. It should have happened thirty years ago, but at least we can still grow old together. What do you say?"

She couldn't help it, the tears started to flow once again. This time, though, they were happy tears. She laughed and threw her arms around her dearest, sweetest, wonderful love. "Oh yes, Liam, yes!"

"You have made me the happiest of men!" he said just before his lips descended on to hers. As his kiss deepened, Christianne remembered only too well the wonderful times they'd had together twenty years ago and all the joy and happiness that had led to Tina's conception.

Sadly, one thought led to another and with a gasp, Christianne reluctantly pulled away. "There's one more thing you should know," she said.

Liam looked disappointed for the merest second. "Please don't tell me there are more children?" he asked with a little laugh.

"Oh, good gracious, no!" Even Christianne had to laugh at that thought. "No, I... I don't know if Tina told you about her predicament with her foster-father."

Liam's face lost its smile. "No, she didn't. What is this?"

"You've got to help her, Liam. Her foster-father is blackmailing her into sending him money. He gave her two months to get her business started and then said she had to send him the amount I had given him every month for her upkeep *plus* fifteen percent!"

"What?"

"If she didn't, he would force her to return and marry his son so that they could keep the money within their family, or else he would put a notice in the paper, announcing I was her mother." She shook her head. "I was so stupid, Liam. I told the man I would support Tina for the rest of her life. I've given him money every month for her upkeep, but now that she's an adult, the money will go to her instead of him."

"And he wants it for himself and more," Liam said, understanding dawning.

"Yes. We've got to do something. We've got to stop this man from bleeding our daughter dry with his horrid threats. If it were to come out... Both Tina and I would be ruined."

Liam sighed heavily. "I'll fix this. I don't quite know how, but I *will* fix this."

"Do you think he can just be paid off once and for all?" she suggested.

"No, he'll just keep coming back for more. There's got to be some other way..." He turned back to her and gave her a little smile. "Don't worry. I'll figure something out."

~May 4~

"I'm very sorry, Your Grace, but the ring wasn't there," Martin said upon his return to London. So, he was still "Your Grace" to Martin and not Warwick.

The duke suspected his friend was still angry at being sent home. That was just too bad. Warwick had enjoyed relaxing a few days while Martin was away, seeing Cousin Sonora back to the quiet of the countryside and looking for his mother's ring.

"Wasn't there or you didn't actually look for it?" Warwick asked, raising an eyebrow. He knew Martin didn't want him giving that ring to Tina, but honestly, Warwick didn't give a damn what Martin thought.

His secretary's jaw worked silently for a moment. Warwick imagined he was working very hard keeping his thoughts to himself.

"What ring is this, Warwick?" Margaret asked. She'd been sitting on the other side of the drawing room with a book in her hand. The duke had thought she was reading but clearly, she wasn't any longer.

"Mother's sapphire and diamond ring," he said as off-handedly as he could.

"I looked in the safe in your study, but it wasn't there," Martin said, having mastered his tongue.

"Did you look in the one in Mother's room?" Margaret asked.

Martin turned and looked at her, his eyebrows rising a touch on his forehead. "No. I didn't know there *was* a safe in her room."

"Yes, it's built into her armoire. The key for it is in the powder jar on the dressing table," Margaret said with a sly little smile on her lips. She was clearly enjoying the fact that she knew secrets even Martin didn't know.

"Thank you, Margaret," Warwick said with a wink. He turned back to his secretary. "It should take you another two days to retrieve it and return. I'll see you when you get back."

That was a clear dismissal. Martin scowled at Warwick but bowed and left the room in silence.

"He was not happy about that," Margaret commented. "What is this ring you're sending him for?"

"It was given to Mother by our father when I was born," Warwick said. He wasn't certain how much he wanted to tell his little sister of his plans. He still wasn't one hundred percent certain he was going through with them himself. He'd been having doubts these past few days about whether this was, after all, the right thing to do, and whether it could harm Margaret's chances at making a good match.

"And why do you want it?" Margaret persisted, nosy little thing that she was.

He turned and looked at her. Yes, that sly smile was back on her lips. She knew he was plotting something, and she wanted to know what it was. To be fair, he'd hardly ever kept anything from his sister—only those things an innocent girl shouldn't know about. But did that include what was in his heart?

Perhaps she could shed some light on his dilemma. She would certainly have an opinion—she almost always had one, no matter what the topic.

"Come on, brother, you can tell me. It's not like I'm going to run tattling to anyone," she said after he'd been silent for a minute.

He sighed. "Very well. I'm thinking—just thinking, mind you—of asking Miss Rowan—"

CHAPTER TWENTY-NINE

"Oh my goodness, Warwick, truly?" Margaret jumped up from her chair and ran to him. Still holding the book in her hands, she pressed them to her chest, her eyes wide with excitement. "You're going to propose to Tina?"

"I said I was considering—"

"But that's wonderful!" She dropped down on the sofa next to him. "I *love* Tina! And I just knew you would too! I have to be honest, I didn't think you'd actually fall in love with her—at least not this fast—but I'm not at all surprised you have. She's wonderful, isn't she? So intelligent! And talented! And beautiful! And funny! And—"

Warwick was laughing when he interrupted his sister. "Yes, yes, she is all of those things. She is also a modiste and the illegitimate daughter of a member of the *ton*."

Margaret's eyes turned a little sad. "But you said that didn't bother you. Do you know who her parents are?"

"I know who her mother is but not her father— and I swore to her that I would not tell a soul and that, my dear sister, includes you. I'm sorry."

"Oh, that's all right. I don't mind."

"But you do see my dilemma."

She sat back, allowing her gaze to wander out the window. "Hmm. Yes. As a duke, you can't marry just anyone. You're supposed to marry someone of high social standing who can take her place at your side as duchess."

"Exactly."

She turned and looked at him. "But Tina is so wonderful. Couldn't an exception be made? What if her father were also a member of society? Would that help?"

Warwick shrugged. "It might if he acknowledged the relationship. But even then, our father would probably turn in his grave. And if we never learn who her father is, or if he's someone of the lower order... She might never be accepted by society. It's that which I'm more worried about, obviously. I would hate for her to be put in an awkward position because of me. And I won't risk your chances for a good marriage either."

His sister turned back toward the window. "Oh, yes, I see."

"But what's the use of being a duke if I can't marry who I want?" Warwick asked. It had been plaguing him for the past few days, ever since he'd sent Martin to Warwick for his mother's ring.

His sister turned back and put her hand on top of his. "Even if society does turn their back on her, I'll stand by her. And please don't give a second thought about me. If she's not good enough for any man I'd marry... Well, then I wouldn't marry him!" She moved closer to him. "We'll make this work one way or another, Robert."

Warwick stared at his sister. She had never in her life called him by his given name. When they were young, it had always been Binton, his father's lesser title. Since their father had died, she'd only ever called him Warwick. Her use of his Christian name made him feel closer to her than ever. "You are the best of sisters, do you know that?" he asked, smiling at her even as he turned his hand over to clasp hers.

She returned his smile.

"But there is still Tina to consider," he pointed out.

"I'm sure she loves you! How could anyone not?" his sweet, innocent little sister said. No one could ever say she wasn't loyal to a fault.

He laughed. "I don't know that she does, and there are many reasons why she wouldn't. But"—he held up his other hand when she started to protest—"if I am so lucky that she does feel the same way, she will still be the one ultimately to decide if she's willing to make this work. It's not going to be easy no matter what."

"No, it's not," Margaret agreed. "But if she does try, it will be worth it. She is perfect for you."

"That I cannot argue with."

~May 5~

Tina looked around the table and could hardly believe it. Her mother sat across from her, and her father sat between them at the head of the table.

Her parents! Both of them. Together. With her.

It felt...amazing. It felt like they were a family. A whole and complete family.

She took another sip of her wine before either of her parents noticed the tears of happiness in her eyes.

"This is probably the most wonderful evening of my life," Lord Ayres said, reaching out and taking Lady Norman's hand in one of his and Tina's in the other.

"I was just thinking the same thing," Tina admitted.

"It is truly incredible. I just can't help thinking this could have happened so much sooner. If only I had had the nerve to tell you, Liam, and make Tina more a part of my life," Lady Norman said, looking from one to the other.

"No recriminations tonight, my dear. We are together now." Lord Ayres paused, then his eyes lit up. "Ah! And we haven't even told Tina our wonderful news yet!"

Tina looked from one to the other of her parents. "What news?"

Lord Ayres let go of her hand and shifted his gaze over to Tina's mother. "Christianne and I are engaged."

"We're going to be married, if you can believe such a thing could happen at our age!" Lady Norman said with a giggle and an incredulous shake of her head.

"But that's wonderful!" Tina raised her wine glass. "Here's to you both. You deserve all the happiness in the world. After so many years of having to be apart, you can finally have your happily ever after."

Lord Ayres laughed as her mother beamed. "Thank you, my dear. It is true it has taken us much, much too long to get to this, but I think it will have been worth the wait," her father said.

As her parents gazed lovingly at each other, Tina basked in their happiness. It was so wonderful they were finally able to be together. She was very happy for them.

She almost shook her head when the Duke of Warwick's smiling face flashed in her mind's eye.

With so much love before her, was it wrong that she should think of him?

The fact she loved him didn't matter. No matter what, she would never have her happily ever after with him. He was a duke, and while she was born of noble parents, they had been unmarried when she'd been born. She would not forget her position. How could she when it kept her from having the slightest hope of being with the only man she'd ever met who made her feel happy.

Yes, she thought to herself as the footmen came in with their dinner and began serving, Warwick not only made her happy, he made her feel special. He respected her and was kind and considerate when no one had ever treated her that way. He made her feel as if she were not only someone but someone who deserved to be treated well. And then, of course, there was simply the thrill of being looked at *that way* by a man so handsome. He made her long to be in his arms.

It was downright depressing to think that she would never—

"Tina, what do you think of that?" Lord Ayres said, suddenly capturing her attention.

"I'm sorry, I wasn't paying attention. What did you say?" she said, picking up her fork and tasting the delicious-looking meat that had appeared on her plate.

Her father laughed. "You were somewhere else for a few minutes there."

"I apologize, my mind was wandering," Tina said, feeling her face heat.

"Quite all right, my dear." He laughed. "I was just saying I would like to introduce you to society. What do you think?"

"Intro—but you can't be serious!" Tina protested.

"Why not?" He lowered his fork and looked at her, losing the smile from his lips.

"Because so many ladies of society already know me—as their modiste! They would never accept I was one of them. I... I'm not one of them."

"You most certainly are! Or you can be. You're my daughter." Lord Ayres said it as if it were obvious.

"I *am* your daughter, but I'm also a modiste, a seamstress. I can't also become a member of society," Tina argued.

"I understand your reluctance, Tina, but you can do this if you want to. You know you'll have the full support of the Lady's Wagering Whist Society," her mother said with a certainty that Tina only wished she could believe.

"That's extremely generous, Lady Norman, but you can't know that for certain."

Her mother stared at her for a moment and then said quietly, "You called me Mother once. When we're in private like this, I would appreciate you doing so."

Tina froze. *Had* she called her Mother? She supposed she had when Lady Norman had been upset at Lord Ayres' reaction to Tina's existence. She'd felt very close to her mother just then. So, yes, why she shouldn't feel close to her now? She nodded her head. "I beg your pardon. I would be honored to address you so...Mother."

"And you will call me Father or Papa," Lord Ayres said, with a broad smile. "I'd like to be called Papa."

Tina laughed. "Of course." She wagged a finger at him. "But that doesn't mean society is going to accept me if you simply tell them to."

He put down his fork and took hold of her finger. "Yes, they will. And as your mother said, you'll have the support of all of her friends as well, and they include some very important and influential members of society. If they say you are a member of society, then my dear daughter, you *are* a member of society."

"No more arguments, Tina. Let your father do this. It will make him so happy," her mother said.

"And there is one other reason—not the main reason, not the primary reason, mind you, but an important one," her father started, his face growing serious.

"What is that?" Tina asked.

"As a member of society, I'd like you to look around for someone who could make you happy. Whether it is the gentleman you told me about or another, I want you to marry—this season, if possible."

"But why?" Tina asked, confused. Why was her father suddenly so intent on her marrying, or was this normal for a father?

He looked toward her mother for a moment, who gave him a small nod of encouragement. "Once I acknowledge you and marry your mother, your foster-father won't have a hold over you. However, if you marry, it will provide that much more security for you from his threats. As a member of society and the wife of a peer, there is nothing he can do to hurt you—ever."

Tina's mouth dropped opened. She'd completely forgotten about her foster-father in the joy of finding her real father and her parent's happiness. But he was right. Once her parents married, even if anyone found out she was Lady Norman's daughter, they would believe Tina was her step-daughter. When Tina married, her foster-father's threats would absolutely hold no water; she wouldn't be able to marry Caleb anyway. With both her parents' marriage and her own, she wouldn't have to pay her foster-father anything ever again.

Tina could only nod. Her mouth had gone dry at the thought of having to find a husband—one who wasn't Warwick. Even if she did become a member of society, she was still illegitimate and therefore ineligible to him. Surely, as a duke, he had to marry someone of impeccable breeding.

No, there was no way he could propose to her. If he could, she was certain he would have so done already.

There was nothing more Tina could say, so she said nothing.

"Good, then it's decided," her father said, picking up his fork again. "I want you to make one of those beautiful ball gowns for yourself, and do it quickly because I'm going to take you to Lady Kershaw's ball next week."

~May 10~

Not a minute after Warwick slammed his study door on another idiot, did it open again slowly...hesitantly.

"Warwick?" His sister's head peeked around the edge of the door. "May I have a word?"

He sighed and dropped into his desk chair. "Yes, of course, Margaret. Come in."

She did so and sat at the edge of the chair on the other side of his desk. She stared at him for a moment, hard enough that Warwick was almost tempted to squirm like a child.

Finally, he said, "What is it, Margaret? I'm extremely busy."

"I'm certain that you are. Being without Martin for so long must be very trying for you. You rely on him such a great deal."

He waited, certain she had more to say—she always did. He tried his best not to scowl at her. It wasn't her fault he was in a foul temper.

"You've been yelling. A lot. And slamming doors. And well, generally being an extremely angry, difficult person these past few days. Can you tell me what's bothering you?" She leaned forward a touch in her chair. The look of concern on her face nearly did him in.

He scrubbed his hand down his face. "I'm sorry. I don't mean..." He couldn't sit still. He got up and began to pace in front of the window behind his chair. "It's been eight days. Eight days! What do you think is taking Martin so long to return from Warwick? Could something have happened to him? There are highwaymen... But he's a pretty stout fellow, and I'm certain he carries a weapon with him when he travels from London just in case." He turned and headed back in the other direction. "Could it be Cousin Sonora? Maybe she's taken ill. Or maybe he's just being obstinate because he doesn't feel Tina is good enough for me. You know how strongly he feels about my position." He paused and turned toward his sister.

She had the faintest smile on her face as she watched him prattle on like a fool.

"I'm being a bloody idiot, aren't I?" he said with a sigh.

Chapter Thirty

Margaret gave a little laugh. "I think you're acting like a man in love, to be honest."

He tried to laugh. Truly, he did, because what she said was absolutely correct. He *was* in love. "The problem is that I don't know how Tina feels. I need to speak to her." He spun away, his anger returning in full force. "But I can't do that until Martin comes back with that damned ring!"

"Why not? You don't need a ring to talk to her. You can ask her how she feels—after revealing your feelings first, of course—without asking her to marry you."

"But you see, I think I've done that. I mean, I feel as if I've done it," he said, trying to keep the exasperation out of his voice.

"What do you mean? When?"

"Before I sent Martin to Warwick for the ring the first time. I, er, when I went to her room to pay her for your dress. I think I might have mentioned it."

"Ah, ha! I knew you'd gone for more than simply a business transaction," she gloated.

"Yes, well, the point is that I showed her how I feel. I'm certain that I did."

"And...?"

"And I think she feels the same way. It was...difficult to tell. How do I know?"

Margaret frowned at him. "You told her you loved her and she said...what?"

"Well, I didn't say it in so many words, precisely," he admitted.

"Then how did you tell her? What did you say?"

"Nothing..." Warwick answered.

"You said nothing, but you feel that she should just *know* that you love her?" She started to laugh. "Do you think she's a mind-reader?"

He scowled at her. "No. I, er, I kissed her. I didn't tell her in so many words, but I showed her how I felt."

"Oh!" Margaret's eyes went wide as her face turned slightly pink. "And, er, how did she respond?"

"She kissed me back." He paused, remembering the evening well. "And then she told me that it was late and I should go."

"I see."

"Yes. So, I really have no idea if she knows how I feel or not. Or if she feels the same way."

"I understand. In that case, you really do need to speak with her, and er, this time using words rather than actions."

"Yes, I suppose I should," he agreed.

"And if you absolutely must propose, tell her that Martin is returning with the ring any day now and as soon as he does you'll give it to her. I'm sure she'll understand." She paused, then added thoughtfully, "And after you do so, I would write to Martin and tell him what you've done because he'll then realize that one man cannot stop the forces of love."

Warwick stopped pacing and turned to look at his sister while she'd been talking. "How did you become so wise? When did this happen?" He came around his desk as she giggled.

Taking her hands in his, he pulled her to her feet. "What would I ever do without you?"

She gave another little laugh and a shrug. "Be miserable, I suspect. Oh, and make everyone around you completely miserable as you've been doing."

He closed his eyes and nodded. "Perhaps I have some apologies to make."

"It's all right. I've already apologized for you and explained you've been under unusual stress without Martin. The staff understands."

He gave her a warm smile. "You truly are a wonder, my little sister." He enfolded her in a hug.

She pulled away after a moment. "Then what are you doing just standing here? Go and speak with Tina!"

He gave a bark of laughter. "Yes! Yes, I will!"

~*~

There was no answer on Tina's door. Warwick had ridden as quickly as he could through the crowded London streets, and now there was no answer. He stepped back and ran a hand down his face. What was he to do now? Where could she be?

He'd seen a draper's shop next door. Maybe she was buying material for a client?

He ran down the stairs and nearly ran over a child, who was hanging around on the footpath. The shop owner just shook his head. "'Aven't seen 'er today, my lord," the man said when asked.

"I see. Thank you," Warwick said, before turning and leaving again. Where else could she be? At a client's home helping them prepare for an evening the way she'd done for Margaret, most likely—in which case, he'd never find her!

The only other possibility was that she was with her mother, Lady Norman—not that anyone was to know the relationship existed, but Warwick had figured it out. He retrieved his horse, then rode once again for Mayfair.

"No, I'm sorry, Your Grace, Lady Norman has already left for the evening," the butler told him in sonorous tones.

"And Miss Rowan? She wouldn't happen to be here, would she?"

The man frowned. "No, Your Grace."

"Thank you." He stopped. "Wait, did you say that Lady Norman had already left for the evening?"

"Yes, Your Grace."

Warwick pulled out his pocket watch. It was nearly eight! Where had the day gone? The evening? Had it really been over two hours since he'd left Margaret? She must be wondering where he was. He was certain he'd promised to escort her to some ball or other.

~*~

"People are going to recognize me," Tina whispered to her father as they stood in line to be greeted by Lord and Lady Kershaw.

"Of course they will, you've got quite a few clients among the *ton*," Lord Ayres agreed.

"And I've fixed hems and what not at Lady Margaret's ball," Tina added.

Her father nodded but didn't seem concerned.

"They know me as a modiste!" She clutched onto her father's coat sleeve.

He pried her fingers loose. "It's all right. They'll get used to your new status quickly enough."

"But—"

He turned to her, cupping her face in his hands. "You are my daughter and I am very proud of who you are. You're a talented, beautiful young woman, and there is nothing you can do or say that is going to make me change my mind about doing this. Yes, it's unusual. Yes, people are going to talk. I don't care and neither should you."

"My business..."

"You are no longer in business. If you want to design clothes for your friends, do so, but I am going to support you from now on. You are going to take your rightful place in society." He leaned down and gave her a kiss on her cheek. "Now, come and let's throw ourselves to the wolves."

Tina couldn't help but laugh. That was exactly how she felt.

"Miss Ayres, how lovely it is to meet you," Lady Kershaw said after her father presented her as such to their hostess. It was strange to be called by a different name, but her father had insisted she take his, and truly, it did make a great deal more sense for her to do so as he was presenting her to society as his daughter.

"It was so kind of you to add me to your guest list at the last minute, my lady," Tina said as she curtsied.

"Not at all. Your father's extraordinary story of finding you will be the talk of the night," Lady Kershaw said with a gleam in her eye. She was clearly thrilled at having her ball be the backdrop of such juicy gossip.

"I'm certain it will," Lord Ayres said with a chuckle. He then took Tina's arm and led her into the ballroom proper.

There were a few eyes quickly on them as they entered the room. Quite a few fans were unfurled as ladies whispered behind them excitedly. Clearly, the rumors had already begun to spread.

"Ah, here is Lady Norman and Lady Blakemore," he said, making a straight line for Tina's mother and her friend. It was good he was starting them out on friendly territory.

Tina curtsied to the two ladies. "How lovely to see you both this evening," she said, doing her best to give them a smile. It wasn't easy considering how nervous she was feeling, though.

"And you, Miss, er, Ayres," Lady Blakemore said.

"You are looking very well," her mother said approvingly.

"Well, I should hope the girl knows how to dress herself," her friend said with a lift of an eyebrow.

Tina gave her a tight smile. "I have to admit, I drew and discarded a number of designs before I came up with this one. It's actually not as easy to design a dress for yourself as it is for others."

"Really?" the lady asked.

"Shop! That's what that smell is, Penelope," said a voice from behind Tina. "Don't you smell it?" the voice drifted away as the person speaking continued walking past.

Tina's spine stiffened and her gaze dropped to the floor.

"Lady Florenton!" her father called out as he turned Tina around and led her away from the comfort of her mother's side.

A woman in a vibrant lavender silk gown with a matching turban paused and turned back. "Why, Lord Ayres, I didn't see you standing there." Her neck practically glowed purple with no less than three strands of amethysts draped around it and resting on her ample bosom.

"Have you met my daughter, Miss Bronten?" the lady said, giving Tina's father a polite smile. "My dear, this is Lord Ayres, from *Ireland*." She followed her words with a significant sniff, letting them all know just what she thought of the providence of his family and title.

He bowed over the girl's hand. She was wearing the prescribed white for a young lady, but it was a horrid shade for the girl, making her round cheeks look florid. It was also possible she was merely embarrassed by her mother's atrocious behavior.

"And may I present my daughter, Miss Ayres," Tina's father said, stepping aside to allow Tina to stand directly in front of the horrid woman.

"Ah yes, I have heard of you, Miss Rowan," the woman said, putting more emphasis on Tina's last name.

"It's Ayres now that Tina and I have found each other," her father said.

"But you were known as Miss Rowan, were you not? You are a modiste, I believe," the woman persisted.

"I was, my lady," Tina agreed.

"Isn't it incredible how quickly things change?" Lord Ayres laughed. "One moment, Tina is a modiste working to make the ladies of society look their best and the next she is a member of society itself. I have to say I am proud of her."

"Proud?" the woman asked incredulously. "How can you be—"

"Oh, quite easily, I can assure you," her father said with a laugh. "How many young ladies here can say they have used their talents to help others, and then had the strength of character to accept such a new and different role than the one they'd been expecting in life?"

"Well, to be sure—"

"None. Absolutely none. Yes, Lady Florenton, I am very proud of my girl."

"And there is no doubt she is, in fact, *your* daughter and not just some interloper attempting to..." Even this horrid woman had the intelligence to see it would be unwise to continue that thought.

Tina's father's eyes were like daggers piercing this woman's thin, aristocratic skin. "I am one hundred percent positive." He softened his gaze. "Why, how could anyone look at her incredible understanding of clothing and how one should dress and not immediately know that she *is* my daughter?" He gave a bark of laughter before taking Tina's arm again. "A very good evening to you my lady, Miss Bronten," he said with a curt nod. He turned his back on the ladies and led Tina away.

"What a horrible woman," Tina whispered as soon as they were out of earshot.

"I believe—I hope," he amended, "that she is the worst of those you will meet this evening."

CHAPTER THIRTY-ONE

"**L**ady Margaret is awaiting you in the drawing room, Your Grace," the footman informed Warwick the moment he entered the house.

"Thank you, Michael." He popped his head into the room. "I'm so sorry, Margaret," he started.

She jumped to her feet. "Did you see Tina? What did she say?"

He sighed and came farther into the room. "She wasn't at home. I searched wherever I thought I might find her, but I haven't seen her. She must be helping a client dress for the evening."

"Oh." His sister deflated a little as she sat back down. "Of course."

"I'll just get dressed then. I did promise to take you out this evening."

"Yes, to Lady Kershaw's ball. Take your time." She gave him a little smile and lifted the book she'd been reading while waiting for him.

He gave her a nod and then disappeared. He was certain he could do with some washing—he smelled of horse. Luckily, he was pretty sure Margaret wouldn't mind waiting a half an hour for him.

Warwick managed to get dressed faster than anticipated, but no matter what he did, he simply could not get Tina out of his mind. Where could she possibly be?

By the time he and Margaret entered the ball, he could barely contain himself. Every possibility had gone through his mind from the idea she'd gotten tired of waiting for him and had left town to return to her home village, to the thought he was being an idiot and she was just busy. No matter what the true reason was, he knew he wouldn't be able to deal with the fawning mothers and their overly eligible daughters in tow. If one young woman batted her eyelashes or fluttered her fan at him, he was certain he would do something very ungentlemanly.

"Oh look, there's Mrs. Aldridge with Lord Ainsby," Margaret said as soon as they'd walked in the door.

"Excellent," Warwick marched over to them, dragging his sister with him.

"Mrs. Aldridge," he nodded to the matron. "Ainsby."

"Ah, Your Grace what a lovely—" Mrs. Aldridge began.

Warwick just didn't have the patience for politeness though. He turned back to Ainsby. "Isn't there a dance forming? I'm certain you'll want my sister on your arm."

"Oh, er, I believe the current dance is about to end, but—" the fop began.

"Brilliant. Here you are." He pushed Margaret a little closer to the fellow. "If you'll excuse me." He gave a nod of his head and strode off to the garden before he snapped anybody's head off.

"But..." the man called after him.

Warwick ignored him. Margaret would work it out and understand his foul mood; he was certain of it.

The garden was blessedly cool. He hadn't realized how heated he was until he stepped outside. He just needed a breath of fresh air, he told himself. He would pull himself together and then make nice in the ballroom.

~*~

"Well, I think you're doing very well," Lady Norman said, soon after her father had left her with her mother and Miss Sheffield. He probably needed some time to himself and Tina didn't blame him one bit. She could use one herself.

"Thank you," Tina said with a sigh.

"How *are* you doing? I can't imagine how difficult this must be for you," Miss Sheffield said. "How funny it is that you know all about society, know so many ladies of society, and yet this is your first foray as a member."

"It is an awkward situation," Tina agreed. "I'm afraid that's probably why I've been getting so many comments—both to my face and, not so discreetly, behind my back."

"What have people been saying?" her mother asked, sounding horrified.

Tina tried to give her a smile but wasn't too sure she succeeded. "Oh, you know, that I'm an upstart, a fraud, a mushroom. I smell of the shop, that it's clear that while I may belong in a lady's dressing room, I certainly don't belong in a ballroom."

"But that's horrid!" Miss Sheffield said, her eyes going wide.

"It is. But I also suppose it's to be expected," Tina said, trying to make light of the hurt that had now moved from being a sharp stabbing in her stomach to something duller but no less painful.

"I am so sorry, Tina." Her mother put her hand on her arm.

Miss Sheffield did too but in an odd way. It was less of a consoling hand than it was a grab. "I'm sorry, but did you just see that?"

"See what?" Tina asked, following her line of sight.

"That man." Miss Sheffield followed someone with her eyes. "That man heading out the door, the one in the gray coat. He just stole two diamond pins from a lady's hair!"

"What? You must be imagining things, Miss Sheffield," Lady Norman said with a little laugh. "No gentleman would steal pins from a lady's hair!"

"No, I'm certain... He's gone," Miss Sheffield said, letting go of Tina's arm.

"He must have just accidentally bumped into her," Tina said.

"Yes," Miss Sheffield said, sounding unconvinced. "Perhaps, it was that." She turned back to Tina and her mother. "Yes, you must be right." She gave a little laugh. "Who would he steal hairpins from a lady at a ball?" She shook her head.

"Perhaps you need some fresh air as much as I do," Tina suggested.

"Oh, no. I'm fine. Truly." Miss Sheffield gave another unconvincing laugh.

"Well then, if you don't mind, I think I'm going to get a breath of fresh air. If one more person insults me to my face, I'm not entirely certain I won't actually scream."

"Oh, dear!" her mother said, looking a little worried.

"It's all right. I'm sure that a brief walk in the garden will make me feel better. If you'll excuse me." Tina gave them both a little curtsy and headed out the French doors toward the garden.

The cool air felt wonderful after the heat of the ballroom. She could feel her head clearing, her stress falling away. She'd had no idea members of society could be so openly cruel!

She wandered down a path enjoying the fresh scents of the newly budding flowers of spring.

She was actually quite proud of herself, she thought. She'd behaved just right. She'd not been rude to one person, no matter how nasty they'd been to her. And she did, after all, belong here just as much as anyone. Yes, it was true she'd been raised in a small village by a poor family, but that didn't change her bloodlines, which were as impeccable as anyone's in society. Hadn't the Duke of Warwick himself said as much to her? He hadn't been at all surprised she'd been illegitimate, nor had he thought any less of her for being so.

If only more people could be as open-minded and accepting of her.

She wondered if he'd heard her news. He had to have. She'd seen a glimpse of Margaret just before she'd left the room, and if Margaret was there, then Warwick had to be as well.

"Tina! Tina!" the sound of the duke's voice pulled her from her thoughts.

She turned and found him striding up to her, a huge grin on his face. "I'm so happy to see you!" he said, taking hold of her hands.

She blinked up at him. "I'm happy to see you too. It hasn't been that long," she laughed. "Only a week."

"It feels like an eternity to me. I've been looking for you."

She stepped back a little. "You have?"

"Yes. I, er, I wanted to ask you something. Now that... Now that things have changed..." He paused and smiled down at her, even running a finger down her cheek.

Things had changed? What had changed? Only her status in society.

He smiled at her, a smile that lit up his whole face and showed through his eyes. "I'm so happy, Tina, that it *has* changed. Now I can ask you what I didn't dare ask before." He held her hands up to his lips. "Would you do me the great honor of becoming my wife?"

Tina's mouth dropped open. She tried to stop it, but...but...

"I know I waited, and perhaps I shouldn't have, but I'm asking now." He hesitated, beginning to look a little worried, perhaps because she wasn't saying anything. "I know you don't know the first thing about being a duchess," he continued before she could say a word, "but that's all right, Margaret will teach you. The one thing my parents did give her was excellent training. She'll help you every step along the way in your new life."

"My new life," she managed to croak out. So he *had* heard. He knew she was now a member of society...and because of her newfound status it was suddenly all right that he propose to her? The week before he wanted nothing more than her kisses and maybe to offer her a carte blanche as his mistress. But now that she was a member of society...

"How *dare* you." She could feel her anger bubbling up within her like a volcano about to erupt. She'd had to endure insult after insult all night, but she'd thought he would support her. He'd always *said* he thought she was more than just a modiste, but now all he cared about was her social position. *Now* she was good enough for him?

"What?"

"Last week all you wanted was to slake your lust with a nobody, but *now* you think I'm worthy to be your wife? Well, to hell with you, Your Grace!" She pulled her hands from his. She could barely breathe she was so furious. "*Now* you think I'm going to just throw myself at your feet? Well, think again, Duke!" she spat. "I *am* worthy and I have been even before this! I am worthy of so much more than you. I don't care about social position and I thought you didn't either. Clearly, I was wrong! You are just as shallow as any of them! So you can take your proposal and... and... sit on it!" She spun around and walked as quickly as she could back to ballroom.

She didn't need him and his empty proposal. Her whole world had just opened up. She'd been acknowledged by her father and properly introduced into society. If Warwick hadn't cared enough about her when she was a modiste, she certainly didn't want him now that she was "good enough" for him. She would find someone else to marry.

~*~

What just happened? Warwick stared after Tina's retreating back. He had absolutely no idea why she'd become so furious. Why she'd turned down his proposal. Was it the way he'd said it? He said he'd be honored. All right, he hadn't mentioned the word love, but surely she was well aware of his feelings toward her.

He was just as shallow as any of them? Any of whom? Society, he supposed, but he had no idea what she was talking about. But the more he thought about it, the angrier he got. He wasn't *good enough* for her? He was a duke! He was being open and accepting of her and her lowly position. She was a dressmaker! And *he* wasn't good enough for *her*?

His fury came hard and fast, tunneling his vision. He had to leave. He had to leave not only this idiotic ball but London. Yes. That was it. He would leave Town. He couldn't deal with these people, the backstabbing, the gossip, the fawning. He didn't want to deal with any of it, and he wouldn't for a minute longer.

He strode back into the ballroom. He spotted his sister immediately. She was standing by the Duchess of Kendell. Good.

"Good evening, Your Grace," he said with a slight bow.

"Oh, Warwick, there you are, I—"

"I beg your pardon, but I have been called away on an emergency. I'm afraid I need to leave town for a few days. Could I possibly ask you to escort my sister home this evening?" he said, cutting her off.

"It's not Martin?" Margaret asked, her eyes becoming worried.

"No. It's not Martin. He's fine. But I do need to leave. Now," he said firmly.

"Well, of course, you can entrust her to me," the duchess said.

"Thank you." Without another word, he turned and left the room, not looking at any one person. He knew if he looked, if he made eye contact, he'd be caught. No, he held his head high and walked straight out of the room. His carriage would take him to Warwick. He would be there long before morning and not have to deal with any of this nonsense any longer.

CHAPTER THIRTY-TWO

Tina was taking a moment to compose herself again just inside the French doors of the ballroom when her mother walked up, accompanied by Lord Ayres. "Tina, what happened? What's wrong?" They both looked very concerned.

"Nothing, I..." Tina started.

Warwick strode past them without a glance in her direction. Well, that was fine with her. She had nothing more to say to the man.

"Did something happen between you and the duke?" her father whispered.

Tina took in a deep breath. "He proposed to me."

"What? When?" Her mother's eyes went wide.

"Just now. In the garden. He said now that I was a member of society, he felt he could do so. I told him... Well, I told him no."

"You turned down a duke?" Her mother squeaked very quietly, clearly aware of where they were and how many ears surrounded them.

"He only was prepared to marry me because of my new status. Last week he nearly offered me a carte blanche," Tina admitted.

Her parents exchanged a worried look.

"I wouldn't accept that then, and I won't accept his proposal now. When I marry it will be for love—or at the very least, someone who respects me. And yes, I know I need to marry quickly," she said to her father, "but I don't have to accept the first man who offers."

"Well, er, no, of course not," her father agreed.

"Clearly, if he didn't love or respect you enough to propose last week, he doesn't now," Lady Norman said and nodded her understanding.

"Yes! Precisely," Tina said, finally beginning to calm down. She was so grateful her mother understood.

"Despite being a duke, as a man, he isn't worthy of you," her father said, glaring in the direction the duke had gone.

Tina nearly laughed, but a moment later was blinking tears from her eyes. "You know, I don't think I've mentioned how lucky and happy I am to have you both. Thank you!"

Her mother put her arm around Tina's shoulders. "We are the lucky ones."

"And we're proud of how strong you are. You deserve love *and* respect and should settle for nothing less," her father said, giving her a warm smile.

Tina thought about it for a moment then said, "It was both of you who taught me that. It's the fact that you both have shown me your love that I've come to realize this."

Her parents shared a smile.

"Well now, I think you need to forget all about that...that duke and have some fun," her father said. "Come, have you met Lord Ainsby?"

He took her arm and escorted her to the side of the room where two gentlemen were speaking with Mrs. Aldridge from the Lady's Wagering Whist Society.

"Mrs. Aldridge," her father bowed slightly to the lady.

"My Lord Ayres, how lovely to see you this evening. And Miss Rowan! Or no, it's Miss Ayres now, isn't it?" The plump woman beamed at them.

"Yes, thank you for remembering, ma'am," Tina said with a curtsy.

"Have you met my son and his good friend, my nephew, Lord Ainsby?" Mrs. Aldridge asked, making the introductions.

"It is an honor, Miss Ayres." Lord Ainsby made a grand leg that had Tina giggling. His friend merely bowed and mumbled how nice it was to meet her.

"Tina, you and Lord Ainsby have something in common," Tina's father said, a twinkle flickering in his eyes.

"If you mean that we are the best dressed of the younger people in attendance this evening, my lord, you are absolutely correct," Lord Ainsby said with a wink.

Lord Ayres laughed. "That was precisely what I meant! You, my dear sir, have exquisite taste and are clearly a man after my own heart." He turned to Tina. "I knew Tina was my daughter the moment we met because we both have impeccable taste and an aptitude for clothes."

Tina felt her face flush. "You are too kind, Papa."

"Kind but not wrong," Lord Ainsby said. "Would you care for a refreshment, Miss Ayres? I would so enjoy speaking with you about fashion and, oh, anything else that should come up."

Tina laughed. "I would like that a great deal, my lord, thank you. Er, if it's all right?" she asked her father.

"Of course! Of course! Go and have fun," Lord Ayres said with a laugh.

Lord Ainsby offered her his arm, and she happily took it. They spent the next half hour laughing over some of the fashions on display that evening and commiserating on what some people—mistakenly—thought was flattering. Tina hadn't had so much fun for what felt like too long. Oh, she was sure she'd had as much fun with Warwick and Margaret only a week or so ago, but she was firmly putting the duke out of her mind for now. She only hoped she wouldn't lose her friendship with his sister now. She truly liked Margaret.

~May 20~

"I hear we may soon become related," Mrs. Aldridge said with a giggle, leaning toward Christianne. In the lady's lap was her little King Charles spaniel, Duchess, her wet, black nose sniffing at the table looking for food.

"I'm sorry? Er, not that that wouldn't be lovely, but I don't know what you're referring to," Christianne said, as she dealt out the cards for their weekly game of whist. The dog gave her mistress's cards an experimental lick.

The ladies were all gathered in Christianne's game room, as always. She was sharing the table with her good friend Claire, Mrs. Aldridge, and Miss Hemshawe, who was, for once, not smelling of horse or dressed in her riding clothes.

"Well, I don't like telling tales," Mrs. Aldridge said, reorganizing the cards in her hand, "but I overheard my nephew, Ainsby, telling my son that he was thinking of popping the question to Miss Ayres."

"They have seen a great deal of each other over the past two weeks," Miss Hemshawe said. "I've seen them together in the park no less than three times!"

"Oh, my!" Claire said, using her cards as a fan. "That does sound serious."

Christianne could only shake her head. "I'm very happy to hear they're getting along so well. Tina hasn't said a word to me. To be frank, I worry she might still be pining for the duke."

"The duke? Of Warwick?" Mrs. Aldridge asked.

"Yes. They had become quite close while Tina was dressing his sister, Lady Margaret. Ayres even thought, from what Tina had told him, that they were quite in love."

"Did he not come up to scratch?" Mrs. Aldridge asked.

"He did, but it was on the night that Tina was introduced to society, and she believes he did so only because of her newfound position and not because he actually held any regard for her."

"*Does* he love her?" Miss Hemshawe asked.

"I don't know for certain, and since he's been out of town..."

Lady Blakemore twisted around in her chair. "Your Grace," she called out to the Duchess of Kendell, who was sitting at the other table.

The lady looked over from her game with a look that let everyone know precisely what she thought of being yelled at, from across the room.

"Have you spoken with the Duke of Warwick recently?" Lady Blakemore asked, ignoring the duchess's withering look.

Her Grace sighed, put down her cards, and then got up and walked over to them after excusing herself from her table. "I have not spoken with Warwick. Why do you ask?"

Mrs. Aldridge gave a little squeak as Duchess jumped from her lap. The dog ran around the table and put her paws up on the duchess's legs.

"Down, you beast," the grand lady said. The dog dutifully sat at her feet, her long, feathered tail wagging furiously against the floor.

"I heard from Lord Ayres that the duke and Tina had, er, a relationship of sorts," Christianne said.

The duchess raised her eyebrows. "Lord Ayres told you this?"

"Apparently, Tina confided in him before she was presented to society. He thought she was in love in with Warwick, but then the duke had the unfortunate timing of proposing to her on the very night she made her debut."

"Oh, er, yes." This clearly was not news to the duchess. She knew more than she was saying. "It *was* very unfortunate timing."

Christianne narrowed her eyes at the woman. "Do you know what's going on with him?"

"No," she said quickly, but then she relented. "I've spoken with Margaret. She told me of...well, of Warwick's feelings for Miss Ayres."

"And?" Lady Blakemore prompted when the woman didn't continue.

The duchess frowned at her. "I don't believe it is something he wants discussed in public."

"We are not in public," Christianne reminded her. "What is said in this room, stays here, right ladies?" she said more loudly.

As the women at the other card table had been obviously listening in on their conversation, everyone nodded or agreed aloud. The dog bounded over to the other table as if to confirm what the ladies had said before trotting back to the duchess content that all was well.

The duchess looked between the two tables, hesitating. She finally relented and said, "According to Margaret, Warwick was very much in love with Miss Ayres and had finally decided to propose to her. Sadly, as you all know, his timing was atrocious. He wasn't aware of Miss Ayres' new status within society."

"And Tina thought he was only proposing because of that and not because he loved her," Christianne said.

"Clearly he botched the job," Mrs. Aldridge said.

The duchess frowned at her. "That is not a proper way to put it, but... Yes, he did."

"Well, we've got to do something about this!" Miss Sheffield said with enthusiasm, having come closer from the other table. "We've got to somehow let the duke know about Tina's new status. We've got to let Tina know he still loves her before Lord Ainsby proposes to her and she accepts, thinking she has no other options."

The dog barked her approval.

"But how do we do that?" Lady Moreton asked from across the room. Duchess, the dog, ran over to her and put her paws on the lady's knees as if to confer with her on her idea. Lady Moreton absentmindedly scratched behind her long, floppy ears.

There was silence as everyone thought it through.

"We need someone who is close to the duke, who can tell him truthfully about his bad timing." Lady Blakemore asked.

"I don't believe he does. He's been at Warwick ever since that night," the duchess answered.

"Could *you* speak with him?" Christianne asked. "You're close to his family, and I know you've been chaperoning Lady Margaret for the past few weeks. Perhaps between you and his sister, he'll understand his error and, well, correct it. Would that be too much to ask? I know you don't have a particular fondness for my daughter."

The duchess lifted her chin. "I happen to like your daughter very well. In fact, I think she's got a good deal of gumption. I like that in a girl."

Christianne smiled. Common sense certainly was something Tina had a great deal of, and Christianne believed Tina had inherited it from her.

"Well then, *would* you speak with him?" Miss Hemshawe asked. "Nothing against Lord Ainsby, you understand," she said to Mrs. Aldridge, "but it would be a terrible shame for two people in love to feel they had to marry elsewhere."

"Oh, I don't believe Ainsby's heart is set. He just likes the girl better than any other he's met, and he's getting some pressure from his mother to marry," Mrs. Aldridge said with a reassuring smile.

"I do believe that a journey down to Warwick with Lady Margaret could be arranged—but only if you remove this animal from my presence," the duchess said, glaring down at the dog who was once again standing on her hind legs, her forelegs against the lady.

Mrs. Aldridge giggled. "She does like you! Duchess and the duchess," she tittered.

The lady merely glared at the dog's owner.

"Oh, very well. Duchess, come here to Mama," Mrs. Aldridge said, relenting.

The dog obeyed her mistress reluctantly.

~May 21~

Warwick came riding in hard and fast. He was about to shoot past the stables for another ride around the south field when he saw the travelling carriage. He pulled up, bringing his horse to a halt a few yards beyond the stables before turning back and guiding his horse to his stall.

Warwick jumped off and handed the reins to the groom, who came running. He normally enjoyed the time he spent brushing his horse down after a good long ride, but clearly, there were guests he needed to see to.

"Brush 'im down, Your Grace?" the boy asked.

"Yes. Do you know who's come?" Warwick asked.

"'Tis Lady Margaret and an older lady," the boy answered with a smile. Margaret was a favorite among the staff. Warwick had been asked any number of times over the past two weeks when his sister would be joining him.

Warwick noticed the crest on the side of the carriage. "The Duchess of Kendell," he said as much to himself as to the groom.

"Fine 'orses she's got. Four of 'em, matched," the boy said, clearly much more impressed with her cattle than her title.

Warwick supposed he should clean up and change before going to greet the ladies. He entered the house but didn't make it to the stair before he heard his name being called from the other end of the grand hall. His sister and the duchess were sitting by the enormous fireplace, a tea trolley between them, clearly enjoying some refreshments while they awaited him.

"Your Grace, Margaret, what a lovely surprise," he said, approaching them. "I do beg your pardon, however, I—"

"It is not *our* pardon you should be begging, Warwick," the duchess said, cutting him off.

"I'm sorry?" he said.

"You should be!" Margaret said with feeling. She looked furious. "I can't *believe* you've hidden here this long! You should have been back in London at least a week ago, if not more."

"Really, Warwick, this is exceedingly irresponsible behavior on your part," the duchess scolded.

"Hidden?" Warwick repeated. "I'm not hiding! What are you two going on about?"

CHAPTER THIRTY-THREE

"**Y**ou, Warwick! You and your atrocious, cowardly behavior!" Margaret said, not mincing words.

Warwick turned and stared at his normally mild-mannered sister. "Why are you so upset? What did I do?" he asked, becoming annoyed with this constant haranguing.

"It is what you *didn't* do!" the duchess said.

"Well, what I *didn't* do is clean up after my ride. I stink, and I'm filthy. I would like to go change, and then perhaps you will have calmed down enough to tell me whatever it is that has gotten you both so annoyed with me." He gave them a curt bow and was about to turn his back to go to his rooms to change when the duchess stopped him.

"You do smell of horse, but this is much, *much* more important. We will speak with you about this now, so you can just stand there in your filth while we say what we have come to say."

With a sigh, he turned back around and waited.

There was silence as the two women looked at each other, seemingly conferring silently. He waited, his patience growing thinner with each passing second.

"That sapphire ring," Margaret said finally. "Can you possibly think of anyone *else* who you might give it to?"

Warwick stopped. He stopped breathing. He stopped moving. He just stopped—as he did every time he thought of Tina. He usually followed this by a great deal of activity—anything and everything he could possibly think of to get her out of his mind. If he didn't, he would think about her again. Replay his proposal. Replay her dismissal of it. He'd lost count of how many times it had happened in the past few weeks. It was too many.

"Warwick?" the duchess said.

He reached into his pocket and pulled out the ring. It hadn't left his possession since he'd arrived at Warwick. He'd retrieved it from the safe in his mother's room the moment he'd gotten here—and hadn't let go of it since. He knew where it belonged, and it wasn't in his pocket.

"Robert." Margaret reached out and put her hand on his arm, her eyes shone with unshed tears as she looked up at him.

"Don't..." It was all he could say or else his own tears might well up, and he would never unman himself enough to cry in front of others, not even his sister.

"You know you want to give it to her. You know she is the only one who should wear it," his sister said, not moving her hand. There was no need to say who *she* was.

"Yes, and she is the only one to whom it has been offered, but she refused it. Well, she refused me," he said, turning and taking a few steps away.

"And do you know why?" the duchess asked.

"She said it was because she was worthy and I was shallow—whatever that means. I still haven't been able to make sense of it." He shook his head and spun back around. "*Why*? I don't understand. What was she thinking? Of course she's worthy! If she weren't, I wouldn't have proposed!"

"Because you missed the most important thing," his sister said with a sad smile on her face. "And she didn't know it."

He shook his head. He had no idea what she was talking about.

The duchess took in a deep breath and gave him a little smile. "Before you proposed, Tina was introduced to society as the daughter of the Earl of Ayres. She's now known as Miss Tina Ayres and will be given a very generous dowry by her father."

"She's been accepted by society," Margaret said. "It was a little rough at first, but she *has* been accepted."

"She thought you were only proposing because of her new position in society, not because you cared for her," the duchess chimed in with the clincher.

"What? But that's...that's..." He stopped and thought about it. He had been about to say it was absurd. Of *course* she knew he loved her. He'd shown her the last time they'd been together. But he'd never been able to find her to *tell* her so, despite the fact he'd looked for her everywhere. And then, instead of saying anything, he'd simply proposed, like a besotted fool.

He began to think of the other things she'd said when he'd proposed—something about his lust the last time they'd seen each other. But she couldn't possibly have thought he'd meant he just wanted... Warwick staggered.

He needed to sit down.

"I think he just got it," Margaret said.

"Yes. Finally," the duchess agreed.

Somehow their voices sounded very far away. He couldn't believe what he'd done. It had been completely inadvertent. He hadn't *known*. How could he have? He'd only just arrived at the ball when he'd seen her and immediately spoken to her.

But could she have known that? What if she'd thought he'd been there all along and she just hadn't seen him?

It explained everything—in a horribly logical way.

~May 22~

Early the following morning, Warwick joined the ladies in the duchess's carriage for the four-hour ride back to town. He could have ridden and made it there in three hours or less, but he needed to know what Tina had been doing for the past two weeks since he'd made a mull of everything.

He simply hadn't been able to face either of the women after his revelation the previous afternoon. He'd been a horrendous host and had taken his dinner in his rooms. He'd been tempted to drink but had endured the night stone-cold sober, rehashing his proposal in light of his new knowledge.

It was all clear to him now. He understood exactly what Tina had meant when she'd turned him down. He knew precisely where the misunderstandings had happened. Partly it had been his fault for not actually saying the words "I love you" the last time they'd met. He'd thought she'd understood, but clearly, he should have been more explicit, more forthcoming.

As for his horrendous timing, it was simply not his fault for how badly he'd bungled it. He hadn't known she'd been presented to society. Yes, if he'd simply taken a few moments to speak to people after he and Margaret had entered the ball, he would have found out, but he hadn't—and Tina had been equally ignorant of his lack of knowledge.

It could all be fixed. It could all be worked out. He just needed to get to London and see her. He'd been tempted to leave then, in the middle of the night, but decided it was ignorance which had led to his inadvertent bad timing. He'd do well to learn all he could about what had been happening while he'd been at his estate nursing his wounded heart.

So now he decided to forego speed and endure the duchess's slow, if comfortable, traveling carriage.

"I'm afraid there's more bad news," his sister began soon after they'd pulled away from the house.

He turned toward her. "How could there possibly be even more?"

"Miss Ayres has not been idle while you were gone," the duchess said.

"Nor has she been continuing her work as a modiste," Margaret said. "Although she has been kind enough to offer to make more dresses for me. She's decided not to entirely give up her occupation but instead to only make clothes for her closest friends."

"That is very kind of her," Warwick said.

"Yes, it is." His sister gave him a little smile.

"If she hasn't been making dresses, then what has she been doing?" He hated to ask, but knowledge was what he was there to gather.

"She has been to a great many parties," the duchess began.

"And for a number of rides in the park," Margaret continued.

"With a particular gentleman?" Warwick had to ask.

"Lord Ainsby," the two women said in unison.

Warwick frowned trying to remember why the name made him want to laugh—and then he remembered. Ainsby was the popinjay who'd been the first to arrive the day after Margaret's ball. He was fribble. A dandy. "You can't be serious!"

"They have a great deal in common, as they're both very interested in fashion and clothing," Margaret said.

"But he hasn't a brain!" the duke argued with a laugh.

"He does! He just bends it toward things that others believe are frivolous," his sister said. "He's actually a very sweet and thoughtful man."

Warwick looked at his sister, hardly believing the words coming from her mouth.

"Mrs. Aldridge, from the Lady's Wagering Whist Society, who is Lord Ainsby's aunt, told us that she overheard the boy tell her son that he was thinking of proposing to Miss Ayres," the duchess said, sounding rather disgusted.

He raised his eyebrows.

"You know how much I hate gossip," she said furiously. "But this was too important. We couldn't *not* act on the information."

Warwick sat back against the seat. "So based on this hearsay, the two of you traveled all the way up to Warwick to tell me what an idiot I've been."

"Yes," Margaret said.

"You needed to know," the duchess said, defending their decision.

Warwick nodded reluctantly. "I did. And I am grateful that you made the journey. But honestly—on a piece of gossip?"

"We have seen Tina in Lord Ainsby's company a great deal," Margaret said defensively. "It's not entirely hearsay."

"Only the part about him proposing," the duchess admitted.

"I couldn't stand the thought of you pining away for Tina at Warwick while she..." Margaret started.

"I wasn't pining away," her brother snapped.

She blinked at him. "Then what do you call it?"

He clenched his jaw in frustration. "I was taking care of estate business. Martin will be following us back to London tomorrow, by the way."

"He can't be very happy about this turn of events," Margaret said, allowing the conversation to drift.

"He's lucky he still has a position. He won't be saying a word against my choice of bride, I can assure you," Warwick said. Despite the fact that he'd been furious with his secretary, he'd been unable to dismiss the man. They had, after all, grown up together. And, he supposed, Martin had simply been looking out for Warwick's best interests. He just hadn't realized Warwick didn't want his personal interests looked after. Martin knew that now.

Silence reigned in the carriage for a few miles before Margaret and the duchess continued to regale the duke with other happenings within society and what they had been doing as well. It was a very long drive back to the city.

"How are you going to do it?"

"Warwick!"

His sister's voice jolted him out of his reverie as he watched the passing countryside. "I'm sorry? Were you speaking to me?"

His sister gave him an indulgent smile. "I asked how you were going to propose to Tina. Have you thought of that yet?"

"Oh! Er, yes, as a matter of fact, I was thinking of that just now," he admitted.

"And?" the duchess asked, clearly intrigued.

"I was thinking if there were a small gathering, I might do it there. I just... I don't want to be the host because that might be awkward," he said.

"You're going to propose in public?" Margaret asked, clearly surprised.

"Well, yes. I thought that the best way to prove I believe she is worthy of my esteem and respect. If I propose in public, then she'll know that I'm not ashamed of her in any way." He paused. "That's what I was thinking. Is it too much? Should I—"

"Oh no, it's perfect!" Margaret cut him off. "But aren't you afraid of demeaning yourself when you do so? I mean, it's not a very respectable thing for a duke to be doing."

"Your father would not have approved," the duchess agreed.

Warwick smiled. "Precisely." He'd had enough of his father's disapproval. He'd had it almost every day of his life while his father had been alive and had continued fighting his ghost since he'd died. But he was not going to do so anymore. Warwick was his own man. He was going to be a duke the way he saw fit.

"My father also would not have approved of my proposing to a woman who is..." He ticked off on his fingers. "Illegitimate. Raised in a small village by a poor family. And a modiste." He returned his hand to his lap. "I no longer care what my father would have thought. I'm through trying to walk in his footsteps."

"Bravo!" Margaret said, beaming at him.

"Thank you." He inclined his head toward her.

"So, you need a social occasion. One that is public, but not too public, is that right?" the duchess said, returning to the topic at hand.

"Yes," Warwick said. "You wouldn't happen to know of something appropriate coming up, would you?"

A small smile lifted one side of her lips. "I think I might."

Chapter Thirty-Four

It was an odd invitation Tina had received. She was requested by the Duchess of Kendell to come to the Lady's Wagering Whist Society meeting. As much as she appreciated the invitation, she didn't quite understand why, though. And why was the duchess making the invitation and not her mother, at whose home the ladies always met?

Still, for someone who was just beginning to make her way in society, she wasn't about to dismiss an invitation from a duchess. She showed up on her mother's doorstep at precisely three.

"Tina, how lovely to see you!" her mother said, amidst the greeting of other members of the Society.

"I'm happy to see you too, although, I have to admit, I'm a little confused," Tina said.

"Confused? What are you confused about?" Lady Blakemore asked, after nodding to Tina's curtsy.

"The invitation. Is someone ill so you need me to fill in a table?" Tina asked.

"What? No, no," her mother said. "At least not as far as I know." She looked to her friend for confirmation.

"Everyone will be here, from what I understand," Lady Blakemore concurred.

"Then..." Tina started.

"Ah, Miss Ayres, you came," the Duchess of Kendell said, coming into the room. "I am so glad to see you."

"Thank you, Your Grace," Tina said, curtsying.

"Are you doing well? Enjoying society?" the lady asked with a pleasant smile.

"Er, yes, thank you," Tina said, becoming even more confused. The duchess had never been so friendly before.

"Good, good. I hear you are rarely passed over for an invitation now that your dear father has introduced you," the duchess said.

"Yes, Your Grace, I have been extremely lucky and grateful that I have been so well accepted," Tina agreed, looking to her mother for some sort of explanation.

She was deep in conversation with Lady Sorrell, however. With a look around, Tina noticed it seemed as if all of the ladies had, indeed, arrived.

"Oh, Miss Ayres, I am so happy to see you," Miss Sheffield exclaimed brightly. "I was wondering if you might give me a little fashion advice."

"Of course, I would be more than happy to," Tina said.

"You go ahead," the duchess said dismissing Tina while giving Miss Sheffield a nod and a smile.

Miss Sheffield took Tina's arm and led her closer to the fireplace on the far side of the room and proceeded to ask her about lace and ribbons and how much of each she might get away with adding to a particular dress.

Tina was doing the best she could to answer her when there was a commotion by the door. Tina turned to see Lady Margaret come in on the arm of... "My God, is that Warwick?" Tina gasped.

She almost didn't recognize the man. He had on the most exquisite cerulean blue coat and a pale yellow waistcoat with blue embroidery. He looked... He looked... Tina sighed, more handsome than a man had a right to look. A knot formed in her stomach.

She'd heard the duke was out of town—had been out of town ever since that fated ball when he'd had the nerve to propose to her.

He caught sight of her. For a moment, his face paled slightly, but then he seemed to pull himself together and left his sister's side to approach her. He stopped a few feet away and just stared.

Tina looked down at her gown to see if there was something wrong or odd with the way she was dressed. She was wearing one of her own creations— a pale pink dress with white lace.

"You look beautiful," he said as if he could read her insecurity.

It suddenly occurred to her where she'd seen the blue of his coat before. She'd made a dress for Lady Margaret and had suggested he get a coat made in the same color. He'd laughed at her, but now...

"I knew you'd look good in that color," she managed to say, despite the fact that her throat and tongue had gone dry.

He smiled. "I'm glad you like it. What do you think of the waistcoat? Is it too much?"

"No! No. It looks perfect."

"I had it and the coat made, thinking of you." He came closer.

"You did?"

"Tina, forgive me?" he said, with a small, pleading lift of his eyebrows.

"Forgive... Wait, are *you* apologizing? I thought dukes never apologized," she said.

He gave a little lift to the corners of his mouth as if he wasn't sure whether he should smile at that or not. "Well, when a man has been as idiotic as I have, I don't believe that even being a duke is enough to absolve me. Only you can do that."

Tina shook her head, confused. She wasn't entirely sure why he was asking her to forgive him. For proposing? For implying she wasn't worthy of his affection? For something else altogether?

He gave a humorless laugh. "It was partly my fault and partly not," he said. "I wasn't paying attention. Margaret and I arrived at the ball late. I was preoccupied and immediately went out into the garden to think. I didn't speak to anyone or even take any notice of anything around me until I saw you standing there in the garden."

Tina began to put the pieces together. "So you didn't know..."

"I thought perhaps you were there to work or... I don't know, I didn't stop to think about why you were there. I just saw you and...well."

Tina took in a deep breath. He hadn't known! He *hadn't* meant to imply that he was only proposing because of her new status within society. He couldn't have.

He came even closer and took her hands in his and then, to her shock, he knelt before her. "I thought I had made it clear earlier, but obviously I botched that up as well. Tina Rowen, I love you. I couldn't care less if you were a modiste or a lady of society. All I want is to spend the rest of my life with you—if you will have a poor fool like me."

Tina swallowed hard trying desperately to keep the tears that had sprung to her eyes from falling.

"Please?"

Please! He'd even said please. The tears began sliding down her cheeks. The word "yes" was just forming on her lips when there was another commotion, and the door to the room was thrown open.

"I don't give a damn about some lady's party," a man growled.

"Let go of me, you bleedin'—" another male voice yelled.

Tina turned to see who was shouting, then suddenly put her hand out on Warwick's shoulder, lest she fall when her knees nearly gave way beneath her.

Her foster-father and Caleb, dressed in rough-hewn shirts and trousers, were standing just inside the room scowling furiously at her. They'd clearly dressed for the city since their shirts were mostly clean, and they'd tied colorful kerchiefs around their throats.

"There she is!" her foster-father said and began advancing on her, ignoring the gasps from the women all around them.

Warwick was up and standing between her and the two interlopers within seconds. "Who are you? And how dare you barge in here like heathens."

"Heathens are we?" her foster-father said with a mean, humorless laugh.

"That's...that's..." Tina whispered. She couldn't even say it. Her tongue was no longer working. Her hands were trembling.

"I'm that girl's foster-father, and this here is my son, Caleb, her intended husband," her foster-father said. "Now who the hell are you?"

"You will watch your language, sir," Warwick said. "We are in the company of ladies."

"I will say whatever the damn hell I please, women or no," Tina's foster-father said, advancing. "And no tulip is gonna tell me otherwise."

Warwick looked down his nose at the man who stood nearly a head shorter than him. "I am the Duke of Warwick, and you will behave properly or be thrown out of this house into the gutter where you belong."

"Now, listen here, your dukedom, I'm the girl's father—"

"No, *I* am Tina's father," a voice said from the doorway. Lord Ayres ambled into the room.

Mr. Rowan and Caleb spun around to face the new threat.

"And I suggest you listen to His Grace and remove yourselves from this property at once," her father finished. Tina had never seen him with such a terrifying expression on his face. Her normally smiling Papa was furious and it showed.

"Now see here," Mr. Rowan began.

"I don't believe we need to see anything more from you," Warwick said, advancing on the men. "Either you leave of your own volition, or I will be more than happy to physically remove you myself."

"That's my wife!" Caleb shouted, pointing at Tina.

"I am not! I never agreed to marry you. In fact, I've been paying your father handsomely to keep from doing so," Tina said, finally finding her voice.

"You've been *paying* him?" Warwick said, half turning around toward her.

"Yes. We made a deal. He wouldn't force me to marry Caleb and allow me to start my business here in London if I paid him two pounds, eight shillings a month. That's what my mother gave him, plus fifteen percent."

"What? She's been payin' you all that money?" Caleb said, turning on his father.

"That's much more than what I paid him," Tina's mother said. "I gave him one and a half pounds a month."

"He told me two and a half," Tina said.

"It sounds as if you have been more than handsomely paid for your services. You may leave," Lord Ayres said with a commanding voice that was impossible to disregard.

Mr. Rowan opened his mouth to argue, but Warwick took another step closer. "Oh, please say you won't. I will so enjoy removing you myself," he growled. He balled his hands into fists at his side.

"I believe, er, that is, well..." Caleb stuttered, taking a step backward toward the door.

"What he means is good luck to you, girl. I hope your business fails," her foster-father sneered.

"She is no longer in business. She has no need to be now that she is under my protection. I know how to treat a child. You help them, you don't hurt them," Lord Ayres said. "You give them what they need, instead of stealing what they have."

Tina watched her foster-father's mouth work as he tried his best to keep his tongue behind his lips. Warwick took another menacing step toward him. Finally, he exploded, "Come on, Caleb. I think we're done here."

The two men left quickly.

"Oh!" Lady Blakemore collapsed onto the sofa just behind her. Miss Hemshawe rushed to her side, taking up her hand and patting it.

"I think we all need some tea," Tina's mother said, moving toward the door to call the maid.

"I think we need something a great deal stronger," the duchess said.

"There's brandy, sherry, and Madeira in the cabinet," Lady Norman said. She rang the bell. Two maids came in a moment, each carrying a tea tray. Clearly, they'd been ready for the call.

Warwick pressed a glass of brandy into Tina's still shaking hand. She'd hardly been able to move her gaze from the door since her foster-father and brother had disappeared through it. "It's all right, Tina," he said gently. "Drink this, you'll feel better."

She looked up at him, feeling the tears well in her eyes. "I'm so sorry!"

"For what? It's not your fault those men came in here just when they did."

"No, but... it's so embarrassing," she whispered. "This whole thing. It's just the sort of display that you hate, isn't it?"

"I can't say that I enjoy seeing you confronted like that, nor having my proposal of marriage so rudely interrupted, but one good thing did come of this," he said, giving her a little smile.

Tina shook her head, blinking away the tears. "What?"

"You won't ever have to worry about them ever again," Tina's father said, coming up to them. "Now, did I just hear you say something about a marriage proposal, Warwick?"

The duke smiled at her father. "Yes, I had just asked the question when those men barged in."

"And did you receive an answer?" Lord Ayres asked nonchalantly.

Warwick turned back to Tina. "No, as a matter of fact, I didn't."

Tina couldn't believe there was a twinkle in the man's eye when he looked at her. "You still want to marry me? Even after, after that?" she asked, incredulous that he would still desire to be associated with her after meeting the man who raised her.

"I would be honored," Warwick answered. "Now that I understand just how far you have come, my respect and love for you is greater than ever. Please say that you will make me the happiest of men." He reached into his pocket and pulled out the most beautiful sapphire and diamond ring. "I'm afraid I've been carrying this around for the past few weeks, but I would like nothing better than to see it on your finger."

Now the tears truly did fall, and there was nothing Tina could do to stop them. Her drink was removed from her hand, allowing her to reach up and caress the face of the man she loved more than anything in this world. "Yes. Oh, yes. I love you too, Warwick."

His smile broadened and his kiss was the sweetest thing she'd felt in a very, very long time. She would, after all, get her own happily ever after.

**Look for the next book in the Ladies'Wagering
Whist Society Series**

JACK OF DIAMONDS

Can the Ladies' Wagering Whist Society help a
young woman with a dark secret allow light and love
into her heart?

Lydia Sheffield is always laughing, always
joking, always charming, always surrounded by
adoring gentlemen. She wants to enjoy the season,
and not yield to Regency society's expectation that
she quickly marry and have children. She also has a
secret lurking within her—one that will keep her
from ever taking a risk on love.

Lord John Welles has a secret of his own, but
Lydia has discovered it. She noticed what no one else
did, that this attractive, upstanding gentleman is
filching diamonds from unsuspecting ladies. Lydia
extracts a price for her silence—a fake engagement
to her for the season. John never expected to want to
make the arrangement real, nor that Lydia would be
so dead-set against it. There's something she's not
telling him, and he's determined to find out what it
is.

Can John discover Lydia's secret in time to save
his heart from breaking? He'll need to convince her
to take a chance on love, on life... and on him.

It will take the Ladies' Wagering Whist Society
to help John win his diamond.

CHAPTER ONE

~**May 10, 1806**~

Lydia Sheffield grasped onto her friend Tina's arm, certain that she had to be imagining things. "I'm sorry, but did you just see that?"

"See what?" Tina asked, following her line of sight.

"That man," Lydia followed the man with her eyes across the crowded ballroom, trying to indicate who she was speaking about without outright pointing in his direction. "That man heading out the door, the one in the gray coat. He just stole two diamond pins from a lady's hair!"

"What? You must be imagining things, Miss Sheffield," Lady Norman, Tina's mother, said with a little laugh. "No gentleman would steal pins from a lady's hair!"

"No, I'm certain... oh, he's gone," Tina said, feeling strangely disappointed. She let go of Tina's arm, but her heart was still pounding. She'd never actually witnessed a crime before.

"He must have just accidentally bumped into her," Tina said.

"Yes," Tina said, not believing it for a second. "Perhaps, it was that." Truly, who would steal hairpins from a lady at a ball? No one could possibly be so brazen! Besides which, everyone here had been invited, and no member of the ton would be so desperate that they would resort to stealing. No, Tina was right. She had to have imagined it.

Lydia turned back to Tina and her mother. "Yes, you must be right." She forced out a little laugh. "Who would steal hairpins from a lady at a ball?" She shook her head trying to dispel the image from her mind's eye.

"Perhaps you need some fresh air as much as I do," Tina suggested.

"Oh, no. I'm fine. Truly." Lydia said, giving another laugh. What she really wanted to do was follow the man and see where he went. But there was no way to do so politely. No, she was stuck right where she was.

"Well, then, if you don't mind, I think I'm going to get step outside for a moment. If one more person insults me to my face, I'm not entirely certain I won't actually scream," Tina said, putting on a brave smile.

"Oh, dear!" her mother said, looking a little worried.

"It's all right. I'm sure that a brief walk in the garden will make me feel better. If you'll excuse me." Tina gave them both a little curtsey and headed out the French doors toward the garden.

Lydia had been doing her best to be a good friend to Tina Ayres when she'd imagined that she'd seen the theft. Tina had just made her society debut that very evening and was having a hard time of it.

Lydia had been half-listening to Tina, and her mother discuss how rude people could be when the man had caught her eye. She'd been casually scanning the people crowding Lady Kershaw's ballroom when she noticed the gentleman move in what almost looked like a furtive manner behind a group of ladies.

The women were probably discussing poor Tina, as every once in a while one of them stole a glance in her direction. It was what nearly everyone at the party was talking about after all. Before today Tina had been known to a number of ladies of the ton merely as a modiste—granted, she was one who made beautiful, extremely flattering gowns, but this evening her father, the Marquess of Ayres, had re-introduced her as his daughter. But for Lydia, it was the gentleman in the gray coat who'd held her attention.

He was incredibly handsome in a rather ordinary way. He was of average height with a mix of dark brown-light blond hair. His clothing was completely ordinary, nothing spectacular or particularly memorable. It was true that his face was handsome and his physique on the athletic side, but other than that he was completely forgettable. Lydia was just trying to figure out what it was about him that captured her attention when she'd seen him pluck the pin from the hair of one of the older ladies.

Lydia's studied the woman's complicated coiffure. It was a maze of braids and curls all held together by a dozen or so diamond hairpins. Had the man—could she call him a gentleman?— pulled a pin from the lady's hair?

"I can't help but wonder who that gentleman was, though," Lydia said to Lady Norman after Tina had left.

"What did he look like, maybe I know him?" her friend said, even though she was still watching her daughter's retreating back. Lady Norman was always so helpful and more than willing to step in as a sort of chaperone to Lydia since her father usually made himself scarce the moment they walked into any party.

Lydia pictured the gentleman in her mind. "He was tall, but not very tall. Brown, maybe dark blond hair. He wore a dark gray coat and a black waistcoat with gray embroidery. Quite elegant, actually, in a very understated way."

Lady Norman turned back to Lydia. "I don't believe I've seen the gentleman."

"Oh, well. It's all right. I'm sure I'll see him again."

"One always does," Lady Norman agreed.

It was less than a quarter of an hour later when Lydia did spy the gentleman again, and oddly enough, he was once again lurking among the ladies. How was it that they didn't notice him, Lydia wondered.

This time she was on her own, so she wound her way through the crowded ballroom, doing her best to keep an eye on the man. It wasn't easy, and she did, in fact, lose sight of him when she was waylaid by Mrs. Aldridge, a member of the Ladies Wagering Whist Society, along with Lady Norman and herself. Mrs. Aldridge was looking quite fetching this evening in a gown of deep pink with matching rubies circling her throat, wrists and hanging from her ears. Lydia complimented her on her attire.

"Thank you, but why are you not dancing, Miss Sheffield?" Mrs. Aldridge said in a good-natured scold.

Lydia gave the woman a wink. "I'm just on my way around the ballroom in the hopes of enticing a particular gentleman to ask me," she said with a giggle before continuing on her way.

The older woman burst out laughing but quickly stifled herself when heads turned her way.

Sadly, when Lydia turned back to where her quarry had been, the man had disappeared once again.

Lydia harrumphed to herself. This was definitely the most elusive gentleman she'd ever seen. She was just about to turn back toward Mrs. Aldridge when there was a small commotion among the ladies by whom he'd been loitering.

"I was certain I had it on when I went into the lady's retiring room," one rather rotund woman in a dove gray silk dress said.

"Perhaps it fell off when you washed your hands?" one of her companions asked.

"But I didn't... er, yes, perhaps that is the case. I'll go back and see if anyone has found it," she said, turning slightly pink.

Lydia stepped up to the lady's friend and asked, "Is everything all right, my lady?"

"Oh yes, Lady Fostler has just misplaced her bracelet." The woman raised a lorgnette to her eyes and peered at Lydia. "Have we met?"

"Yes, the Duchess of Kendell introduced us at Lady Bradmore's ball a few weeks ago," she said, lying straight through her teeth but knowing no woman would ever deny knowledge of an introduction by a duchess. "I'm Lydia Sheffield. My father is Lord Daniel Sheffield,"

As expected the woman nodded slowly as she lowered her eyepiece. "Oh, yes, of course, Miss Sheffield. How lovely to see you again this evening."

"And you, my lady. I do hope that Lady Fostler finds her bracelet," Lydia said.

"As do I. It was apparently given to her by her husband for her birthday only last year. A beautiful diamond confection," the lady said.

"Oh, dear," Lydia said, tsking sadly. That gentleman in the gray coat... he wouldn't have... he couldn't have... Lydia shook her head. No! It would simply be too outrageous if he had stolen a bracelet right off a woman's wrist.

But Lydia was more determined than ever to discover the identity of the man.

~*~

John, the Viscount Welles, didn't like hiding behind potted plants. It made him feel ridiculous, and yet he had to make sure the girl who had been heading directly toward him a moment ago didn't see him. It wasn't that he didn't want to speak with her, goodness knows he'd love to, but not this evening. Not while he was working.

The girl was not only beautiful but, if he wasn't mistaken, she was the famous Miss Lydia Sheffield, considered one of the "diamonds" of the season. She was funny and charismatic—or so he'd heard. He'd never been introduced, and he knew that he didn't want to be. She was precisely the sort of girl he avoided at all costs.

He wasn't quite sure how he'd drawn the attention of the lovely Miss Sheffield. He was dressed as always in his most unmemorable clothes. Black and gray, he'd found, usually encouraged eyes to slip right by him. His waistcoat was as understated as the rest of him, and carefully cultivated to be so.

Only a few years ago when he'd been at University, he'd dressed better. He'd been more outgoing and enjoyed his excursions to London as much as anyone in his group of friends. Then, the world was his to discover and enjoy.

So much had changed since those carefree days.

He no longer enjoyed being social, or so he told himself. He didn't have the time or inclination to stand about and discuss silly things like who danced with whom or who was seen riding in the park with another. No, now he simply hid behind plants, avoiding beautiful women instead of seeking them out. Now, he was stealing jewels straight out of the hair of ladies and off their wrists without them even realizing what had happened to them.

In a way, he hated what he'd been reduced to, but in another, he rather enjoyed the challenge, and it allowed him to make more of his life than so many of his peers.

But in order to continue with his chosen occupation, he had to avoid the likes of Miss Lydia Sheffield, no matter how much he'd much rather be laughing and dancing with her.

ABOUT THE AUTHOR

Meredith Bond's books straddle that beautiful line between historical romance and fantasy. An award-winning author, she writes fun traditional Regency romances, medieval Arthurian romances, and Regency romances with a touch of magic. Known for her characters "who slip readily into one's heart," Meredith's heart belongs to her husband and two children.

Meredith loves connecting with readers. Sign up for her monthly newsletter at http://meredithbond. com/blog/newsletter-sign-up/ to receive free short stories and get all her news before anyone else. And don't forget to find her on-line:

Website: http://www.meredithbond.com
Facebook:
https://www.facebook.com/meredithbondauthor
Twitter: https://twitter.com/merrybond
Pinterest:
http://www.pinterest.com/merrybond/
Instagram:
https://www.instagram.com/meredith_bond/
Bookbub:
https://www.bookbub.com/authors/meredith-bond
Newsletter:
http://meredithbond.com/subscribe/

Please don't forget to leave a review wherever you buy books.

Sign up for Meredith's Newsletter!

Would you like to get a free short story every month? How about the chance to beta read (get a book before it's been published for free in exchange for your honest opinion about the book)? Keep up to date on my writing, get advanced notice of new books and be the first to see the covers? **Then sign up for Meredith's newsletter!**

As a special thanks, you'll receive a copy of the *Ladies' Wagering Whist Society Short Story Anthology* – an exclusive volume of short stories only available to Newsletter Subscribers!

To sign up just go to
https://meredithbond.com/subscribe/

Follow all of the women of the Ladies' Wagering Whist Society

1806 Season
A Hand for the Duke
Featuring Christianne Norman, Lady Norman
The Jack of Diamonds
Featuring Miss Lydia Sheffield
The Games She Played
Featuring Miss Diana Hemshawe

1807 Season
A Trick of Mirrors
Featuring Claire Tyne, Lady Blakemore
A Bid for Romance
Featuring Alys Russell, Duchess of Kendell
Gambling for Hearts
Featuring Mrs. Penelope Aldridge

1808 Season
Love in Spades
Featuring Cynthia Montley, Lady Sorrell
coming: 2021
A Token of Love
Featuring Ellen Aston, Lady Moreton
coming: 2021

Bonus
The King of Clubs
Featuring Joshua Powell, Lord Wickford
coming: 2021

Other Books By Meredith Bond

The Merry Men Series
An Exotic Heir
A Merry Marquis
A Rake's Reward
A Dandy in Disguise
My Lord Ghost
My Gentleman Thief
Under the Mango Tree
A Spanish Dilemma
When Hearts Rebel

The Storm Series
Storm on the Horizon
Bridging the Storm
Magic in the Storm
Through the Storm

The Children of Avalon Trilogy
Air: Merlin's Chalice
Water: The Return of Excalibur
Fire: Nimuë's Destiny

Falling
Falling for a Pirate

Chapter One: A Fast, Fun Way to Write
Fiction
Self-Publishing: Easy as ABC
The Writer's Journal
"In A Beginning", a short story featuring Lilith